MONSTROUS
DEVICES

With a *whirrrrr,* the head turned,
until the face seemed to be looking at him.

MONSTROUS DEVICES

DEVICES

— by —

Damien Love

VIKING

VIKING
Penguin Young Readers
An imprint of Penguin Random House LLC
375 Hudson Street
New York, New York 10014

First published in the United States of America by Viking,
an imprint of Penguin Random House LLC, 2018

LIBRARY OF CONGRESS CATALOGING-IN-PUBLICATION DATA
Names: Love, Damien, author.
Title: Monstrous devices / by Damien Love.
Description: New York : Viking, [2018] | Summary: Alex, nearly thirteen,
flees with his grandfather across snowy Europe to escape the human and
mechanical assassins that pursue them, trying to retrieve a powerful object.
Identifiers: LCCN 2017053893 | ISBN 9780451478580 (hardcover)
Subjects: | CYAC: Assassins—Fiction. | Adventure and adventurers—Fiction. |
Robots—Fiction. | Grandfathers—Fiction. | Golem—Fiction. |
Supernatural—Fiction.
Classification: LCC PZ7.1.L7293 Mon 2018 | DDC [Fic]—dc23
LC record available at https://lccn.loc.gov/2017053893

Printed in U.S.A.   Book design by Jim Hoover   Set in Fairfield Lt Std

1   3   5   7   9   10   8   6   4   2

TO ALISON

FOR NORAH

AND IN MEMORY OF DREW

MONSTROUS
DEVICES

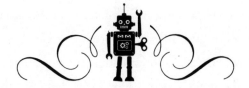

A PROLOGUE IN PRAGUE

SNOW IS FALLING on the city of Prague.

Soft white against a sharp black skyline, it dances around the castle spires and wisps past the patient statues of the church of St. Nicholas. It flurries over fast-food restaurants' glowing signs, drifts down on cobblestones, tarmac, and tramlines. Old women in headscarves shiver, and street vendors selling hot sausages stamp their feet in Wenceslas Square. Bleary young tourists' teeth chatter outside bars in the Old Town.

A tall man and a small girl stalk through the snow. The man wears a long black coat and a homburg hat. He clutches a cane. The girl's black coat reaches her ankles, where purple-and-black-striped socks disappear inside heavy black boots. She looks nine or ten, with a pale, round face framed by long black hair.

They cut briskly across the Old Town Square: past grumbling workmen struggling to erect a huge eighty-foot Christmas tree; past the house where a famous writer lived an unhappy life long ago; past an ancient cemetery crammed with graves like a smashed mouth filled with broken teeth.

For each of the man's long strides, the girl must take three, yet she easily matches his angry pace. The city grows older around them as they walk. The light is fading, the day turning blue beneath a heavy slate sky. The snow is beginning to lie. It crumps under their feet. It frosts her hair like icing sugar. It gathers in the nooks and crannies of the strange metal straps that encase each of his boot-heels like heavy surgical supports.

They come eventually to a narrow street, barely more than an alley between aging buildings, dark, save for a single yellowy light burning in a shop window bearing a sign painted in cheerful red:

> BECKMAN'S TOYS

Behind the words, heavy red curtains frame a dusty display. Monkeys wearing fez hats brandish cymbals. Ventriloquists' dummies leer secret smiles at blushing Victorian dolls. Black bats hang from black threads alongside ducks with propellers on their heads and wooden policemen with bright red noses. Machine guns and ray guns, farting cushions, furry spiders, and fake bloody fingers.

A line of robots marches through this chaos. Tiny cowboys

and cavalrymen battle rubber dinosaurs at the feet of fat tin spaceships.

The man in the long black coat pushes open the door, ushering the girl in ahead. A bell actually rings, a pleasing old sound of polished brass in the musty dim as they step inside. Around them, the little shop is a cluttered cosmos of toys. Squadrons of fighter planes and hot air balloons swarm the ceiling. Sailboats and rocket ships patrol shelves. Teddy bears are crammed into corners with rocking horses and dogs on wheels. Bright things new and old, of plastic, lead, and wood, fake fur and cheap metal.

When they are certain there is no one else in the shop, the girl flips the sign from OPEN to CLOSED. Snapping the lock, she stands with her back to the door and folds her arms.

The man strides to the counter, heading on toward the back room, when a figure emerges from in there, pushing through the rattling hanging beads holding scissors and a roll of brown tape. A small man with severely cropped gray hair and big, round glasses, thick lenses reflecting the light, shabbily dressed but for an incongruously bright-yellow-with-black-polka-dots silk scarf knotted at his throat. A torn-off strip of brown tape hangs from the end of his nose.

"Snow is falling," this little Beckman sings in a high burble, still frowning down at the tape in his hands. "Christmas is coming—"

Looking up to blink happily at his visitors, he stops abruptly.

The roll of tape drops from his hands. He swallows with difficulty.

"Eh . . ." He licks his lips. "Did you get him?"

The girl solemnly shakes her head. Pouting a frown that mockingly mirrors Beckman's own, she twists her knuckles at the corners of her eyes in a *boo-hoo* pantomime, before refolding her arms.

Beckman swallows again as the tall man leans across the counter.

"You had it."

"No. Please. I—I can explain," Beckman begins, backing away.

The man looms farther over him, reaching out a sharp, pale hand. Beckman flinches, grabs protectively at the scarf around his neck, and lets out a girlish shriek—it could be the word *no*—as the man rips the tape from his nose. Beckman laughs, a nervous and treacly too-loud giggle. He pretends to relax as the tall man rubs the tape into a ball between his slender gray fingers and lets it drop.

"Tape," Beckman babbles. "On my nose. Always I'm putting it there. Forgetting. Packaging up a gift. A horse. Going to a little girl in Germany. Near my old hometown. A lovely little horsey. For a lovely little girl."

He tries a grin on the girl. It curdles and dies as she glares back. She picks a toy revolver from a shelf. Still unsmiling, she aims at him, pulls the trigger. Without a sound, a tiny flag unfurls from the snout bearing a single word: BANG.

"Now," Beckman stumbles on, faster. "Please. I can explain. Yes, you just have to believe me . . ." He trails off. In the toy shop silence, he has heard a small, distinct *click*.

Now the girl starts smiling.

"You *had* it," the tall man in black says once more. "And you let it *go*." He raises his arm again, and there is something small and sharp, silvery and slivery in his hand, arcing down through the warm reddish air as all the monkeys and cowboys and ducks and dogs and dolls look on with their glass and painted eyes.

For the next few seconds, the sounds inside this toy shop are muffled and breathy, desperate, wet, and horrid.

Outside, snow is falling on the city of Prague.

Lights are flickering on in the streets and squares and up in the mysterious windows of the high castle. White globe lamps glow along black bridges over the river, reflections restless in the cold, dark water.

The snow falls.

People hurry through the streets, and it covers all their tracks.

I.

THE GIFT

"THIS ONE IS special," his grandfather had told him. And it was.

Alex sat at his desk, alone in his bedroom, gazing at the old toy robot that stood beside his laptop, when he should have been looking at the screen.

The cursor blinked impatiently at him from his unfinished composition on the symbolism of the novel they were reading in English. He had started to write about decaying teeth, then given up. He didn't know what decaying teeth were supposed to symbolize, except maybe decay. He couldn't stretch that to eight hundred words.

The computer's clock showed 11:34 p.m. He leaned and pulled back the curtain. Outside, snow fell from a low and heavy British sky, gray clouds stained orange by drab suburban streetlights. A thin, gray-looking fox ran into the small back garden, something white in its mouth. The animal stopped, dropped whatever it was carrying, then lifted its head and barked out its harsh and awful cry.

As always, whenever he heard that shriek, Alex felt a chill crawl up his spine, over his scalp. The loneliest sound in the world.

The fox stood, head cocked. It screeched again. Faintly, Alex heard another, higher, answering bark. The fox picked up its food and trotted off. The friendless sound was not so friendless after all.

His computer chimed and his phone vibrated. On each, eight new messages. From eight different people. All saying the same thing:

YOUR GETTING IT PATHETIC FREAK

He deleted them, looked at his essay, typed some words, deleted them. He leaned back heavily in his chair.

His eyes settled on the photograph of his father on the wall above his desk. The only photograph he had ever seen of him. "Never liked anyone taking his picture," his mum always said when she looked at it, in the same sad, apologetic tone.

It showed the two of them, his dad and mum, caught in a red-black party haze. His mum young and happy, with bad hair. His dad behind, half turned away, blurring in the shadows. A vague, tall man, black hair pushed back from a high forehead. For the millionth time, Alex found himself squinting at the picture, trying almost to will it into focus. For the millionth time, the man refused to become any clearer.

His gaze returned to the robot. A small, bright army of these things lined three shelves above his desk, tin and plastic toy robots of all shapes and sizes, from all corners of the world. Battery-operated and clockwork, some new, the majority decades old. Many still in their deliriously illustrated boxes, or standing proudly beside them.

A few he had found himself, in thrift stores and online auctions. Most, though, the oldest and strangest, the most fantastic, had come from his grandfather, his father's father, who had started his collection, and his fascination.

The old man picked up these toys on his travels around the globe, and this newest robot—or rather, this oldest, for Alex sensed it was very old indeed—had just arrived out of the blue a few days earlier: a brick-shaped package in the post, brown paper tied with string, his grandfather's spidery scribble across the front. The parcel bore stamps and postmarks Alex didn't recognize at first—*Praha, Česká Republika*—and when he tore it open, he discovered newspaper scrunched up as wrapping inside, printed in a language that made no sense to him.

There was a plain white postcard, too, with his grandfather's scrawl, elegant yet somehow hasty:

> *Greetings from sunny Prague!*
> *What do you say to this ugly little brute?*

This one is special. Take good care!
See you soon.
I hope.

The toy stood about five inches tall and was wonderfully grotesque. Angry and pathetic-looking, it was made from a cheap, thin gray-green tin, with a bulky torso resembling an ancient boiler, held together with tiny rivets. Little dials were painted on its chest, as if it ran on steam. It grimaced with a mouth like a tiny letterbox, filled with a jagged nightmare of ferocious metal teeth. Its eyes were two holes, framing a hollow interior blackness.

Alex picked it up and brought it into the light from his desk lamp. Angling the lamp, he turned the robot, carefully.

Not carefully enough.

"Ow."

In places, the rough edges of old tin were sharp enough to draw blood. Dark red pulsed in a sticky stream from a scratch in his thumb.

Setting down the toy, he hissed and sucked at the cut while he hunted for tissues, wrapping one around the bleeding finger. He noticed he had left a thick red smear on the robot. Blood formed a bubble-like skin over one of its eyes. He poked another tissue in there, hoping not too much had leaked inside.

"If you only had a key," he murmured, rubbing more blood

away from the hole where the key to wind the clockwork mechanism would go. Often, keys from one old toy would fit another, but none in his collection had worked. He squinted into the inky eyeholes. In the space where the robot's head was welded to its hollow body, the tiniest dark edge of something was just visible. Part of the clockworks, he guessed, but when he tried to look directly at it, it faded from his sight.

Looking deeper, he was seized by something like the same icy, tingling sensation he had felt when he heard the fox crying. The room got heavy and cold. The robot's empty eyes stared up. At the periphery of his vision, Alex sensed the room beginning to dim, beginning to flicker, beginning to change, becoming like a room in some old, scratched sepia film.

Frozen, eyes wide, he saw himself now as if from above, saw himself sitting in this strange, changed room, saw things moving in the shadows. The world grew woozy. A dim figure, enormous and misshapen, stepped from a dark corner down there, stood hulking, unmoving, right behind him.

A cold white glow shone now from the toy robot's eyeholes, growing starker as the light around began to fade, until blackness and the glowing white eyeholes were all there was.

And then, there was only black.

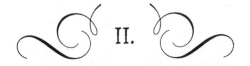

II.

THE UNEXPECTED GUEST

"ALEX."

A voice, gentle.

Then not so gentle: "Alex!"

He woke with a start, lifted his head too fast, sat dazed, surprised to find himself still at his desk, stiff from a night spent sleeping slumped over the computer keyboard. A small puddle of drool shone by the space bar.

His mother stood over him, trying to smooth down the strange quiff of hair that stuck up where he had been sleeping on it. In the other hand, she held a bowl of cereal.

"I've been shouting at you for half an hour. I keep telling you: get your homework done when you get in, then you won't have to stay up all night. Here." She handed him the bowl. "That, then shower. You've got about ten minutes before the bus."

After she left, Alex sat blinking, still stunned by sleep. He began to spoon cereal automatically into his mouth, then stopped, frowning, as half-caught memories started playing at the edges of his mind. His mother's voice from downstairs brought him back.

"Nine minutes!"

He shook his head, spooned faster.

His mother's shout halted him again as he was halfway down the street. Looking back, he could see her in her bath-robe, leaning over the gate, waving sheets of paper at him.

"You stay up half the night writing it," she said as he ran back, "then you leave it lying in the printer."

"What?" Alex puffed, reaching to take the pages. "What's this?"

"Honestly." She shivered, pulling her robe together at the neck. "About to turn thirteen, you'd think you'd be able to pack your own schoolbag. And now, if you don't mind, I'm going back in before I catch my death."

"But . . ." Alex stood staring at the pages. "But, I didn't," he tried again as the front door closed. He started reading. His English composition. Completed and spell-checked.

"But I didn't write this. At least, I don't think . . ."

A sharp rapping made him look up. His mother stood at the living room window, sipping tea from her Johnny Cash mug. She raised her eyebrows and made a shooing motion with her hand, turning it into a smile and a wave as he set off at a trot.

Slipping through snow, Alex reached the corner in time to see his bus signaling to pull away.

"No!"

He sprinted to the stop, where his right foot hit a patch of ice and skidded from under him. Going into a tumble, he landed hard in a sitting position, kept moving, sliding, watching in interested horror as his legs, splayed before him, headed directly into the path of the bus's very large back wheel as it started rolling forward.

The air under the bus was warmer, he noted. It smelled terribly of spent oil and rubber. He was about to watch his legs get crushed, he thought, weirdly calm.

The wheel stopped. He heard the hiss of brakes, the other hiss of the bus's door. Scrambling up, he walked shakily to the front of the vehicle, feeling his face flood red. The driver shook his head as he mounted the stairs.

"Honest to God, Alex. There'd have been another bus seven minutes from now. It's not worth it, mate, it's really not."

The doors hissed again as the bus lurched off.

"Loser," a girl named Alice Fenwick muttered as Alex passed up the aisle.

"Loser," her friend Patricia Babcock chorused.

"Thank you for your messages of last evening," Alex chirruped back, dusting snow from his trousers. "Your thoughts are always appreciated."

"Loser."

He swung into an empty seat and busied himself with the pages from his bag. His essay, just as he had started it, and, he realized as he read, just as he would have *finished* it, had he been able to marshal all his vague thoughts. It was pretty good.

He thought back. He remembered sitting at the computer, fuggily deleting and retyping the same lines. He remembered looking at the clock. The fox. The toy robot. Then waking this morning, slumped over his desk.

He must have woken and finished the composition during the night without remembering. Either that, or he had typed it while he was asleep. That was a thought. That would be fantastic. Auto-homework. Maybe he could train himself to do it.

His reverie was interrupted by his friend David Anderson sliding onto the seat beside him, already chewing the bubblegum he would keep working on for the rest of the day.

David leaned over, blew a green bubble, letting it pop before sucking it back in.

"God, did you get that done? I forgot until this morning. Let's have a look."

He lifted the pages easily from Alex's hand, read them over, frowning, cracking gum.

"Yeah," Alex began. "I'm not really sure about this, see—"

"Shut up," David said. "Your stuff's always brilliant. Miss Johnson loves you." He read on, blew out an impressed puff. "Yeah, man. That's brilliant. She's going to love this all over the place. I can't understand a word of it."

Alex began to say something, decided not to, shoved the pages back into his bag. As he did, his fingers touched something cold. Peering in, he saw the toy robot gazing up from the darkness with its empty eyes.

"Hey, how did you get in there?" Pulling it out, he offered it for David's inspection. "Check this dude out. This is the one I was telling you about."

As he handed it over, Alex felt something cold creep across his scalp. For half a second, he recalled the weird, woozy sensation he had felt the night before. But this was a much more familiar, much more mundane feeling.

Looking up, he saw the potatoey face and porcupine hair of Kenzie Mitchell leaning over from the seat behind, Alice Fenwick and Patricia Babcock at his shoulders, giggling. Kenzie was in the process of letting a long, thick loogie dribble from his mouth into Alex's hair. Across the aisle, the five other members of his little group sat snickering, interchangeable boys whose names Alex had never bothered to remember.

"All right, toy boy?" Kenzie said, slurping what was left of his spit back in and wiping his mouth. "You and your girlfriend playing with your dolls again?" He lunged and plucked the robot from David's hand, then swung back across the aisle.

"Look at this, boys," he said, holding it aloft. "Little freak's brought another freaky little toy to school."

Alex stepped into the aisle. "Give me that back."

"Whoa, look." Kenzie snickered. "It's getting angry. What's the matter, toy boy? Daddy never teach you to share? Oh, wait: don't have a daddy, do you? Just mummy and her boyfriend."

"Give me it."

"Or what—Jesus!" Kenzie stopped. The hand that held the

robot was running red. "Poxy thing's dangerous," he said. "Too dangerous for little toy boys like you. Not suitable for children under three. Reckon I'll have to keep it out your reach. In fact," he went on, rising and yanking open the window above his seat, "best thing would be to destroy it for your own safety."

"No, you won't. You'll give it back." Alex swallowed, mouth dry, copper-tasting, trying not to stutter. "Now."

"Will I? Or what?" Kenzie held the robot out the window, dangling above the cars swishing through the slush in the other direction, enjoying it. "What you going to do about it, fetus?"

It was the eternal Kenzie question. Alex had been pondering it for years.

A couple of grades ahead of him, Kenzie had been a leering cloud on his horizon since primary school. Alex retained the sharp memory of their first encounter, a jeer in the playground, a stubby finger pointing down: "Look! It's a wittle *BABY*-boy!"

When Alex had started there, he was small and young-looking even for a five-year-old. *Closer to three*, one teacher had murmured to another above his head. As it happened, she was wrong. In the same album from which he'd lifted the photograph of his mum and dad, there was a picture Alex particularly hated: himself at three, balanced bewildered on his mother's knee, a frail, pale, underdeveloped little creature, gazing out with owlish black eyes, oversized round head still bald, save for a few fragile wisps of downy baby hair.

Eventually, though, the puzzled prophecies of the endless doctors his mum had taken him to during those years proved true. None could find anything wrong, all promised everything would be right in time, and at around nine, his body had taken a sudden stretch and caught up with his classmates. His mother's constant worry gradually lifted and, with the older boy gone, his last two years at primary had been a happy, Kenzie-free zone.

But when he went to secondary school, he found Kenzie waiting. By now, the taunts—"It's the Umbilical Kid!"—were meaningless. Nevertheless, Kenzie's crew took it as gospel: he was a little freak. Whenever Kenzie rounded on him, Alex felt he was looking at that photograph of himself again. Or rather, still trapped *staring out* from that picture, still that strange, frozen little creature.

What you going to do about it?

Blood hammered in his ears. He felt his face burn, his hands tremble. He looked out at the spiteful staring faces swimming before him. Kenzie's hand waggling the robot out the window.

"I'm not going to do anything, Kenzie," he croaked. "All I'm saying is, I'd like you to give me that back, please."

As he spoke, Alex dimly felt a small, odd sensation, like something shifting slightly in his mind. And something curious happened. Kenzie grew silent. Color drained from his already pale face. He suddenly looked very young, and very sad—lost, even. He pulled the robot back in and, to the bewilderment of his gang and everyone else watching, solemnly handed it to Alex, before sitting down without another word, staring at his knees.

Sitting, Alex pulled a tissue from his pocket and wiped Kenzie's blood from the robot. He put the old toy back in his bag and zipped it shut.

The seats around remained silent for a spell, but, as the bus rumbled toward school, the usual morning buzz gradually grew again, although Kenzie's seats remained uncharacteristically subdued. After a while, David leaned to Alex.

"What was that? Jedi mind magic?"

"I don't know," Alex replied.

"Big respect, man." David whistled. "You need to teach me that stuff."

"I don't know," Alex said again, looking out at the grimy white streets rolling past the window.

"TOLD YOU SHE'D love your essay, man." David cracked a triumphant pop on his gum.

"Yeah, well, I wish she hadn't loved it."

"She went nuts! She was making classes two years above us read it this afternoon."

"And I wish she hadn't done that, either."

They were walking across the path worn into the grass toward the stop to catch the bus home.

"That bit about 'the bleached angst,'" David continued. "Awesome. What does that even mean? I'm going to use that. When I form my band, I'm going to call it the Bleached Angst." Then he said an odd thing. "Look out."

Alex looked at him, then the world lurched on its axis and grew dark.

His jacket had been pulled savagely over his head from behind. His bag pressed against his face. He couldn't see. Breathing was getting hard. He was pitching forward, hands tangled, helpless to break his fall. What felt like punches rained on his back on the way down. A muffled voice: ". . . bad enough we have to read Shakespeare, now she's got us reading *you*?"

Sprawled on the grass, Alex felt a few misaimed kicks glance off his leg. He braced himself for more but none came. He rose to his knees and pulled his head free from his jacket.

The first thing he saw was Kenzie. Kenzie lying on the ground. Kenzie lying on the ground with all his friends standing around him. All of Kenzie's friends looking up, looking angry but uncertain. And standing over Kenzie, a tall, elegant figure in a long dove-gray coat, a hand in a dove-gray glove holding a long black cane with a silver tip. The silver tip pressed hard to Kenzie's throat.

"Oh, God," Alex moaned. "Grandad."

"Hello, Alex," the old man said cheerily, ignoring the bulky fifteen-year-old gasping at his feet. "Just got into town, dropped in on your mother. Figured I'd come see if I could catch you, maybe have some fish and chips and a catch-up."

"*Gttthhhhhhh,*" said Kenzie.

"Shall we do that?" Alex's grandfather went on. "Fish and chips? And a catch-up? With mushy peas? I've not had decent chips for months."

"Hssssstthhh."

"Grandad, could you let him go?"

"Let him . . . ? Oh, you mean this?" He stepped back, lifting his cane. "There you go, young man, up you pop."

Kenzie hauled himself to his feet, rubbing his red neck.

"Big mistake, Grandad," he seethed in a strangled voice. His staring friends crowded forward. "Don't go walking around on your own. And, you"—he pointed at Alex—"I'll see *you* later."

He turned and started to walk away, but then he was lying on his back again, having tripped somehow over the old man's cane. Alex's grandfather leaned over him, pressing the stick gently to his chest. But not so gently, apparently, that Kenzie could move it.

"That's no way to talk." He grinned.

"I'm going to have the cops on you!" Kenzie spluttered.

"Let you in on a little secret, old chap." Alex's grandfather bowed lower, voice suddenly cold. "I *am* the cops, son. And I'll go walking anywhere I please, on my own or not. And you had better hope that I don't see you later, or even hear about you."

He stood back, let Kenzie to his feet, and watched with a pleasant smile until he and his friends had sloped out of sight. "Now," he said, "fish and chips?"

"Not for me," David said, grinning, beginning a backward jog toward the bus stop. "*Serious* respect, man," he called to Alex's grandfather as he turned.

"Much appreciated." The old man beamed.

"Why did you tell him you were a policeman?" Alex asked as

they trudged between snowdrifts in the direction of the chip shop.

"Did I say that?"

"You know you did."

"I have no idea why I would say that." His grandfather frowned. A meager new snow had started, soft white flakes mingling with his crown of thick white hair. "What a strange thing to say."

They walked in silence for a while.

"Uhm," his grandfather said eventually. "Back there. Has that been happening a lot? Does your mother know?"

"It's nothing," Alex said, looking away. "Just a moron. Don't have to worry Mum about it."

"Oh, you don't have to worry about Anne. Bravest person I know, your mother. Tougher than all of us put together."

They trod on without speaking again, but Alex could sense the old man struggling to leave the subject alone.

"You know," his grandad finally burst out, "people like that, you really should stand up to them. I mean, you were raised never to start a fight, I know that. But it doesn't hurt to know how to finish one."

"Grandad." Alex concentrated on staring at the snow under his feet. "A kid in my year got stabbed in a fight last month. He's still in the hospital. I know what you're saying, but things have changed. It's not like when you were young anymore. I can handle it. I just try to keep my head down. I'd rather not get involved."

"Well, yes, but sometimes . . ." His grandfather stopped. "No. I suppose you're right. Times have changed." He smiled. "A wise old head on those young shoulders. Whereas I'm more the other way around."

"That's not such a bad way to be." Alex smiled back, glad the subject was changing. "So long as I'm around to keep you out of trouble."

In the restaurant, Alex munched a small portion of chips and watched happily as his grandfather demolished the biggest plate of battered haddock and chips the waitress could bring, unbuttoning first the jacket, then waistcoat of his immaculate suit to accommodate extra peas and buttered bread, washed down with pots of stewed tea.

"This stuff," the old man mumbled through a full mouth, holding up the remains of a slice he'd been using to wipe his plate, "is extremely bad for you. White bread, and what's worse, with butter. You should never, ever eat this. It's far too late for me, of course. When I grew up, none of us knew any better. But you should take care of yourself. Never eat it." He popped the morsel, dripping with pea juice and ketchup, into his mouth, making a contented noise that actually sounded like *yum*. "Quite ridiculously bad for you. Now, how's your mother?"

"She's doing okay."

"Um-huh. And the Idiot?"

"Carl's not that bad," Alex replied.

"Ha! *You* were the one moaning about him to *me*!"

"That was months ago. That was the time he said, 'Don't you think you're getting too old to be playing with toy robots?'"

"And what was it you said to him again?" His grandfather leaned in, grinning conspiratorially. Anticipation played about his face.

"I told him I didn't play with them. And I told him a robot like one I bought for five pounds had sold for six hundred dollars on eBay. That seemed to change his mind about it."

"No, no, that wasn't it," his grandfather said, petulant. "That wasn't it at all. What was it you said when he said, 'Don't you think you're getting too old . . .'?"

Alex sighed. "Okay, I said: 'And don't you think you're getting too old to be wearing T-shirts of bands who are all half your age?'"

"Splendid!" his grandfather roared, clapping his hands. "Excellent!"

"Really, though. He's okay. He's okay to me, and he makes Mum laugh and he looks out for her. You should give him a chance."

"I know," his grandfather said, quietly now, gazing down at his empty plate with eyes looking much further down than that. He smiled back up. "Wise head. Come on, let's get home."

"YOU OKAY?" ALEX said as they stepped from the bus. His grandfather stood glancing around the street.

"Hmm?" The old man was looking off over his shoulder. He turned and peered ahead again, flashed a grin, and started walking. "Yes, fine. Oh, now tell me, how's that new, well, that old robot I sent you?"

"See for yourself." Alex rooted in his bag and held the thing up.

His grandfather stopped, suddenly serious and cross.

"You had it *out*? You took it to *school*?"

"No. Well, yes, but—"

"Goodness' sakes, Alex," the old man snapped. "It's not a toy. Well, of course, it is a toy, but you know what I mean."

"No, but listen. I didn't take it out with me. I mean, I didn't mean to. It must have fallen into my bag, I just found it in there this morning."

"Oh." His grandfather pulled at his bottom lip as they resumed walking. "I see. I'm sorry. May I?" He held out a hand.

Alex gave him the robot and watched as he inspected it, turning it carefully, squinting as he held it up to the street-lights.

"Uh-huh. Well, no damage done." He handed the toy back. "Maybe pay to have a look in your bag before you leave the house, though."

"Yeah," Alex said, pushing open the gate. "Mum was saying the same thing."

"Clever woman, your mother." His grandfather nodded, adding, as the door opened to reveal Carl wrestling out a bulging bag of recycling, "most of the time."

A little later, they all sat at the kitchen table. Alex watched his grandfather decimate a plate of biscuits and pretend to be interested in what his mother and Carl were telling him about their plans to extend the room by four feet when they got the money together. He could tell there was something on the old man's mind. When his grandad rubbed his chin, drummed his fingers, and said, "Well, now, so," Alex knew he was getting around to it.

"I was thinking"—he beamed at Alex—"that old robot. It's rather a curiosity. I can't quite place it. Now, I have to pop over to France, and I have a friend there—a dealer, in Paris—who might be able to help identify where and when it comes from. Would you mind terribly if I took it with me for him to have a look at? I'd be sure to take care of it, old chap.

"I mean," he continued, pulling at his ear, "ideally, I'd love for you to come along and see his place. He has wonderful pieces, has Harry, amazing old toys and gizmos. But, you know, can't have you missing school. But next time, for certain—"

"But we only have a couple of days of school left," Alex interrupted. "The holidays start next week. I could come with you. Couldn't I, Mum?"

He looked at his mother, who turned to his grandfather with the beginnings of a nod, a smile, and a yes, all of which faded as she saw the worried look on the old man's face, the slight shake of his head.

"Well, no, son," she said, looking back to Alex. "You can't

just take days off school. And your grandfather won't want you in the way; he'll have his work to do."

"Next time, for definite." His grandfather smiled sadly.

"Yeah. Sure, okay." Alex knew he hadn't concealed his disappointment. "I should go up and do my homework."

BY 11:34 P.M. on the computer's clock, he had finally admitted to himself he had long given up on the last three math questions. He would ask David about them on the bus tomorrow. David was miles better at math.

Sitting chin in hands, staring idly at the old robot, Alex noticed a small black spot beside the hole where the key should go. Licking his finger, he rubbed at it, looked at the red smear. A little dried blood. He used his sleeve to polish it clean.

The bus tomorrow. He winced.

Things had taken on a more serious edge with Kenzie the past week. Alex's project "Like Clockwork: An Illustrated History of the Toy Robot, from Postwar Tin to Tomorrow's Tech" had been voted winner at the end-of-term Christmas exhibition, beating Kenzie's glossy, multiscreen presentation of "Soccer Stars' Sports Cars." Kenzie's father had paid a lot of money for a former soccer player to make an appearance and bring his car with him, but people had been more interested in winding up Alex's old toys and watching them walk.

There had been a hard punch to the back of his head in the

corridor the next day, the promise of more to come. After his run-in with Alex's grandfather, Kenzie would be out for serious revenge. Maybe that's why he'd felt so keen to get away on a trip with the old man.

Alex sighed and turned to the window. Pushing back the curtains, he was surprised to see his grandfather in the dim garden below. He stood silent and alone with his back to the house, leaning on his cane, watching the night. He looked almost as though he was on guard. A thin line of smoke rose from a cigarette in his right hand.

Alex pushed open the window, letting in the knifing air.

"I wish you'd stop," he called as the old man turned sharply at the sound.

"Huh? Oh." He waved the cigarette. "Quite right. Absolutely disgusting habit. What I'm doing here, Alex, is vile and stupid and unimaginably bad for you. You really must promise me that you will never, ever do it. Seriously. Of course, it's far, far too late for me. When I grew up, none of us knew any better. But never take this up. Or, if you do, wait until you're about seventy-four before you start. And take care of yourself until then."

"You could stop if you really wanted."

"Ha. Well, let's see." He puffed again at the cigarette, let it drop to the snow, snubbing it out with his cane.

"Well, look at that." He grinned. "True enough. I've stopped. Alex, you don't mind me not taking you with me, do you? You know I'd love to have you along. It's high time we took a trip again. It's just that things will be a little hectic this time out."

"It's okay." Alex forced a smile. "Watch you don't get cold. I'll see you in the morning. Good night, Grandad."

"G'night, Alex."

III.

A RUDE AWAKENING

HE BECAME AWARE he was awake.

Alex lay on his back in bed, eyes focusing on the thin, dim orange line on the ceiling, where street light squeezed in through the curtains.

Something had woken him. He lay listening, trying to work out what it might have been.

The room was dark, silent. The house around it dark and silent, save for the slow tick of the clock in the hall downstairs. His eyelids wanted to close. He let them.

Seven ticks later, his eyes popped wide. He had definitely heard something. A small *click*. Followed by a smaller *whirr*. Frowning, fully awake now, he strained to catch it again.

Click. Whirrrrr. Click. Whirrrrr.

Alex sat bolt upright, peering in the direction of the noise. The noise stopped. Reaching out, he pushed the switch on the reading lamp above his bed.

Click. Whirrrrr.

The sound came from somewhere around his desk. He couldn't think what could be making it. His eyes ran over the pile of math books, the unlit desk lamp, his laptop, the old toy robot beside it.

His jacket hung over the chair, his schoolbag over that. He thought about his cell phone, in his jacket, but he knew he had turned it off—the usual evening's worth of texts from Kenzie and crew would be waiting in the morning. Anyway, it wasn't that sort of sound.

Alex wet his lips. Kenzie. Maybe his grandfather had pushed the bully over the edge. Maybe instead of virtual harassment, Kenzie had come in person tonight, to finish him off.

Alex turned to his window in alarm. Nothing. He looked back at the door, his desk, the chair.

And there.

Just visible, behind the chair leg, the edge of . . . something. Something that shouldn't be behind the leg of his chair.

He angled the lamp to shine on that spot, sending long shadows shifting around the room. He stared at the thing, trying to identify it. The small shape remained mysterious and, the longer he stared in the dim yellow light, somehow more threatening.

Click. Whirrrrr.

The whatever it was edged back out of sight.

Puzzled, Alex stepped one foot out of bed. There came a furious little run of many clicks and whirrs, and the something came out from behind the chair, moving fast, into the middle of the floor, where it stopped.

Startled, Alex pulled his leg quickly back under the covers and sat blinking at the thing on the carpet.

A toy robot.

One he had never seen. It looked old, like clockwork. Red mottled tin. Boxy and square, with tiny vents in its chest and a sad little face painted onto a cube head topped with a flimsy wire hoop, like an ancient TV antenna. With a *whirrrrr*, the head turned, until the face seemed to be looking at him.

Alex sat transfixed.

Whirrrrr. Click.

This time, the robot on the floor hadn't moved. This sound was coming from somewhere else.

Lifting his eyes with effort, Alex looked behind it.

There were two.

This one was much the same design but silvery blue. It was somehow climbing, *whirrrrr, click, whirrrrr, click*, up the leg of his chair, as though heading toward his desk.

The red robot stood, looking disconcertingly like it was watching him. The blue robot climbed higher, scrambling onto the seat of the chair with awkward little movements that would have been funny, were they not so weird.

Keeping his eyes fixed on the red robot, and with no clear plan in his suddenly empty mind, Alex, moving very slowly, started gingerly to lift the bedcovers away.

A sudden, fast *click-click-click-click-click* made him freeze. This sound was angry, and very close.

Alex turned toward the bottom of his bed, where there now stood a small, thin, white robot with a head like an elongated egg and sharp silvery arms. The face on this one was frowning.

Eyes wide, Alex sat motionless, watching as this thing pulled itself steadily up the bed toward him. He opened his mouth to shout but found he couldn't remember how.

Click, click, click, click, click.

He felt it click and clamber along his leg.

Click, click, click, click, click.

Onto his belly.

Click, click, click.

Onto his chest.

Click, click.

It finally stopped where Alex's folded hands lay on top of the quilt. There, with a *click*, it cocked its head, frowning its painted frown.

Neither of them moved for what felt like a long time.

Click.

The thing shook its head from side to side.

Click.

One of its little arms raised. Alex saw that it tapered to a point as sharp as a needle. A thin brown liquid dripped from the tip.

Click.

Only when the robot's arm came down with a violent jabbing motion did he realize it was trying to stab him.

Several things happened almost at once. The robot's needle-arm plunged through the sleeve of his pajamas, narrowly missing his skin, down on into the thick quilt, which Alex, finally managing a cry not nearly as loud as he had wanted, threw violently away from him, sending the white robot flying clicking backward through the air.

Beyond the foot of the bed, his door was thrown open, and his grandfather came bursting in. With one fluid motion, the old man brought his cane up and neatly caught the white robot on the end, plucking it from the air and redirecting its momentum toward the floor, bringing the tip of the cane down onto its belly and pinning it there while its spiky arms whirled.

"Alex. Window," he said.

"Buh—" Alex managed.

"Alex," his grandfather said, with a firm but pleasant nod. "Open the window, there's a good chap."

Flinging himself from bed, Alex ripped back the curtains and pulled the window up as far as he could.

"Now, stand back, if you don't mind." Wielding his cane like a golfer pitching in the rough, his grandfather scooped the flailing white robot up in a smooth arc that sent it sailing *click-click-click-click* out into the night.

"Buh—" said Alex again. He gestured wildly at the red robot whirring over the carpet toward his grandfather's feet, and at his desk, across which the blue robot was now clicking at surprising speed.

"Yes," the old man said. "Good point."

Reaching into his coat pocket, he scattered what looked like white powder over Alex's desk. As the stuff fell around it, the blue robot stopped moving.

The red robot almost at his foot, Alex's grandfather kicked out, sending it flying toward the window but not quite making his target. It bounced off the frame, falling writhing at Alex's feet. With a surge of panicked inspiration, he dropped to his knees and heaved his bed up, dragging it over. Just as the old man said something like "Alex, no!" he let the leg drop heavily onto the little robot's chest, crushing it, splitting it open as its arms and legs whirred and clicked.

On his desk, the blue robot was trying to walk again, but with erratic movements, stumbling in ragged circles closer and closer to the edge, until it finally fell over, at which point, swinging his cane while it was still in the air, Alex's grandfather batted it surely out through the window.

Kneeling, the old man raised Alex's bed and pulled it off the crushed red robot, which had stopped moving.

"It's . . ." Alex said.

His grandfather produced a large white handkerchief and spread it on the floor, delicately beginning to place the jagged, glistening remains of red robot on it.

"It's . . ." Alex repeated, pointing. "It's wet. Inside it . . . Wet."

"Yes," his grandfather murmured, knotting the handkerchief into a loose, messy bundle. "I'd rather hoped we might avoid that part. I really don't like to kill them if I can help it."

"What—" Alex began, waving his hand at his desk, trying to catch hold of at least one of the scramble of thoughts racing around his mind. "White stuff? The—the white stuff. You threw."

"Huh? Oh, salt. Just salt." His grandfather stood, handkerchief dangling sadly from his hand, looking damp, a little pink. "I stocked up on packets at the chip shop. They don't like it. Confuses them."

"What—" Alex tried again.

"Never mind that right now. I need to check outside."

He turned—then stopped and turned back, stood considering Alex. Gripping him by his shaking shoulders, he steered him gently to the bed and sat him down. Dropping to one knee, he waited until Alex's eyes locked on his, brown on brown.

"Alex," he said softly. "You know, you look very much like your father did when he was your age? Listen, now. I'm going to check outside. Then we're going to write your mother a note to say we've changed our minds, and you're coming to Paris with me after all, off for the early connection. I don't think you should stay here now. We can phone her later. Now: pack a bag. Not too much. You have a bag?"

Alex nodded.

"Good man." His grandfather patted his shoulder and left, leaving Alex sitting openmouthed.

He stared at the scattered salt grains shining on his desk. He shivered at the touch of icy air from outside. He looked at the window, his mind replaying the image of the white robot flying through it, rattling out its clicks. He shivered more.

His grandfather leaned his head back in the door.

"Chop-chop. Train to catch. And make sure you bring *that*."

He pointed his cane at the old toy robot on Alex's desk.

STATION TO STATION

DUMPING HIS HASTILY packed rucksack on the kitchen table beside the old man's gray Gladstone bag, Alex found his grandfather in the back garden, bent over his cane, studying the ground.

There were two small dents in the snow beneath Alex's bedroom window. Two frosty little lines of square tracks led woozily off toward the missing plank in the fence with next door's garden, crossing over a fresh set of fox prints.

"They've gone? *They've gone?!* Where've . . . Did you . . . ?" Alex looked frantically around. An image from an old *Tom and Jerry* cartoon flashed strangely in his mind: the legs and feet of a woman standing on a stool, screaming because the mouse was loose. He strained to reel his thoughts in, stay calm. "Where've they gone?"

"Not far, I shouldn't think." Still bent, the old man strode to the fence, Alex at his heels. Peering over, they could see the tracks ended just beyond, beside two sets of human footprints that led off from where they had come, into the darkness. One set had been made by shoes a bit bigger than Alex's. The others were smaller, the feet of a child.

His grandfather straightened and looked at the sky, now cloudless, a deep indigo dotted with pinpoint stars, no sign of a moon. Throwing back his head, he inhaled a lungful of the biting air, let it out in a long, contented sigh of steam, beating his chest lightly with both fists. "Now. You've got the, ah, robot?"

Alex nodded.

"Splendid. Taxi's on its way. I've written a note for your mother. You should add something. And tell her you'll call her later. And a kiss."

"But—"

"Come on. Time's a-wasting."

As Alex sat scribbling at the kitchen table, the old man strode through to the front of the house, watching the street. "Think this is our cab," he called softly. "Now. Sure you have everything you want?"

Alex nodded. Then: "No, wait."

Grabbing his rucksack, he ran as quietly as he could back up to his room, took the picture of his mum and dad from the wall, and tucked it deep inside his bag.

At the door to the bedroom where his mum was sleeping and Carl was snoring, Alex hesitated. He raised a hand to the door. He dropped it. He padded quickly downstairs.

His grandfather stood impatient on the front step. A black

cab puttered at the gate, framed by exhaust fumes that hung like a wreath in the air.

"If we're quite ready."

As they glided through dim, empty streets, Alex's racing pulse slowed. His mood settled from swarming confusion to something like irritation as his grandfather refused to answer any questions, electing instead to strike up a long conversation with the cabdriver about the government.

"Interesting fellow," he said to Alex as the taxi left them in the forecourt of the local train station. "Mad as a loon."

In the deserted waiting room, heat pipes coughed gently while Alex's grandfather waved his questions away again, preferring to spend his time wrestling with a spattered drinks machine. Turning finally with two cups, he proffered one to Alex.

"Hot chocolate. Allegedly. Most likely hideous, but drink it down; sugar'll do you some good." He sipped gingerly at his own. "Ye gads."

On the almost empty early train to London, his grandad stubbornly continued to refuse to address any of Alex's questions. "We've got about two hours," he said settling back opposite Alex. "Should grab some sleep."

"*Sleep?!* I can't—"

The old man shushed him. "I think you'll find you're feeling very sleepy. Very sleepy, indeed." He spoke as lightly as ever, but his eyes seemed to burn, boring through the air between them. Alex sat staring back with a tight, angry frown. But after a short while, he felt his eyelids grow heavy.

The sleep was deep and punctured by fragments of a vivid, jumbled dream. He was a very small boy again, and his grandfather was taking him and his mother on yet another journey to see yet another doctor. Hospital corridors and hospital rooms. Weighing machines and measuring tapes, needles and wires. Blood samples and strange fingers testing his skin. The old man watching gravely from the corner, grim concern in his eyes. His mother trying to keep her anxiety hidden as she sat forward, listening to results that solved nothing, squeezing Alex's hand.

He woke only once before London, opening his eyes barely a second, to see his grandfather sitting up very straight and very awake, staring bleakly out the window at the shadowy world falling away from him.

BY THE TIME they were walking through St. Pancras station, hunting for their platform, Alex had almost begun to doubt anything of the night before had actually happened.

The station was already busy in the early morning. People wearing harassed expressions pushed past in all directions. Advertisements and TV news blazed on bright screens. A group of nursery workers struggled to keep a small, excited line of children together. A girl of around ten with a pale moon face and long black hair stood holding a red balloon beside a small man wearing a startlingly bright yellow scarf with black dots. His eyes were lost behind the shining lenses of large, round glasses. As Alex looked, the girl, returning his stare with a frown, calmly let go of her balloon. It floated straight up in the crystalline shafts of light pouring through the high glass ceiling.

Place names and numbers flickered and flashed on display boards. Indecipherable messages echoed over the loudspeaker. His grandfather moved beside him at a happy stride. The day, the planet, all seemed deeply normal.

As the train to Paris pulled out, Alex's grandfather popped the cork on a small bottle of champagne.

"Drinking alcohol in the morning is a very bad idea," he said as he poured himself a healthy plastic glassful and pushed Alex's orange juice to him across the tabletop. "Drinking during the day at all is a bad idea. You should never do that. Seriously. But especially in the morning. Then again, it's not every day you catch the train to Paris. And there is a school of thought that says champagne doesn't count."

He raised the glass in a toasting motion, swigged a little, smacked his lips, and sighed in satisfaction. "Splendid. Now, then. Questions. One at a time."

Alex put both elbows on the table and rested his forehead on the heels of his hands, fingers working at his scalp as he tried to think where to begin. He pushed back his hair and took a deep breath.

"Okay. Right: was I just attacked in my bedroom by three toy robots last night?"

"Mm. More or less. Yes."

"Where did they *come* from? Why were they after *me*? How—"

"Hold on. One at a time, I said. But we can take those two together. They weren't after you, not really. They were after . . . Well, I'm sure you've guessed what they were after by now. And *they* weren't really after it; they were sent by someone who is. So, ah, that's where they came from."

"After *it*?" Alex, the events of the previous night suddenly tumbling vividly through his mind again, heard his voice rise in outrage, but he didn't care. He opened his rucksack and pulled out the old toy robot, shaking it under his grandfather's nose. "After this?"

"That's right. Don't wave it around like that, Alex, there's a good fellow. In fact . . ." He pulled his Gladstone down from the overhead rack, started rooting through it. "Yes, here we are."

He produced a sturdy white cardboard box, about half the size of a shoebox, lifted the lid, and pushed it to Alex. Inside was another, smaller box of thinner card. Picking it up, Alex noted that it was slightly worn at the edges, but still in generally excellent condition. The same bold illustration was printed on all four sides: a cartoonish painting of the robot he held in his other hand, stalking angrily down a dark street of jagged buildings. Blue steam rose from its rusted-pipe ears, forming a cloud that framed a single word in thick red letters: ROBOT.

"The box," Alex said, thoughts of the thoroughly bizarre

circumstances he was in momentarily fading as his collecting reflexes took over. "Wow. Where did you find that?"

"Ah-ha. Isn't it wonderful? I finally tracked this down in a little shop in Austria. Next door to the most wonderful bakers in the entire world, as it turns out. The woman there, she makes this bread, and, oh, these cakes. Well, not quite *cakes*, they're like horns of sugared pastry, filled with shavings of apple and—"

"No. Stop that. Wait." Alex shook his head, trying to clear it or shake something loose. He was getting nowhere.

Outside, a brown-and-white blur of flat English fields mottled with snow rolled silently past. His grandfather poured himself a second glass of champagne, emptying the last drops from the little bottle by holding it upside down.

"Who's after it?" Alex asked, trying to focus and stay calm.

"Hmm? Ah, well, now, of that, I'm not sure."

"You're not sure?"

"Not entirely sure, no."

"But it's someone who . . ." Alex trailed off, feeling ridiculous. "Someone who sends . . . toy robots out . . . to do things."

"It would appear so, yes."

"And you've seen these . . . robots before."

"Well"—his grandfather paused, glass held to pursed lips—"yes, there's no point denying that now."

"Okay, wait a minute, let me think."

The notion of asking his grandfather where he had seen the things before seemed appealing. But he needed to stay on track. "Okay. So, when you've seen them before, did you know who they belonged to?"

"Ah . . . yes. I had a good idea."

"And you don't think it might possibly be the same person who sent them last night?" Alex shouted.

"Simmer down, Alex."

His grandfather raised his drink in a salute to a portly couple across the aisle, peering down sharp, wrinkled noses at Alex as though he was the source of a bad smell. "Adolescence!" He rolled his eyes. "Hormones! You remember, eh?"

The couple aimed their noses at him, before turning away, each raising a large pinkish newspaper. Alex's grandfather turned back.

"Okay, yes, it might have been the same person, but I can't say that for certain, now, can I?"

"Oh, no, I suppose not," Alex fumed quietly. "No, because, I mean, there must be *hundreds* of people out there with . . ." He stopped again, running up against the ludicrousness of what he was saying. "Little gangs of . . . toy . . . Right, I get it. You're just not going to tell me who it is, are you?" He crossed his arms and threw himself back in his seat.

"What difference would it make, old chap? You wouldn't know the name anyway. All you really need to know is that it's someone who wants *that*." His grandfather pointed at the old robot. "And rather badly. And who, as you know, has peculiar methods."

"*Peculiar methods?* That . . . *thing* tried to kill me last night."

"Oh, no." His grandfather drained his glass and looked at it with a melancholy half smile. "No, I shouldn't say it was trying to kill you. Although, of course, I didn't get a chance to find out what was on its needles. But I'd say it was more likely something that would have put you to sleep."

"Oh." Alex swallowed the shout he was about to let out and leaned in, speaking in a furiously reasonable whisper. "Oh, *well* then. That's *different*. If it was just a toy robot who was there to *knock me out* while its other toy robot *friends* stole another toy robot from my *bedroom*, that's a whole different situation. You're right, I don't know what I'm making all this *fuss* about."

"Sarcasm, Alex"—his grandfather frowned—"is the lowest form of wit."

"But how . . ." Alex searched the questions now jumping for position at the front of his mind. "How did they work? What were they . . . like, radio-controlled?"

"Well, something like that."

"Wait. I remember: that one, it was wet inside."

"Ah." His grandfather gave a sickly smile and turned to the window. "Yes."

"And you said you didn't like to kill . . . They weren't *alive?*"

"Alex." The old man tutted. "That would be ridiculous. Although, on the other hand, you do raise a very interesting philosophical point. How do we define life? Do we even have the right? Tell me, did you ever get around to watching that film I bought you, *2001: A Space Odyssey*?"

"*What?!?* No. I fell asleep. It was really dull."

"Alex, you really should try and stretch yourself a little more when it comes to cinema. I mean, you read all kinds of books, and, well, anyway. There's a computer in that film, you see, called HAL. Actually there's a very interesting story about why he's called HAL—"

"No. Please. Stop. Okay. The robot last night. It was wet inside. What was that . . . battery acid or . . . some kind of oil . . . like hydraulics?"

His grandfather sat gazing out the window at nothing in particular. He tapped a finger at his bottom lip, drew it thoughtfully along his chin. His eyes dropped to the table, then rose to meet Alex's again.

"As I said, I had hoped not to have to go into any of this, Alex, old chap. But here we are, you're asking, and there's no way around it. So. It's not hydraulics, no. It's pieces of . . . well . . ."

"Pieces of what?"

"People, Alex. Pieces of people."

The train rushed on into the tunnel beneath the sea.

ALEX WAS LYING in bed. If he opened his eyes, there was the ceiling. There was the orange paper lampshade he hated, hanging thick with dust. If he turned his head to the right, he would see his posters. If he turned to the left, he would see the pile of unfinished homework on his desk.

It had all been a dream. Any moment, his mum was going to come in and shake him and tell him he was going to be late for school. He'd need to remember to ask David about the math. And then there was Kenzie to be avoided somehow. Here Mum comes now. There's the knock at the door. There she is, leaning over him. She opens her mouth, she opens her mouth, she opens her mouth, and she says:

"I wonder, do you think you could find me some decent coffee and a couple of croissants on there? And for you, Alex?"

Alex opened his eyes and stared at his grandfather, who sat across from him, half-turned to the man pushing the trolley up the aisle of the train. He had been trying hard to will himself to wake up from this dream. But it seemed that he was awake, and this was the reality he was stuck with.

"Alex?"

He didn't know how long he had been sitting like that, but his face had set in a sore, frozen grimace.

"Alex." The old man leaned forward, tapped a finger on his sleeve.

"Huh?"

"Fancy a spot of something to eat?"

Alex frowned harder at him.

"Just my coffee and croissants," his grandfather said, turning back to the trolley. "Oh, and some of that jam. And I'll have a few of these, if you don't mind." Leaning around the cart, he came back brandishing a bulging fistful of salt packets. The man pouring his coffee raised an eyebrow in mild disgust.

"Can never have too much salt." The old man beamed up at him.

"Okay," Alex said, watching the trolley trundle slowly off down the carriage. He leaned forward again, rubbed at his forehead, tried a breath. "So. Pieces of . . . people." He watched his grandfather lather jam onto a torn-off corner of croissant. "You mean dead people?"

"Ew," his grandfather said, pulling a face. He popped the croissant into his mouth. A dollop of jam dripped off and landed thick, wet, and red at the feet of the toy robot on the table between them.

"Dear me. How does your mind work, Alex? That would be hideous. No, living people. You know: a single donor for each robot. Just patches of skin and blood and . . . such. Hair, maybe. Some spit, and perhaps, if they're really serious, little scrapes from inside of . . . Well, you get the idea."

"Single donor," Alex repeated, nodding pleasantly, as though they were discussing his biology homework. "And that would be the person who's wanting to steal my toy robot?"

"No." His grandfather slurped his coffee and winced. "Muck. No, I shouldn't say so. Those things last night were rather too easily dealt with. Just two little lookers and a stinger. No, if they'd come from him, we would have known all about it. More likely someone working for him."

Alex nodded again, noting the *him*. At least he knew it was a man. He opened his mouth, closed it. Trying to think, he glanced up past his grandfather.

In other seats, people sat talking and reading, tapping laptops, prodding tablets, staring at phones, nodding to earphones. The man pushing the refreshments cart was almost at the end of the carriage. As Alex watched, the door down there whished open. A small, dark figure pushed in past the trolley, a girl in black. She came walking carefully up the carriage, turning her round, milky face left and right, searching the seats. She wore a sleeveless black top, with long black-and-purple-striped arm warmers covering from wrists to pale elbows.

No one seemed to be thinking about flesh-powered robots coming at them in the night. The sheer weight of normality around their table struck Alex forcefully.

"Right," he said, looking back to his grandfather. "I've had it."

He glanced up at the girl, halfway along the carriage now. Her gaze swept over Alex, returned to him, and locked. She stopped, stood staring at him. There was something about her face. He recognized her as the girl from the station with the red balloon. That must have been it. He wondered if she was lost. Automatically, he started scanning around for the little man he had seen with her, but when he looked back, she had turned, leaving the carriage the way she had come.

"All this," Alex went on, "is just nonsense. People with little robots filled with bits of skin that they can control somehow. It's just nonsense."

His grandfather had twisted around to follow Alex's gaze, looking off up the carriage. Turning back, he frowned, a little hurt. Then he grinned.

"Good show, Alex. That's the stuff. Skeptical mind. You're quite right. Everything I've been telling you is utterly ridiculous. Plainly, it can't possibly be what's going on. There must be some other, more rational explanation. And someday very soon, I hope that you and I can sit down over a good long lunch and have a proper conversation about it, see if we can't thrash it all out."

Leaning forward, he picked up the robot from the table and deftly slipped it inside the old box, putting that back inside the other box and closing the lid.

"For the moment, though," the old man continued, standing, "the nonsense is what we're stuck with. Sometimes there isn't time to think things all the way through. You just have to accept what's happening and get on and deal with it."

Reaching over, he picked up Alex's rucksack, shoved the box inside, and zipped it shut. He stood, holding the bag out to Alex.

"Now. It's about time we got you to the toilet."

"*What?*" Alex was genuinely outraged all over again. "I'm not a little kid! I don't need to *go* to the toilet."

"Yes. You do." His grandfather had one hand in Alex's armpit, hauling him up, slipping the rucksack over his shoulder. "Now. And quickly."

Lifting his Gladstone and ignoring Alex's rising complaints, he began bustling him backward out of the carriage.

Alex started another round of protests, but as he looked past his grandfather's elbow, the words died in his throat.

At the far end of the car, two big men in black suits with heads as bald as cue balls were coming through the door, walking very quickly and very grimly.

And very definitely coming straight for them.

"KEEP GOING," HIS grandfather said.

"Who—?" Alex started.

"Quick as you can now, Alex."

He trotted faster, looking wildly about at the blurring, oblivious faces in the seats as they passed. They had already gone through two carriages. As they came to the next set of doors, Alex looked back to see the men already entering the car behind them. He hurried on.

They came out into a different kind of carriage, no seats, more like a corridor. A toilet was set into a curving wall on the left. The sound of the train rushing over the tracks was much louder in here. His grandfather opened the toilet door and pushed him inside, tossing his Gladstone onto the sink.

"Now. Lock this behind me. Don't open until I knock. I'll knock like this." He rapped sharply with his cane, three rapid taps, two longer ones, then stepped quickly back out and pulled the door closed, leaving Alex alone in the small gray room.

Alex pulled the door open again. "But—"

"Alex!" his grandfather snapped. Beyond him, the two men were coming into the corridor. "Lock it!"

He felt himself being pushed back. The door ripped out of his grasp and slammed shut. He leapt to the lock and turned it. He stood looking at his hands on the lock.

The copper taste in his mouth. A small, pallid version of himself, panicking in the mirror above the sink. The sounds of the train's steel wheels rattling furiously.

He stood back, examining the door for a way to see out. Nothing. He pressed against it, listening.

All he could hear was the train.

He pushed until his ear got sore, listening as hard as he could. Muffled seconds dragged past. Suddenly, the door shuddered mightily against his cheek as something crashed into the other side, sending him jumping back in fright.

Rap-rap-rap. Rap—rap.

He rushed to pull it open. Something large and black came tumbling into the room, falling heavily past him to the floor.

"Lock it!"

His grandfather's voice. Alex slammed and locked the door again.

He stood with his arms folded, hugging himself, backed into the corner. He stared down at the large bald man lying crumpled in an uncomfortable-looking heap at his feet.

The rushing sounds of the train roared around his head. He poked the man with the toe of his shoe. Nothing. He looked at the door. He looked back at the big man. He looked at the door again.

The train's roar shifted to a howling new pitch. Alex thought distantly that he would quite like to go to the toilet now. But the big man's face was pressed nose-first against the seat. *Clackety-clatter* screamed the train, over and over and over again.

"*Uhhhhhhhhrrm.*"

Alex actually felt his heart jump inside him, then slam into the pit of his stomach. A cold feeling.

"*Ohhhhhhhhhrrrr,*" the man grunted again. The eyelid Alex could see was flickering.

The eye opened, rolled to stare at the floor, closed.

Then opened.

"*Uuuuuuuuuuurrrrfffff.*"

The sausage-link fingers of one huge hand twitched. The hand spread itself flat on the rubbery floor, beginning now to push, lifting his unimaginable bulk into a kneeling position. He held that pose for a moment, swaying gently over the toilet seat, eyes closed, looking like he was considering being sick into the bowl.

Not taking his eyes from him, Alex edged toward the door.

Slowly, the man raised his quite enormous, square-looking head and blinked. He turned to Alex, staring confusedly at him. He lifted a hand and pointed.

Alex scrabbled at the lock. The catch slipped out of his sweaty grasp as though it had been buttered.

The man was on his feet, rocking slightly with the motion of the train.

Rap-rap-rap. Rap—rap

Alex twisted uselessly at the lock.

Rap-rap-rap. Rap—rap

He felt a heavy hand land on his shoulder, pulling him back.

Rap-rap-rap. Rap—rap

Alex kicked back hard with his heel. The grip on his shoulder loosened. It was enough for him to lunge forward. With the last desperate brush of his straining fingertips, the catch clicked. The door swung open.

"Goodness' sake, Alex, what took you so— Oh, hello."

His grandfather stepped in past him, cane twirling, a black-and-silver blur. Alex saw the other bald man lying facedown in the corridor. He heard a blunt thwacking noise close behind and turned to see the man in the toilet crumbling to his knees again.

"Give me a hand, would you, old chap?"

His grandfather had stepped back into the corridor and was lifting the man from the floor.

"Going to see if I can't drag him in." He nodded toward the next carriage. "Could you keep a look out?"

Alex stood looking dumbly at him.

"Alex? Look out?"

Alex stepped over to stand hovering by the carriage entrance, shifting unconsciously from foot to foot. His head felt empty.

Behind him, with a lot of huffing and grumbling, his grandfather maneuvered the hulking figure into the little toilet and dropped him on top of his colleague.

Through the glass panels of the sliding doors, Alex watched a girl of about sixteen in a gray sweater and jeans rise from her seat halfway down the next car. She was, he thought vaguely as she began walking toward him, about the most beautiful girl he had ever seen. Even from here, her eyes, which now glanced up and caught his, were an astonishing green. Long chestnut hair.

Walking toward him.

"Right, then," his grandfather grunted in satisfaction. He stood in the toilet doorway regarding his handiwork, the men on the floor, rubbing his lip with his thumbnail. He broke off as Alex jumped back, spluttering.

"Someone! Coming!"

His grandfather grabbed him and shoved him into the toilet with the men.

"Lock it," he whispered urgently, stepping out and pulling the door shut again.

"*What?* No!"

"*Lock it.*"

Fingers trembling, Alex turned the lock.

He was actually standing on top of the men now, he noticed, his feet on the uppermost one's massive chest. With glum fascination, he saw that he bobbed up and down a little as the man snored quietly under him.

Outside, his grandfather had started cheerfully whistling a loud, ornate tune.

"Afternoon!" the old man's voice suddenly sang out. "Lovely journey, eh?"

Alex stood listening, staring down at the unconscious man he stood on.

"Grandson's just popped back in," his grandfather's voice bubbled on. "Shouldn't be too long now. Least I shouldn't think so. I mean, he's been running in and out of there constantly getting on for twenty minutes already. Quite horrendous case of diarrhea. Can't imagine there's too much left to come now. I did warn him."

The eyes of the man under Alex's feet were flickering, eyeballs moving rapidly left to right behind thin eyelids.

"Dodgy-looking portion of jellied eels. I said to him, 'Those things just don't *smell* right.' But you can never tell anybody anything, eh? That's one thing I've learned. Hmmm? How's that? Oh, yes, now, I think there is another one, yes. Just back down through the carriage toward the other end of the train. Can't miss it. Well, you have a lovely trip now, miss! Lovely talking to you! Watch out for those eels!"

The whistling started again, fading gradually to silence.

Rap-rap-rap. Rap—rap

Alex pulled the door open as far as the legs of the men he was standing on allowed.

"'Horrendous case of diarrhea'?"

"Look out," his grandfather said, leaning past him, swinging his cane briskly. There came another thunk, another sighing groan.

"Now," he said, stepping in, pulling the door closed. "Let's see what we can do here."

With the four of them in there, there was barely room to move. Feet straddling the men on the floor, elbows in Alex's face, his grandfather swayed from side to side with the train as he rummaged in his bag at the sink, hemming and hawing. When he turned, he had several ties draped over his arm.

"Handmade. Awful shame to waste these. But needs must. Now, Alex, help me get them on their sides, face-to-face."

Grunting in the hot little room, Alex's grandfather bent over the men, working swiftly, binding each man's hands together behind his back with intricate knots, securing their ankles, then tying the bonds at wrists and ankles together. Alex was reminded of a film he'd seen, cowboys roping up at rodeo.

Patting his pockets, his grandfather produced four cotton handkerchiefs. Scrunching two into loose balls, he stuffed them casually into the men's mouths. He twirled the others into thick strands, then tied them firmly around their heads, gagging them.

"Promise they're clean," he said, patting one of the sleeping men on the cheek.

"Is that . . ." Alex swallowed. "Him?"

"Him? Him who? Oh, I see. No, no. Just a couple of his pets. Now, then." The old man pulled the door open a crack, peered into the corridor. "Coast's clear, out you pop."

Alex stepped gladly from the stifling room, nervously watching the door to the next carriage. His grandfather stood behind him, bent fiddling at the lock, then jumped out into the corridor, wrenching the handle up and slamming the door hard. He tried the handle, and turned with a triumphant smile.

"Et voilà," he chirruped, pointing at the lock with a flourish. The sign had been flipped to red, ENGAGED. "Handy trick," the old man said. "Teach it to you sometime. Now would you look at that!" He gasped, pointing to the window behind Alex.

"Paris. Isn't she lovely?"

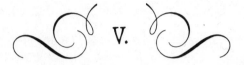

THE TROUBLE WITH HARRY

THE TRAIN SITS *idling in Paris's Gare du Nord station. Most of the passengers arriving from London have long since left. But in a carriage toward the rear, the small man and the moon-faced girl stand beside the closed toilet door. They do not speak. For a time it seems as though nothing is happening.*

A banging begins behind the door. It trembles. Finally, with an enormous splintering, it is ripped open, wrenched off its hinges.

The two bald men stand crammed in the doorway, panting, bruised, and shamefaced. The girl shakes her head. Beside her, Beckman makes a small, empty giggle, devoid of humor. He sighs. With great reluctance, he begins removing the bright scarf from his neck.

"And so," he says, weakly.

Beneath the scarf, his neck is a horrible red and sore-looking network of scars, some still fresh. From a pocket, he produces a small piece of thick, waxy white paper and unwraps it to reveal a shiny new razor blade. He lifts the blade to his throat.

"No."

The voice stops him. Silhouetted in the gray light streaming through the window, the tall man in the long black coat steps into the carriage. He puts a hand on Beckman's arm, pushing the blade away.

"Something more, I think."

He turns to the girl. Smiling eagerly, she reaches into her coat and pulls out a battered old pouch containing an empty syringe, a rubber tourniquet, cotton wool swabs, and a small bottle of clear alcohol. Shrugging one arm free from his coat, the tall man pushes up his shirtsleeve, locates a clear spot amid a mess of old scars and scratch marks that mottle the skin from wrist to elbow. He inserts the needle and begins drawing out his blood.

A train cleaner has the bad luck to enter at this moment. He splutters at the broken toilet door.

"What the—?"

He stops, words dying, as he notices what the tall man is doing.

The girl whips around, glaring. There is a strange stirring inside her coat. As she throws it open, the cleaner catches sight of something: some silver blur, moving fast through the air.

And then he sees nothing more.

FOR ALMOST TWO hours, to a commentary of muttering, sighing, and shrugging from the driver, Alex's grandfather made the taxi drive this way and that through busy, drizzling streets, while he sat studying the traffic behind them through the rain-smeared rear window. Beside him, Alex wondered if the numbness in his head was shock.

By the time the old man gave the driver a definite destination, it was midafternoon. The day was already dark. Lights glowed softly along blue boulevards as they pulled up outside a hotel that managed to look both grand and comfortably ramshackle.

The porter cursed quietly while he wrestled to erect a camp bed for Alex in the corner of their top-floor suite. His grandfather sat at a table beside doors leading to a small balcony, flipping through street maps in a guidebook.

"Here we are." He pointed out to Alex. "That's us. Métro station just around the corner, see? Very handy. And my friend Harry's place is just"—his finger traced a short wavy line across the page—"here."

He handed Alex the map, then crossed the room and dialed room service, excitedly ordering an ever-larger late lunch.

"Bed okay?" he asked Alex as the porter left, pocketing a tip.

"Huh?" Alex stood staring in the general direction of his feet. He looked at the bed and sat, halfheartedly patting the mattress. "Yes, fine."

"Important thing, a decent bed," the old man said over his shoulder, disappearing into his own room. There was a pause, followed by a sudden, complaining squeal of mattress springs. "Oh, yes. That's just the ticket."

Sighing, Alex wandered over. His grandfather lay spread-eagle on his back on a huge white bed, looking very much as though he had flung himself backward onto it straight from the doorway. He bounced contentedly up and down, one hand clicking a remote control at a large TV on the wall.

"Two thousand channels," he said, flicking through a great number of them at a blur. "Nothing on, of course."

"It's really valuable then?" Alex said.

"Hmm?" His grandfather had stopped on a talk show. Two large teenage girls sat on either side of a larger woman, shouting at each other. "'Sister, Take Your Cheating Face Out of Our Mom's Man,'" he read from the onscreen caption. "Good lord."

"Our robot," Alex tried again, wondering distantly if he was growing more patient, in shock, or simply too tired to get worked up. "It must be really valuable?"

"Ah," his grandfather said. He sat up, clicked the TV off. "Yes. Quite possibly. And possibly even more valuable than that. Invaluable, you might say."

There came a polite knock.

"Excellent," the old man said, springing to his feet with one eager bounce. He squeezed past Alex, rubbing his hands. "Luncheon."

They sat at the table by the balcony, Alex dimly surprised to find he was prepared to set his questions aside for a moment as he concentrated on spooning down a wonderfully hot and thick brown soup.

"Cream of mushroom." His grandfather slurped happily. "Rivaled only by cream of tomato as the king of soups. Don't believe what anyone else tells you. Although, there are those who follow the cream of chicken path. And leek and potato is never to be sniffed at."

Bowls scraped clean, Alex picked at the spread, assembling a sandwich from cheeses and salads. His grandfather did likewise, but with considerably more ambition, then further set about a platter of biscuits and pâté, polishing off another small bottle of champagne in the process.

"Now," the old man said, eyeing the stand of cakes. "I'm feeling rather warm after that. I think coffee on the balcony. Care to join me?"

It was bracingly cold outside. The rain had stopped. His grandfather stood balancing his cup on the iron balustrade as he popped the remains of something sugary into his mouth and buttoned his coat.

"Ordinarily, around this point," he said, "I'd have myself a cigarette. But, of course, I've stopped."

"Have one if you really want," Alex said without looking up, staring out at the soft and mysterious city, the black traffic swishing along the gold-and-orange street seven floors below.

His grandfather reached an eager hand inside his coat, hesitated, brought it back empty.

"No, you're quite right, Alex." He sipped his coffee and sighed. "Lovely. You know, just around the corner there"—he pointed off toward the end of the building—"you can see the Eiffel Tower. There are rooms on the other side of the hotel that have the most ravishing views of it by night. But, I don't know, I thought that would have been a bit touristy. Although,

I rather wish we'd taken one now. I think it's going to snow."

He turned back to Alex, watching him closely over his cup as he drank.

"So. Our robot. Yes, if it's what I think it might be, then it is very valuable. Very valuable indeed. Alex, you remember what I told you about the first and best toy robots, where most of them came from?"

"Japan," Alex replied automatically. It was a basic collector's lesson, drummed into him long ago. "After the Second World War, when they were trying to get their industries going again. They used scrap tin from the canning factories."

"Very good. And we're talking around about when . . . ?"

"The 1940s, the end of the 1940s."

"Excellent." His grandfather beamed. "Now, what if I told you *our* robot might date from *earlier* than that, maybe even the early 1920s? And what if I told you it didn't come from Japan, but from Europe? From what we used to call Czechoslovakia. Prague, to be precise. Tell me, Alex, do you know where the word *robot* comes from?"

"Um." Alex frowned. This was a new one. "No. I thought it was just . . . you know . . . the word." He winced at how lame it sounded.

"Really." His grandfather tutted. "Words all come from somewhere, Alex. Okay. *Robot* comes from a play, *Rossum's Universal Robots*, by a man named Karel Čapek, a Czech writer. Wrote it in Prague back around 1920. There's a Czech word, *robota*, you see, which means drudgery, menial work, and his play was about a factory that makes these artificial people—these robots—to do all the boring work for humans. But the robots, they begin to think for themselves, you see, and . . . well, that's another conversation. Although, actually, it ties in with what I was telling you before, about that film with the computer—"

"Okay," Alex broke in, feeling himself dangerously near the edge of one of his grandfather's massive, swampy lectures, and keen to get away from it. "So, our toy robot."

"Oh, yes. Now, there was a man in Prague, a watchmaker and toymaker on the side, name of Benjamin Loewy. Sometime soon after Čapek's play, he was inspired to make his own little clockwork robot toy, probably the first in the world. Strange thing: in the play, Čapek's robots looked more like humans, so we might even have Loewy to thank for coming up with the idea of making them look like metal machines. But it's not such a stretch, I mean—"

"So, he made these toy robots." Alex sighed.

"Oh. Yes, well. Story goes, he only ever made three. Two are known to be in the hands of private collectors—rather odd chaps, actually, hate each other, and never show any of their stuff to anybody—and both those are in badly damaged condition. *The third*, though, has never turned up. Most people believed it was destroyed long ago. But recently there were rumors of a big find: a cache of old toys discovered in an old woman's basement in Prague. She had died and her family were selling the stuff off and . . ."

He raised his eyebrows meaningfully.

"And you think this is it?" Alex asked.

"Well, it's tricky. There have been copies made over the years. But yes. I've spent a long time looking, and I really think we might have found Loewy's robot. But that's why we're here. The only man I can trust for a second opinion is my friend Harry. Which reminds me, I need to call him."

Walking back inside, his grandfather stood holding the room's phone to his ear.

"Ringing out," he mused, tugging at his bottom lip. "Well, it's not far; we can go over, see if we can't find him." He nodded to Alex. "But first, you should call your mother, let her know you're all right."

"Okay," Alex piped back innocently. "Shall I tell her about being attacked on the train and you locking me in a toilet with the men who were attacking us?"

"Yes, very amusing."

Alex pulled out his cell phone. He realized it had been off since the night before. It shuddered in his hand. Nineteen new messages.

"Now, don't use *that* thing," his grandfather groaned. "Curse of your generation, Alex. I mean, you all go on about being so *individual*, and the whole time you're all chained, addicted to these devices, shuffling around with your faces bent to all these little screens, like some science-fiction cult. Reading live updates of one another's thoughts before any of you have had a chance to think about anything. Use a proper telephone, man, one that was simply designed for talking like a civilized human being."

Alex rolled his eyes, scrolling quickly. The daily horror from Kenzie and his minions. Three from David: where are you? you ok? remind me the diff between simile and metaphor again and what even is an allegory? Eight from his mum. Increasingly terse. CALL. ME. NOW.

He put away his phone, took the chunky old receiver his grandfather held out.

"Dial a nine to get an outside line. Yes, just put your finger in, and pull it around . . . There you go. Well, what's wrong now?"

"I can't remember the number," Alex said. "Can I read it from my cell phone?"

"Unbelievable."

"Oh, hello stranger." His mother's voice sounded stern but relieved through the crackling connection. "I've been leaving you messages all day."

"Yeah, sorry, Mum."

"Is something wrong with your phone?"

"No, it's fine, I just . . . forgot to switch it on."

"Could you make sure it's on now then, please, so you can hear if I call you?"

Alex fumbled one-handed with the settings as she went on in the old phone at his ear.

"Is your grandad with you?"

"Uh-huh."

"Yes, well, I'll be wanting a word with him." Her tone softened. "Are you okay? Where are you?"

"We're in Paris, Mum. A hotel. We're fine, just a bit tired. The journey, uh, took a bit longer than we expected."

"Have you eaten anything?"

"Yes, Mum."

"So, then. Having a nice time?"

"Uh, yeah. Yeah, it's . . . good. We only just got here, though."

"And what are you going to do now?"

"We're going to go visit this friend of Grandad's, the one he was talking about."

"And do you know when we can expect you back? I mean, you know, just so I can have your pajamas ironed and warmed, peel some grapes, get the red carpet out of mothballs."

"Uh . . ."

"Can you put your grandad on, please?"

"Right, Mum. Um . . . Love you. Bye."

He handed over the phone and lay on the camp bed, staring at the ceiling, listening to his grandfather's increasingly cowed voice.

"*Hello*, Anne, and how are y— How's that, now? . . . Eh? . . . Eh, no. Yes, I can see that. Yes. Yes. Well, we *did* leave a *note*, my dea— No, you're quite right. . . . No, absolutely. Of course you would. But, in my *defense*— No . . . None at all. No, you're absolutely right. Yes, but, *Anne* . . ."

The old man dragged a chair from the table and sat, looking suddenly weary. He passed a hand over his eyes and on back through his hair. The room grew silent, except for the angry buzz of Alex's mother's voice in the telephone receiver his grandfather now held slightly away from his head. He winced at Alex.

"Yes, Anne . . . Absolutely, and I do apologize . . . Well, a few days. Week tops . . . Yes. Of course I will. Yes, I'll tell him . . . Yes, I'll make sure he does. You have my word on . . . Yes, I know I have . . . Yes, Anne. Yes. Good-bye, my dear, good—"

He stopped talking mid-word, sat looking humbly at the receiver, then dropped it back in its cradle, slapped his hands briskly, and smiled at Alex.

"Right, well, that's that all smoothed over. But, really, Alex, you should keep in touch with your mother a little more often. I mean, just a text every now and then, not much to ask, is it? Just to let her know you're okay and where you are? What's the point of having a cell phone if you're not going to use it?"

THEY TOOK A taxi to a grand terrace overlooking the river. The buildings loomed pale in the night, caught in a swaying net of shadows cast by trees along the street. Alex's grandfather stopped before a black wooden door set behind a wrought-iron gate, looked around carefully, then pressed a buzzer. The little plaque above the button read simply H. MORECAMBE.

"Harry's a dealer," the old man said. "Only topflight stuff. Doesn't have to advertise. By appointment only, that sort of thing."

He pushed the buzzer again.

"Ah," he said after several seconds of silence. "Must be out.

Well, not to worry." Digging in his trouser pocket, he produced a set of keys, used one on the gate, another on the door.

"Here we are." He waved Alex inside. "Third floor is his."

A small silver lamp with a shade of thick, dimpled glass glowed on a wooden table beside a door on the third-floor landing. On the other side of the doorway stood a tall cabinet. The top half was glass. Trapped inside could be seen the stern wax figure of a man with unsettling staring eyes, dressed in white tie and tails. One veined and knuckly hand rested on a large ball glowing yellow white. The other was held out, palm up, as if waiting for something to be placed in it. Decorative letters unfurled around the top of the cabinet:

It's amazing—know your future—true!!!

"That," said Alex, "is creepy."

"Ah," Alex's grandfather said behind him. "Meet Marvastro. *Marvastro the Mysterious Oracle: his stare can penetrate the mists of time!'* From about 1904. He'll tell your fortune. Here." He reached over Alex's shoulder to a bowl-like metal lip protruding from the machine and picked out a large blackened coin.

"Harry leaves these for visitors. Have a go. Curious thing: he has hundreds of fortunes in there, but, once you've tried him, he'll always tell you the same thing. Never could figure it out."

Alex hesitated, glancing up into Marvastro's unseeing eyes. He dropped the coin into the slot, heard it roll and fall inside.

Hidden gears started turning, a ticking, pulling noise. Little bells chimed. Suddenly, Marvastro lurched to life. His nostrils flared. His gray head twisted slightly, horribly, side to side. His shirt began to move in and out at the chest, as though he was breathing. His eyes opened wider, seemed to burn brighter, rolled in their sockets, and then glared fiercely down at Alex.

With a painful, far-off grinding, the automaton's outstretched hand twisted over, palm down, and slammed onto the wooden counter inside the glass. When it lifted and flipped over again, a small white card had appeared in it. The hand dropped forward, and the card slid off, disappearing into a slot in the counter, then shooting out into a tray on the front of the machine.

Alex picked it up. The card was thick and pearly white. He turned it over. One word, typed in simple black letters.

POWER

"Oh, that's a good one." His grandfather sounded distracted.

Alex fumbled in the change bowl, held out a coin. "Are you going to have a shot?"

"Hmm? Oh, no. No, he's told me my future lots of times. Like I said, always the same."

His grandfather was staring at the door, holding a key, but making no attempt to use it.

"What did it say?" Alex said.

"Hmmmm?"

"Your future."

"Let's see. Can't quite remember. *Long life and happiness,* eh? Something like that. Now"—he frowned flatly—"don't much like the look of this."

Raising his cane, he pushed softly at the door. It swung open. The lock had been ripped out of the frame.

Inside, Alex could see what had been a very elegant suite of offices, filled with what had been lots of wonderful things, mechanical toys and gizmos, large and small. Automatons the size of Marvastro and little white rabbits with drums. Smoking bears and iron monkeys drinking beer. Acrobats and clowns and intricate music boxes with tiny birds atop them. Rayguns and rocket cars, robots and Grim Reapers.

All smashed and broken, strewn around as though a war had been fought in the room.

As his grandfather stepped in, picking a way through the wreckage, Alex saw several powdery white lines stamped here and there into the carpet. His scalp crawled.

He didn't have to examine it to know it was salt.

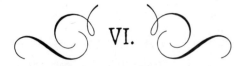

VI.

A SCENE BY THE SEINE

"I THOUGHT HE would have tried to follow us," his grandfather said, more to himself than Alex. "Didn't occur to me he'd go straight to Harry. I'm just not thinking. I'm sorry, Alex. Sorry, Harry," he added in a murmur.

They had left the trashed offices and were hurrying through an inky maze of dark, wet streets. His grandfather led the way, picking an obscure, twisting path through only the smallest and emptiest backstreets, glancing over his shoulder every few steps, stopping at every corner to press to the wall and peer ahead before going on. Alex had never seen him look so worried. It was maybe this more than anything that made his own heart race.

"This man," Alex said. "The man who's after the robot. Couldn't we just . . . give it to him?"

"How's that?"

"Couldn't we just give it to him?"

His grandfather stopped. A horse's-head sign hung from a

butcher's shop behind him, sad and sinister. A few snowflakes drifted down.

"*Give* it to him?"

"Well, yeah. I mean, this whole thing, it's dangerous. I don't like it. It's not worth it. I just want things to be normal again. I mean, look what's happened to your friend. Do you think he . . . he's—?"

"We don't know what's happened to Harry," his grandfather snapped, turning on his heel, stalking off. "Harry can take care of himself; don't you worry about that. And I'll tell you this, young man"—he stopped again, raising his cane and pointing back the way they had come—"*whatever* happened back there just makes me more determined to make sure he never gets his hands on it."

He abruptly sagged and sighed, stood staring silently at his feet.

"Look, Alex, I'm sorry," he eventually continued. "All of this, there's more to it than money. I should never have brought you. I thought it was safer than leaving you at home after last night, but that was a mistake. Maybe the best thing to do is get you back on a train out of here in the morning. I'll put you on it, we can let your mother know, and she and the Id—she and Carl can meet you at the other end. But, right now, we need to get back inside the hotel."

He strode off, beckoning Alex to keep up. Alex stood, turning over the idea of taking a train back to home and safety. He couldn't decide if he was relieved or disappointed. A little of both. Another thought occurred:

"But what about you?" he called at his grandfather's back, to no reply.

"Okay, so what else?" he tried again, trotting after him.

"What else?"

"'There's more to it than money,' you said. What else?"

"I'll explain, Alex. But later. Right now we need to . . . Shhh."

He stopped, whirled, listened, and then pulled Alex off the street, into the darkened doorway of a tobacconist's.

"Very quiet now," his grandfather whispered.

Seconds of nothing crawled past, measured out in the thin but slowly thickening fall of snow.

His grandfather lifted one gloved hand, pointed to the end of the street, the corner they had been heading for.

A lone iron lamp flickered there. As Alex watched, a large figure stepped under it. Light bounced from his shaved head like a cold halo. The man stood stock-still, staring down the narrow street toward them.

Alex felt his grandfather's grip tighten on his shoulder, pulling him farther back into the shadows. He found himself staring at a display of black pipes in the tobacconist's unlit window. His grandfather patted his shoulder reassuringly.

"Hasn't seen us," he said in a whisper Alex could barely hear. "Just have to wait till he goes."

They heard footsteps from the other direction, the way they

had come. Alex stopped breathing. The steps grew louder.

The other bald man emerged from the gloom across the street, walking toward his partner, shaking his head.

"Just sit tight now," his grandfather breathed. "Not a sound."

The second man was directly across from them, raising his arms in a shrugging gesture, passing by. Alex felt his grandfather's grip relax.

That very moment, many miles northwest, Kenzie Mitchell lay on his stomach in his sweaty bedroom, working his cell phone with thick thumbs. With a satisfied snort, he hit SEND with a chewed and grimy fingernail.

In the small street in Paris, the snowy silence shattered as Alex felt his phone vibrate, and a rousing, tinny version of the theme tune to the 1960s *Star Trek* came blaring from his pocket.

"Unbelievable," his grandfather muttered as Alex fumbled to shut the phone up. "Stay behind me, Alex."

The nearest bald man had started toward them. He was in the middle of the road, peering toward their darkened doorway. As Alex's grandfather stepped out, his colleague started running.

"Small world!" the old man called. He raised his cane and held it ready. The man closest made a lunge. A blade glinted dully in his hand.

Alex's grandfather stepped into the blow, turning his chest almost casually at the last moment. Finding only empty air where his target had been, the man was carried stumbling forward by his momentum. Standing directly behind his grandfather, Alex now had a crystal-clear view of a knife coming fast at him, straight for his face.

A gray blur crossed his vision and the blade and the man were gone. Looking down, Alex saw him curled in the gutter. The knife hand was empty, jerking in a useless spasm.

"Behind me, Alex."

His grandfather kicked the knife scattering across the street and retreated a few steps. He stood tall in the road, cane loose by his side, watching with curiosity as the other man came running. When he was a few steps away, the old man ducked in a fluid motion, bringing his stick scything forward. It made no sound as it connected with the charging man's knees. He made no sound as he was sent flying into a helpless dive that landed him heavily, face-first, a few feet behind Alex.

Coat curling out, Alex's grandfather leapt nimbly. His cane's silver handle flashed, slashing down across the jaw of the first man, who had climbed to his feet and was now sent reeling back into the gutter.

The old man landed lightly between the two groaning figures, looking from one to the other with a quizzical expression, as though turning over the possibilities of what further damage to do them. A sound of running footsteps made him look up sharply.

Three figures came around the corner at the end of the street, quivering silhouettes echoing in the light from the streetlamp, breath coming off them like smoke in the cold air. One tall, one shorter, one small.

Abruptly, still some distance away, the tallest stopped. The other two came on. Bewildered, Alex recognized the girl from the train and the little man in glasses. Behind them, another man was crouching low, gathering himself oddly.

His grandfather grabbed his arm, and they were running. Alex heard a weird metal creak from behind. Glancing back, he saw the crouching figure leap.

This tall man launched eerily from the cobblestones, high into the air, so far up, the streetlights almost lost him. Then he came curving down, fast, falling out of the night right at them. He spread his arms cruciform as he fell. In one hand, something sharp caught the lamplight.

As his grandfather dragged him around the corner, Alex heard the figure land just behind them with a harsh metallic judder.

The old man pulled him along a thin black alleyway that ran the crooked length of a block. Sprinting hard, they came out onto an empty street, darted across the road, into another alley. Halfway along, his grandfather motioned Alex to stop and stay silent. They listened. Snowflakes wisped. Seconds passed. Alex's blood pounded. Then running footsteps. Getting closer.

The snow stirred and grew heavier yet as they set off again, sprinting faster, changing directions, losing themselves in a darkness of alleys that ended finally in the bright, soft light of a larger thoroughfare. Exploding onto a broad boulevard of shops and restaurants, they sent the evening strollers scattering and kept on running, straight out into a busy road.

Cars with horns blaring swerved around them. Alex had a vivid, frozen snapshot glimpse of the inside of a bus as it whipped past an inch from his nose, sleepy blue and black faces staring out in the aquarium light.

He had lost all sense of direction, but as his grandfather dragged him dodging through traffic, he saw they were somehow back by the riverside. Once across the road, they sprinted down a steep flight of stone steps to the river walkway, the old man taking stairs two at a time as Alex stumbled to keep up.

The dim path was empty. They charged along it. A tourist boat floated slowly along the glassy black water, lit up like Christmas.

"Not far now," his grandfather said. He slowed, looking back, then stopped. "You know? I think we lost them."

Alex staggered to a halt. He turned, following his grandfather's gaze. No one. The empty stairs they had come down looked ominous in the night.

"We'll just take those steps up ahead," his grandfather said, pointing off with his cane, "and we're only a few streets from the hotel."

"Okay," Alex wheezed. His lungs burned. His legs trembled. Leaning forward, hands on knees, he thought he might be sick. "Give me a second." He stood gasping, glancing up at his grandfather, who didn't even seem to be breathing heavily.

"Who," Alex panted, "*was* that? That *man*. He . . . *jumped*."

"Yes," his grandfather muttered, watching behind them. "He does that."

Over his ragged breath, Alex heard a high mosquito-like buzz. Something smashed into his ear.

The blow sent him stumbling toward the river, legs buckling. He pitched forward. All the lights of Paris came rushing upward in the water to meet him as the rest of the world grew slow and silent.

His grandfather caught him before he fell in, held him by the shoulders, gazing urgently into his eyes. "Alex. Can you hear me?"

Alex shook his head to try and clear it. His ear was ringing, a hot, stinging ache. "I'm okay. What happened? What hit me?"

His grandfather grunted, stepped back, looking warily around, looking up. "Flier," he said.

"What—?" Alex began, when he heard the whirr again.

"Head down." The old man pushed Alex roughly behind him, swinging his cane at the dim air. The noise went streaking past, close. "Nasty little blighters," the old man grunted. "Try and get you with their propeller blades. Go for your eyes. Now, come on. Keep your head down."

He drew Alex under his arm, and they set off at a crouching run for the stairs ahead.

The noise came shooting at them again. His grandfather threw Alex to the side, spun wildly, swiping his stick blindly at the night.

Hunkered down where he had been flung against the wall, Alex heard the high sound shudder, saw the old man's head whip back from an unseen blow. Blood spouted from a deep cut on his forehead, just above his eye. The buzzing noise moved off.

"Grandad!"

"I'm okay." His grandfather held a handkerchief to his head. "Stay down."

The old man crouched alert on the walkway, studying the empty night. He hurriedly peeled off his coat. Alex heard the high whine coming again, somewhere over the river.

"Stand up, Alex," his grandfather said, still squatting. "But don't move."

Alex stood, hearing the noise grow louder.

"Grandad?"

"Shhhh."

The angry whine screamed closer.

Alex squinted desperately toward the river. The tourist boat bobbed smoothly along out there.

"Just stand still, now, Alex."

He could see people moving on the boat's open deck. They seemed happy. A grand church floated above them on the opposite bank, lit by spotlights, looking like a stately white slice of cake. The whirring intensified to a livid new pitch.

He felt it coming, like an arrow between the eyes. Something was rippling in the dark now. A tiny, orangey glow.

"Grandad?"

He somehow forced himself to stay standing. He felt the leading tip of an air current brush his forehead. A gray blur filled his vision. Then there was only the silent river, the happy boat floating on by.

His grandfather knelt before him, strands of white hair stuck to the blood on his forehead. He was wrestling oddly with his coat. Alex thought he could smell burning.

"Caught it," the old man grunted. "Give me a hand. Hold that side down."

Alex dived at his grandfather's coat, helping him pin it to the paving stones. The fabric bulged and started to tear as something struggled under it.

"Pocket nearest you," his grandfather said.

"Huh?" Alex gasped. He could definitely smell burning.

"Salt."

Alex grabbed inside, pulling out a bundle of the salt packets his grandfather had picked up on the train. The old man ripped them open with his teeth, fed his hand inside the empty coat sleeve, pulled it quickly back, sucking at his fingertips.

"Ow."

Between them, the coat was bucking so violently that Alex could hardly hold it. Gradually, though, he felt the vibrating force ebb until, finally, whatever was in there seemed only to be rolling around in a gentle little circle.

"Okay," his grandfather said. He sat back on his heels but

still held the coat tightly down. "That should have done it. Let go your end, Alex, then stand back."

Alex did as he was told. His grandfather waited and watched, then took his hands from the coat and scratched at his neck. The little lump continued rolling this way and that.

"Right." He whipped the coat away like a magician pulling a cloth from a table. Before him on the walkway, a small, dark gray toy robot was walking in tiny, aimless circles.

Two metal wings, in a shape akin to those of a housefly but honed to a razor-sharp edge, hung dejectedly from its back. Four similarly sharpened propeller blades sagged limply from its head, like a hat made of leaves that had blown apart in a storm. One hand was a vicious hook, the other a scalpel blade. Its eyes were two tiny, dim orange lamps.

"Look at that." His grandfather was inspecting his coat. Alex could see a ripped scorch mark inside, where the thing had tried cutting its way out. "Lining's ruined."

"What'll we do with . . . that?" Alex said, pointing at the robot, now teetering drunkenly toward the river's edge.

"Hmmm? Oh, whoops." His grandfather hurried across, picked the robot carefully up by its head and set it gently back down, stumbling safely toward the wall.

"Well, we'll just leave him. I told you, I don't like to kill them. He'll wander off somewhere."

"Won't it just come after us again?"

"Oh, he won't be much use for a couple of days. Fliers are

hard to catch hold of, but if you can manage it, they really don't like salt."

"But how do they work? How do they control them?"

"Just reverse engineering on your basic voodoo, really—" The old man stopped, wincing. He considered Alex's baffled frown, then shrugged. "Ever hear stories about people making wax dolls to control others? Jabbing them with pins and all that? Same thing. More or less. Only in reverse. But with modifications. Now," he continued, pulling on his coat and nodding off behind Alex's head, "time to go."

Alex turned. High behind, the shadowy figure of the girl stood at the top of the stairs they had come down. She whipped her arm in a pointing gesture. A small piece of darkness dislodged itself from the night at her shoulder and came shooting toward them.

The tall man and the bald men were already halfway down the steps. As Alex watched, the tall man curled in his curious crouch. The creaking noise carried on the freezing air as he sprang into another high, uncanny flying jump.

"Who *is*—" Alex managed as his grandfather hauled him into a sprint for the steps ahead. Alex took them two at a time. His grandfather managed three. As they reached the top, the old man already had his cane high, hailing a taxi, sending more oblivious passersby stumbling.

A cab flashed its headlights as they darted into the road. Bundling in behind the old man, Alex heard the high whine coming. He slammed the door. Something thumped off the side. His grandfather waved a fistful of notes at the driver and told him to drive fast.

Twisting to the back window, Alex flinched as he saw the tall man complete a leap that landed him at the top of the steps behind them. He stood staring after them through the snow as the car sped into traffic.

Alex pulled out his phone. He snorted a bleak laugh at the message.

Your DEAD.

He turned it off, checking twice before he put it back in his pocket.

VII.

A MUCH OLDER STORY

AS THEY WENT charging through the hotel lobby, the desk clerk called out to them, waving a small blue envelope.

Alex's grandfather ripped it open in the elevator, unfolded a sheet of the hotel's stationery, and frowned. Then he grinned, flourishing the page.

"Message from Harry! He's okay!"

He handed the note to Alex, rubbing his hands together:

> *He's here.*
> *Managed to get out. Not hanging around.*
> *Gone to my country place. Come when you can.*
> *If you can.*
> *—H.*

"Excellent. Harry has a lovely little place just outside Fontainebleau. Not too far. Good cook, is Harry. Has an arrangement with the woman who runs the farm down the road. Free eggs. Makes the most wonderful soufflés."

He hummed happily as he unlocked their door.

"Do you think you should get someone to look at that?" Alex asked.

"How's that?"

Alex rubbed a finger across his own forehead.

"Oh. Ah." The old man stepped into the bathroom, clicked the light above the sink, and pressed gingerly at the cut on his head. "Not too bad. Deep, but the bleeding's stopped. Looks clean enough. Could you fetch me my bag, old chap?"

When Alex came back, his grandfather had his coat and jacket off, and stood with one bloody shirtsleeve rolled up, holding his arm under the running tap. There was another large gash across his forearm.

"Our friend with the knife. Just a scratch."

Rooting through his Gladstone, he came out with several handkerchiefs, a bottle of aftershave, and a small white tube. He held up his haul.

"Something else your generation has forgotten: chap can never have too many handkerchiefs." Dousing one with after-shave, he set to cleaning and dressing his arm, wincing and hissing. After dabbing at his forehead, he squeezed a line of puttylike cream from the tube and smeared it over the wound.

"Plastic skin." He smiled. "Of course, everything you've just seen me do, you should never do it. If you have a cut like that, you get it treated properly. And never run into traffic either, the way we did back there. That's just stupid. Now"—the old man drummed the sink with his fingertips, then walked past Alex to the table bearing the remains of their lunch—"we should get going. Tonight. Right away."

He slathered pâté onto a biscuit.

"Are you packed?"

"I hardly unpacked." Alex gestured at the pile of clothes he'd dumped on the camp bed.

"Good chap," his grandfather mumbled through a mouthful of crumbs. "Be prepared. And that reminds me." Pulling out a fistful of bills and coins, he handed it to Alex.

"What's this for?"

"Oh, just to have. Spending money. Save you bothering me if you see something you want to buy. I don't know, a comic. Postcards, perhaps. Now, I just need to change my shirt."

He strode into the bathroom and rummaged through his bag, producing a crisp white shirt, still in its wrapper.

"You said you'd tell me what was going on," Alex said, stuffing money into his pockets. His mind was racing. "Who are those people? That little man, the girl, they were on the train. And that tall—"

"Look at this. Suit's almost ruined," the old man muttered, dusting the knees of his trousers. He straightened to inspect his jacket, hanging on the bathroom door. Tutting, he turned to the mirror, unknotting his tie. "But I left some clothes at Harry's last time I stayed, said he was going to have them cleaned for me."

"Grandad."

The old man sighed. He gazed down into the sink, shoulders slumping, then straightened and turned.

"Okay, Alex. What's going on. Well, let me see." He rubbed a hand over his face, clearly reluctant to go on. "Okay: have you noticed anything odd happening?"

"Have I noticed anything *odd* happening? Is that supposed to be a joke?"

"What? No, no— I mean, before I showed up. Have you noticed anything odd happening?"

"Uh, no. I mean . . . how do you mean?"

"With the robot, man, with the robot. Look, remember, when I met you, you had it in your schoolbag? But you said you hadn't put it there? Anything else like that?"

Alex frowned.

"Well . . ."

"Yes?"

"There was a moment." He thought back, amazed to realize it had only been two nights before. "I was in my room; I was looking at it and . . ."

"Yes?"

"I don't know. I started to feel funny."

"Feel funny?"

"I was looking at it . . . into its eyes, and I started feeling weird. Kind of sick."

"Okay." His grandfather had come out of the bathroom, stood retying his tie, listening intently. "What else?"

Alex's frown deepened as he thought back. So much strangeness had occurred since that night he'd almost forgotten. "Well, I was trying to write an essay, for my English homework, right? But I wasn't getting anywhere with it? I had it started, but I couldn't finish it . . . I *didn't* finish it."

"Fascinating insight into your life as a writer, Alex." His grandfather scowled as he buttoned his waistcoat. "But if you could get to the point?"

"That's rich."

The old man raised his eyebrows at him as he pulled on his jacket. "We'll ignore that. Look at this." He held out the sleeve the knife had slit. "Barbarians. And so, there you were, struggling with your essay?"

"Nothing. It's stupid."

"No." His grandfather came over and put a hand on his shoulder. "Sorry, Alex. Believe me, whatever you tell me, I won't think it's stupid. Go on. Please."

"Well, next day . . . it was finished."

"It was finished?"

"My essay. Someone had finished it. I thought maybe I had done it during the night and not remembered. But I know I didn't. At least, I think . . ."

"Ah."

His grandfather turned away, stood gazing out the balcony doors. The dark city pulsed in shades of blue.

"Now, that's interesting." He spun again, pointing at Alex. "That's very interesting." The old man's eyes glittered. He seemed to be trying to hide a smile. Then all traces of a smile disappeared.

"Yes, interesting," he repeated gravely. "And more than a little worrying. Get your bag packed, Alex."

"Grandad, you need to tell me what's going on!"

"I will. You can pack and listen at the same time, can't you? We have to get a move on."

Alex stomped to his bed, took the robot in its boxes out of his rucksack, and started shoving clothes back in. His grandfather approached, arm outstretched, as if to pick up the toy, then snatched his hand away. He stood watching Alex pack.

"What's that?"

Alex paused. The old photo of his mum and dad. He handed it over.

"Oh. Yes," the old man said softly. He stood looking at the picture, momentarily lost. "Sorry I never had a better photograph of him to give you myself, Alex. He never liked having his picture taken. Got that from me. I'm the same way."

He gazed at the fuzzy image another few seconds, then handed it back. Wandering to the table by the window, the old man shook the empty champagne bottle as though hoping it might make more appear, then started unpeeling a banana.

"So. Where were we? I told you about *Rossum's Universal Robots*, the play. Remember?"

"Uh-huh."

"Well, there's another story from Prague, you see. A much older story. It's maybe where Čapek got his idea in the first place, actually, because it's also about people who made . . . well, artificial creatures to work for them."

"Uh-huh?" Alex kept working at his bag, keeping his answers short in the hope his grandfather might get to the point.

"Yes. Now, Alex, tell me: have you ever heard of a golem?"

Alex frowned, turning. "Like in *Lord of the Rings*?"

"Hmm? No, no, no. That's G-O-L-L-U-M. Golem. G-O-L-E-M."

"Oh. No. Oh, wait, there used to be a Pokémon called Golem. I used to have the card when I was a kid."

"A what?"

"You know, from the video game?"

His grandfather scowled. "Really, Alex, I'm trying to teach you something here. Listen. Golem. Word comes from the Bible, Old Testament, the Hebrew Bible. It means . . . an unfinished creature. A creature made of clay. There used to be stories, you see, that very wise men, or very holy men, could create these things, rough men of clay, and bring them to life, as their servants."

"Like magic?" A sudden image of the little flying robot popped into Alex's mind, blades outstretched.

"Well, that depends on your definition of magic," his grandfather said. "And your definition of holiness. The idea, basically, was that these were people who had studied so hard to get close to God they had picked up some of his wisdom and power, and so they could create a kind of life. But, yes, let's say magic. That'll do as well as anything. The legend goes that sometime in the 1500s, there was a holy man in Prague. Rabbi

Loew. This was a time when the Jewish people of Prague were under a great deal of threat. There were attacks, and there was worse coming. And so, Rabbi Loew went to the river, and he used the clay from the banks to make a great and mighty golem who would protect his people. The Golem of Prague. And he did defend the ghetto, at least at first—"

"Hang on," Alex said. "Did this really happen?"

His grandfather took a deep breath. "All I'm telling you, Alex, is that this is the story. It's a story. Stories all come from somewhere, and sometimes they get bent out of shape over the years. But this is the story."

"Okay. But what's all that got to do with this?" He held up the toy robot's box and shook it, before stuffing it into his rucksack. "And that . . . tall man."

"Well, if you'd let me, I was getting to that. Now—"

There came a knock at the door.

They looked at each other. The old man raised a finger to his lips, tiptoed quickly across the room, and lifted Alex's rucksack, shoving the robot deep inside before zipping it shut. Opening the balcony door, he stepped out of sight, returned empty-handed, closing the door quietly behind him.

"Who's there?" he called.

There was another knock.

"What do we do?" Alex whispered.

His grandfather pulled on his coat and took up his cane. "Why, we answer it," he said brightly.

VIII.

A MODEST PROPOSAL

THE LITTLE MAN stood in the hallway, large eyes swimming almost invisibly behind thick glasses lenses. The shabbiness of his coat made the vividness of his scarf all the more incongruous. Alex's eyes were drawn helplessly to it. As he stared, he noticed wounds on his neck showing beneath the bright yellow material, some looking raw. A sweet smell came off of him.

"Uh-huh," Alex's grandfather said.

Cane held ready, the old man stepped out past him, glanced around the empty hallway.

"Just yourself, is it?"

"Please," the little man said in an unctuous whine. "If I may trouble you to allow me to come in for a moment."

"Mm-hmm." Alex's grandfather pushed past him back into the room, crossed to the table, and sat, beckoning. "By all means. Make yourself at home."

As Alex backed away, the man crossed the threshold, then stood with his back against the closed door. Reaching inside his jacket, he pulled out a small black gun. Alex froze.

"Oh, you *are* joking," Alex's grandfather groaned, piling pâté onto another biscuit. He held it up. "Here. Put that away and try some of this. You won't believe it."

"Please," the little man said with an apologetic snicker. He gestured almost sadly with the gun at Alex, waving him toward the old man. "If you could also go over there, please."

Alex did as he was told, staring at the snout of the pistol as it followed him. The only sound was biscuit crunching between his grandfather's teeth.

"I said to them that there was no need for any of this." The man made a weak, remorseful gesture. "I said we could avoid all this unpleasantness. We could just talk, you and I. That you would see sense now—now that you have the child to think about."

He turned to Alex. The round glasses lenses seemed perpetually to reflect the light, making his expression impossible to read. Still, Alex had the creeping sense of being under intense study.

"A strong resemblance," the man finally said.

Alex's grandfather's smile vanished. "Just get on with what you came to say."

"I told them," he continued, "that you could be *persuaded*. So. Just give it back to me, now. Then I can give it to him, and you can take the boy safely back to his home. It was I who found it, after all. I. After all these years. And you stole it from me."

"Now, now." Alex's grandfather said, wagging a finger. "I bought it, old chap. Bought it. All fair and above board . . . ish. And just to be clear: you didn't find it. After all these years, it popped up in the cellar of this woman none of us had ever even heard of.

"Alex"—the old man flourished a hand in introduction—"meet Hans Beckman. Owns a very nice toy shop. In Prague, as it happens. Little dusty, but very nice.

"Now, as soon as Beckman here heard through the grapevine about the discovery of all these toys in the basement, he had rather a crafty idea. He called up the family, before the auction, and made them an offer they couldn't refuse for the robot. Not really the done thing, but they agreed to sell it to him. The thing *was*, though, at much the same time, I'd had much the same idea myself—only I went around in person to make my offer. And when I showed up and said I was calling about the toy robot, well, you know, they might *possibly* have just assumed that I was the Herr Beckman they had spoken with on the telephone, and I might *possibly* have failed to correct them and then put on a German accent. But, anyway, they sold it to me. For less than I was going to offer at first, actually. Had it all nicely packaged up, waiting. Even gave me a receipt!

"Trouble was"—Alex's grandfather shrugged—"just as I left their house, I ran into Hans here along with those shaven-headed thugs you've already met, in rather a hurry to collect it themselves. That got a little sticky. There was quite the most unseemly chase, and by the time I'd made it to the center of town, ah, our jumping friend and the girl had got involved, too.

"I'll admit, I started to worry I might get caught. So I decided that if they were going to get *me*, the only thing left to do was make sure they didn't get *it*. I made for the post office— wonderful building, actually, Alex, we should visit there some-day—and I slipped it in the mail to you. That's an old trick. The mail is like the poor man's safe. Or the man in danger and in a hurry. But then I got away after all. It was very busy in the post office, what with Christmas, and they didn't want to draw too much attention and have anyone calling the police, and I managed to give them the slip. Or I thought I had. Although, as you know, it turns out they were never far behind me.

"But, Beckman"—he turned back to the little man, ignoring the gun—"my dear fellow: less of the 'stealing,' if you please. You can't blame me because you didn't get in there in time. You're a collector. Rules of the game. Anyway, who's to say that it's even the toy we think it is?"

"*I'm* to say," Beckman whined. "I know it is. Now, don't do that, please."

Alex's grandfather had reached for the pâté knife. "No?" He pouted. "No, I suppose you're right. Very rich, Alex, not at all good for you."

"Will you give it to me?" The little man was almost pleading.

Alex's grandfather leaned forward, elbows on the table,

made a steeple with his fingers, and touched the tips to his nose.

"No," he said after a moment's consideration. "I don't think I will."

"Then, please, I must make a search of these rooms. You"—the gun pointed at Alex, then the open bathroom door—"bring that bag, please."

Alex looked at his grandfather, who shrugged. He got the Gladstone from the bathroom.

"Now, please, empty it onto that bed there. Slowly, please."

Beckman took a few steps back, so he could see both Alex and his grandfather, but the bed and the table were too far apart to keep watching both at once. Behind the shining lenses, Alex could glimpse his eyes darting nervously side to side.

The Gladstone was amazingly heavy, and, as Alex tipped it out, there was an amazing amount inside. Shirts, shorts, and socks. Many mysterious little bags and pouches. Old books, maps, a tin of hard candies, salt packets. A few spools of electrical wire, a coiled length of rope with a grappling hook on the end. Lots of string.

As he sorted through the junk, Alex saw from the corner of his eye that Beckman was looking more and more intently at the growing pile on the bed, shifting his weight from one foot to the other.

"Please. What's that? Open that, please."

Alex held a thick brown leather bag, about the size and shape of a brick, zippered shut. Inside was an ancient shaving kit, complete with brushes and shaving soap, wicked-looking razor blades, and a dusty jar of talcum powder. As he held it open for Beckman to see, at the periphery of his vision, Alex thought he saw his grandfather's hand flash forward and back from the table.

"Ach," Beckman groaned, stepping across the room to him, spinning awkwardly on his heel to keep Alex's grandfather in his sights. He grabbed the Gladstone and held it upside down. The few remaining contents rained onto the bed. A pack of playing cards was the last thing to drop out.

"Oh, I'd been looking for those!" Alex's grandfather piped happily.

"Ach," Beckman said again. Glancing rapidly around the things on the bed, he picked up the note from Harry, left lying where Alex had tossed it. Reading, he smirked, then folded it away into his pocket. He gestured toward the main bedroom.

"Now, please." The gun pointed at Alex's grandfather. "In there. Hands up, please."

The old man stood and, with a sigh, raised his hands loosely. He started toward the bedroom.

"No. Wait. Please."

Beckman was smiling. Something was visibly bulging from the inside pocket of Alex's grandfather's coat.

"Please. If you would show me what you have there?"

"Hmmm? What?" The old man glanced vaguely down. "Oh, that?" He smiled. "That's nothing, my dear fellow. Just a badly cut coat is all. The line is off, the hang's all wrong. Been meaning to have a word with my tailor about it, actually. Don't know if you know him, little basement just off Savile R—"

"Please. If you would show me what it is you have there."

"But— Oh, okay. There's no fooling you, I can see that."

Alex's grandfather reached quickly toward the pocket. Beckman's gun jerked up in alarm.

"Stop. Please. Hands up."

The old man raised his hands again.

"You think I am not so smart." Beckman snickered softly. "This is fine. No one thinks Beckman is smart. But this is a strength for me. So, please, if you wouldn't mind turning around, I shall get it for myself."

The old man spun slowly on his heel, offering his back, hands still up. Alex's eyes darted around the pile on the bed, searching for something usable.

"Keep still, please."

Beckman crossed the room and stood close behind the old man. He held the gun in his right hand, aimed at Alex's grandfather's shoulder blade, and reached around with his left, fishing blindly inside his coat.

With a savage, yet strangely lazy movement, Alex's grandfather whipped back his raised right arm, going into a turn. His elbow smashed into Beckman's temple, sending him reeling. At the same time, the old man stamped hard on Beckman's foot, pinning it down. Unable to steady himself, Beckman started falling backward. The hand with the gun swung up, to be met hard by Alex's grandfather's now straightened right arm.

The gun jerked out of Beckman's hand, twirling. Alex's grandfather picked it casually from the air, lifting his foot, allowing Beckman to fall in a crumpled heap.

Alex leapt across and threw the contents of the jar of talcum powder into Beckman's face. The little man started sneezing, sending up delicately perfumed clouds.

Alex's grandfather turned with a look of incomprehension. "What on earth did you do that for?"

"I was helping you!" Alex shouted.

"That's expensive stuff, that." The old man frowned. Then, seeing the fury breaking across Alex's face, quickly added, "But quick thinking."

He stood considering the little man, weighing the tiny pistol in his hand, then slipped it into his pocket. Reaching inside his coat, he brought out the remains of the loaf they had been eating for lunch. He bit off a corner and chewed.

"I was saving this for later," he said.

"Please," Beckman moaned. "Please give it to me. You don't want to do this. You don't want this to happen. Please." He sounded almost in tears.

"Now, now." Alex's grandfather bent forward, offering his hand. "None of that." He pulled the little man to his feet and dusted at his shabby coat lapels. Talcum rose off him in drifts.

"Look at that, you'll be the best-smelling chap in town. So. Where are they?"

"Downstairs." Beckman was kneading his hands together. "In the lobby. I told him I could talk to you. Please."

"Well, then." One arm around Beckman's powdery shoulders, Alex's grandfather steered him to the door. "You shouldn't keep them waiting. Tell me, though, before you go. Does he have the key?"

Beckman said nothing, staring at his feet.

"Okay." The old man sighed. "Off you go. Be seeing you in a few minutes, I'm sure."

He stood leaning in the doorway, watching the little man slope toward the elevator. As Beckman disappeared around the corner, Alex's grandfather jumped across to the camp bed, searching through the scattered contents of his Gladstone.

He pocketed a couple of leather pouches, some string, the wire. Gathering up all the salt he could find, he stepped into the hallway, spreading a thick line over the carpet from wall to wall. Coming back into the room, he locked the door, lifted the salt-cellar from the table, and emptied it along the foot of the door.

"Don't have much time," he said. "Push your bed against the door, Alex, then see if you can't drag that table and chairs over, and pile them up."

"But—"

"Alex. Seriously. Move." The old man disappeared into the bedroom.

"Want me to pack your bag?" Alex shouted as he hauled the camp bed across the room.

"No, no time. I have everything we need. Actually"—his head popped back around the door frame—"if you could grab that tin of sweets."

The mattress from the big bed appeared in the bedroom doorway, followed by Alex's grandfather, grunting. Leaning it against the wall, he helped Alex with the table and chairs, set the mattress against them, then finally pulled the sofa from the center of the room and upended it heavily against the pile.

Standing back to contemplate their work, he took the candies, popped one into his mouth, then offered the tin to Alex, who shook his head.

"I'd hoped I'd be able to get the bed frame out," his grandfather said, sucking sadly at his candy. "But I'd need to take it apart. No time. Ah, well, that'll have to do. It'll only slow them, anyway. Just depends what they have with them. Mmmm. Black currant. Very, very good."

Stepping to the bathroom door, he leaned in, fiddling at the handle, then jumped out, slamming it shut, repeating his trick from the train, as though it had been locked from inside. "Keep 'em guessing." He beamed at Alex and slapped his hands together. "Now. Time to go."

"Go?" Alex nodded at the barricaded door. "Go where?"

"This way, of course," his grandfather said, heading toward the balcony.

SNOW WAS COMING down thick and fast now, spiraling prettily in the biting Paris wind.

Alex's grandfather stood poking with his cane at the lintel above the balcony door. After a few seconds of fruitless fishing, he brought it back down, the rucksack hooked over the end.

"Never liked a rucksack much," he said, holding it so Alex could slip both arms through the straps. "You see people walking around town with them, always thought they looked rather silly. But, if you need your hands free, handy things. As it were. Now."

Turning, he bent to the door handles, wrapping wire from a spool tightly around them, binding them shut. Satisfied, he walked to the end of the balcony and stepped casually up onto the thin iron rail.

Alex felt his heart stop, then start again, faster, in his throat. "Grandad!"

The old man stood balanced above the street like a tightrope performer, inspecting a ledge that ran along the front of the hotel at waist height from his position. It led from their balcony to the next, about thirty feet away.

"Looks fairly easy," he said, smiling down at Alex. "Although, I really must stress this, Alex: you should never, under any circumstances, do what we are about to do."

"I'm not doing that! This is insane!"

Alex looked around desperately. Far below, traffic moved along the shining road. The lights made the snow pale gold, shot through with blue. Across the street, the small figures of two grown men pelted each other mercilessly with snowballs. As he watched, they launched an attack on a man and a woman who had just passed beneath Alex's balcony. The man's annoyed curses came drifting up, sounding far away.

Back inside the bright hotel room, the pile of furniture against the door seemed an odd and dreamlike assemblage. As he stared at it, Alex saw it shudder slightly.

He looked back up at his grandfather, balanced on the railing.

"You could take it," Alex said, voice hoarse. "I could stay here."

"True. But then, he would take you, to make me give it to him. So, Alex. Time to choose. What's it to be?"

In the room, a muffled thump came at the door. Then another, accompanied by a weird, high buzzing.

"Mum's going to kill you," Alex muttered, moving stiffly to the end of the balcony.

"Good show," his grandfather said. "Nothing to worry about. This'll be a walk in the park."

The old man hoisted himself up onto the snowy ledge. Facing in toward the wall, it was just wide enough for his feet. He crouched, extending a hand.

"Now, up you come, onto the railing first, then a jump up here. Don't worry, I won't let you fall."

Alex looked at the railing, the long drop beyond. His heart was hammering. He didn't feel he could trust his arms or legs.

"Just take my hand."

Grabbing his grandfather's hand, he felt himself lifted more than climbing. Then, almost without realizing, he was standing on the narrow ledge high above the street, his forehead against the hotel wall. He heard faint crashing noises coming from their room.

"So." His grandfather had one hand firmly grasping Alex's collar. "We'll just shuffle along over here. You know what they say: don't look down."

Alex had no intention of looking down. He moved his feet sideways without lifting them. The ledge was slippery with snow. He moved his right foot to the right, then dragged the left over to meet it.

Then again.

His grandfather's hand reassuring at his neck. He moved one foot to the right, then dragged the other to meet it.

And again.

Wind whipped his ears.

One foot, then the other.

And again. And again.

"Now, then. Here we are. Just you balance there while I climb down."

The hand at his neck was gone. He stared into the sandstone at the end of his nose. Small things glittered there in the faint light. He closed his eyes, pushed his forehead harder against the coldness of the wall. He felt a sickening sensation, warm gravity reaching up, pulling him backward. He had to keep his head pressed against the wall.

"Alex?"

He opened one eye, turned as much as he dared. It was like looking through binoculars the wrong way. His grandfather stood on a balcony about a hundred miles below, holding up a hand.

"Just have to bend your knees slowly and take my hand, son," the old man said, voice gentle on the whistle of the wind. "Think you can manage that?"

Alex turned back to the wall, closed his eyes, and swallowed, trying to push down the nausea climbing from his stomach.

"I think I'll just stay here for a while," he managed. It was very cold.

"Not such a good idea, old chap. Come on, now."

Alex swallowed again, forced his eyes open. Gingerly, he began bending, felt himself swaying out, lurched desperately against the wall.

"Almost there, old chap."

He bent farther, toward his grandfather's hand, reached out his own, felt strong fingers close around it.

"Excellent work. Now just step your right foot down onto the railing here, and then it's just a little push forward."

Alex looked at the railing, about two hundred miles away. With strange clarity, he could see his grandfather's shoeprint in the soft snow piled up on the black iron. He stretched his foot out— He stretched his foot out— He stretched his foot out— And he slipped and fell.

His grandfather held him caught by one arm.

Hanging there, Alex thought that this would be a good time to look down. It was very odd. There was just nothing beneath his feet for a long, long way. Down there, a thousand miles below, a few funny little people were walking through the pretty snow. He found the word *dangling* floating into his mind. His feet were dangling. He was dangling. Dangle.

"Just give me up your other hand, Alex."

His grandfather sounded worried. Why was he worried? The whole world was soft and dreamy. Little robots were on the prowl with bits of people in them. Beckman must have cut those little wounds in his neck to feed the little robots. That seemed obvious now. Single donor. The little robots in his bedroom, maybe they had little bits of little Beckman in them. Dangle, dangle.

"Give me your other hand."

Kenzie Mitchell was going to kill him. Not actually kill him, just beat him up. The little flying thing, that might have killed him. Really killed him. He wondered what his mother was doing. This was another thing he would probably never tell her about. What time was it, anyway? Men were making snowballs out of salt. Men were making men out of clay hundreds of years ago. It was funny when you thought about it. *Dangle* is a funny word. Maybe he should start laughing.

"Alex. Hand."

He looked up. Robots. Clay men. Snowmen. Salt. There was his grandfather, reaching out for his hand, snow falling around his head from the deep blue night. He should give him his hand up. But then he might have to stop dangling, dangling over all the snow and all the funny little people. And it was so peaceful.

"Alex."

Alex reached up.

His grandfather heaved him roughly over the railing. They collapsed together onto the balcony. Alex pulled himself into a sitting position, feeling snow seeping into his trousers, but also feeling the firmness of the balcony beneath. He started laughing, a high, loud laugh that stopped as his grandfather clamped a hand over his mouth.

"Shhhh." The old man nodded toward the new balcony doors. Thin white curtains were drawn. There was a light on in there. A droning TV. The silhouette of a figure in a chair. Just someone living a normal life.

"Don't want them calling the management."

"Won't they hear all the crashing at our door?" Alex whispered.

"Let's hope not, for them."

"What do we do now?"

"Ah. Well."

His grandfather lifted his cane, pointed toward the far end of the balcony, then off at the next balcony along, just visible through the quickening, thickening snow.

"If you're feeling up to it, we do it again."

Alex closed his eyes, opened them. His head was pounding, but his shock was melting. He swallowed hard, nodded.

They did it again.

IX.

THE ROOFTOPS OF PARIS

THE NEXT BALCONY, when Alex tumbled onto it, was dark. The curtains in the doors were open, no sign of life in the room beyond.

"Empty room," the old man said. "Or they're out. Or they're in bed. Or they're sitting there in the dark, watching us. Although, that would be odd. Well, anyway."

He produced a small leather bundle, which he unrolled on the snowy balcony floor. A row of thin, sharp metal rods glinted. Alex was reminded of instruments his dentist used for scraping and picking.

His grandfather's hand hovered above them, fingers wiggling. Finally, he selected two, one needle sharp, the other with a tiny hook. He began working at the door.

"You pick locks."

"Much-maligned art," the old man grunted, holding one pick still while twisting the other. "Handy skill to have. Never worry about losing your house key again. Ah."

He turned the handle. The door opened.

"Quiet now," he said. He bundled up his picks, and they went inside.

The dark room was very like the suite they had just left, except all the furniture was still in its proper place. Alex's grandfather stood with his ear to the main door, listening intently. Finger to his lips, he opened it slowly, enough to poke his head around. He pulled back quickly, closing the door.

"Still crashing about down there," he said, gesturing in the direction of their room. "They'll be through in a minute. Now, we're right at the corner where the corridor turns. The corridor to the elevator and the stairs leads off straight in front of us. Time it right, and we can just sneak out and away." He pressed his ear back to the door. After a minute, he eased it open again, glanced out.

"Right. I'll go first. Ready?"

Alex nodded.

"When I give the signal. Straight ahead. Quick and quiet."

He slipped out. Alex watched him cross the corridor in three stork-like steps. Once across, his grandfather flattened himself against the wall and looked back around the corner, toward their room. He held up a finger, brought it down sharply.

"Now."

Alex ran. Halfway across, he couldn't stop himself from looking toward their door. There was a great mess. Sheets of what looked like tinfoil had been laid over the salted carpet. As he looked, the little girl came out into the hallway. Her large eyes rounded, then narrowed. She raised her arm and pointed.

"Get."

Four small things came shooting from the room, trundling fiercely over the floor toward him.

His grandfather peered around the corner. His eyes widened. He dragged Alex into a sprint. As they reached the elevator, he stabbed furiously at buttons, almost without breaking his stride, then pulled Alex along again.

"No use. It's on the ground floor. Need to take the stairs."

The stairs were straight ahead, beyond double doors at the end of the corridor. They ran on.

Alex looked back. The four things were hurtling after them. They were mostly a mottled silver in color, each roughly the size and shape of a model train engine. They lined up in formation, two in front, two behind. The front pair had round, smiling blue faces and flat backs. The two behind had no faces, simply ended in savagely sharp points, like vicious metal stakes. They were gaining rapidly.

Alex and his grandfather were almost at the doors.

With a sudden loud clicking, the two machines at Alex's heels stopped dead. Their flat backs snapped up, forming ramps. The two behind came racing on, hitting the ramps at furious speed.

"Down!" his grandfather yelled, diving forward, pulling Alex with him.

They hit the floor hard. Alex felt carpet burn his nose, sensed something shooting over him. Lifting his head, he saw the two metal stakes impaled deep in the doors ahead. He calculated the one on his side would have hit him in the spine at the small of his back.

As he watched, thin metal arms popped out from their sides. They began struggling to pull themselves free from the doors. Behind him, the little machines with the ramps were churning their wheels in the carpet, almost in frustration. Back behind them stood the small girl, stamping furiously with a heavy black boot, actually shaking her fist. Beyond her, the bald men and the tall man were rounding the corner. As they passed her, the girl shook open her coat. Two fliers darted from inside and took up formation, hovering close around the tall man's hat.

"Come on." His grandfather was on his feet. Alex needed no encouragement.

Through the doors, into the stairwell. His grandfather stooped, urgently wrapping wire tight around the handles. Starting down the stairs, the old man suddenly stopped.

Turning onto the landing below came the tall, broad figure of a man wearing a long black coat and large black hat. When he lifted his face to them, Alex, struck numb with horror, saw it was made of dull metal. Painted eyes. A wire grid for a mouth. It began climbing the stairs.

"Life-sizer," his grandfather grunted, turning back up.

There was only one more flight of stairs. It led up to a small, bare half-landing, containing a cupboard door and an iron ladder bolted to the wall, beneath a ceiling hatch. His grandfather was up and through it in a flash of gray, hauling Alex after him.

A huge attic, old and dark, musty and empty. They crouched under high slanting roof beams while his grandfather worked with another spool of wire, tying the hatch shut as best he could. He twisted on his heels, searching the dim space around them.

"Nothing to block it with," the old man muttered, running a hand over his brow. He took Beckman's little gun from his pocket, weighed it for a second, then threw it far off into the shadows.

"What are you doing?" Alex gasped. "We need that!"

"Never liked guns. C'mon: onward and upward. This way."

Alex already knew where they were headed. Halfway along the attic, a single skylight glowed dimly, just low enough to reach. Just big enough to fit through.

Snow was falling steadily as they climbed out onto the enormous roof.

His grandfather made him go first, crawling away from the window up the steep slope. The cold black tiles were slippery under Alex's feet. There was little to get a grip on. But, clawing and scraping, sliding back then scrabbling on, they made it to the pitch of the roof, where they stopped, sitting facing each other on the peak, breath misting the sharp air. A frail full moon pushed through the wisping clouds, staining the rooftop silver.

Freed from concentrating on the climb, drawing breath, Alex's mind flooded with panic, then a stunning sense of disbelief. He became aware of the raw ache in his throat, his shaking limbs. The sky was enormous above him.

"What did I tell you?" his grandfather said. He was pointing off behind Alex's shoulder.

Turning his head, across the stretching roofscape Alex saw the Eiffel Tower, not far away, strangely clear, lit up gold and black, its blue searchlight strafing the swollen cloudbanks.

He turned back. The scream he felt building came out as a sigh. He sagged.

"Yes. That's very pretty. Tell you what, shall I get my phone out and you can take a picture with it behind me? We could send it to Mum. That would be a nice surprise for her."

"That's the spirit. Have to keep your sense of humor about you. Now." The old man dug in his coat pocket. "Sweet?" He held out the open tin.

"Well, why not. We're on holiday. Thanks."

"Sugar'll do you good. Much-maligned stuff, sugar." His grandfather squinted, tilting the tin in the weak blue light. "Bit of a Russian Roulette, taking a hard candy in the dark. Can't see what you're going to get. Ah well, nothing ventured."

He popped one in his mouth and rattled it around his teeth. "Black currant again! Must be my lucky night. What did you get?"

"Lime," Alex said. It tasted surprisingly good.

They sat there in silence, sucking candies on the high snowy roof in the Paris night, smiling stupidly at each other.

"So, now," his grandfather said. "I should probably tell you the plan, give you something to look forward to."

"Oh, do we have a plan?"

"Of course! Now, listen, Alex. Once we get away from here, we're aiming to get to Harry's place, okay? Harry lives just outside Fontainebleau. Can you remember that? Just outside Fontainebleau, there's a little town called Barbizon. A beautiful little village. Barbizon. Got that? And Harry's place is just outside that. House called Dunroamin'. Harry has a terrible sense of humor, but it's an easy name to remember. Okay? Now, you tell me."

"Just outside Fontainebleau, just outside Barbizon, a house called Dunroamin'. And, um, how do we get off this roof again?"

His grandfather pointed. "If we go along behind you, then slide down toward that corner, I can see a ladder. Leads down to a flat section, like a catwalk. Once we get there, it should be easy living."

Alex said nothing. In the fragile light, the arm of his grandfather's coat was heavily stained, soaked through. A trickle of blood ran from beneath the sleeve, shining blackly on his hand.

"You're hurt."

"Hmm? Oh, that's nothing. That cut has opened up, that's all. Looks worse than it is. This coat is past saving, though. Now." The old man nodded back the way they had come. "Probably an idea to get moving."

Following his glance, Alex stiffened. The bald men and the tall man were out of the skylight already and coming at them. The tall man led, looking like some terrible long insect crawling over the roof tiles in the moonlight.

His grandfather helped Alex into a crouching stance.

"Don't try and run, just walk fast. Bend forward, keep your balance. Make sure one foot has a grip before you lift the other. Watch out for the snow. Go."

Powered by desperation, Alex went as fast as he could. Below him to his left, though, he could see one of the bald men had almost drawn even with him and was now beginning to move stealthily upward in a diagonal, aiming to cut him off ahead.

"Almost there, old chap," his grandfather said reassuringly in his ear. "Now, can you see the ladder?"

Alex peered down. He could just see it, poking up at the edge of the roof.

"Uh-huh."

"Good man. Now, start making your way down there. I'll be right behind you. Remember. Dunroamin'. Where wonderful food awaits."

Alex crouched, grabbed at the peak of the roof, and started lowering himself slowly down the other side on his stomach, crawling backward toward the gutter. He had a glimpse of his grandfather's shining black boot, stepping after him, pausing.

The going was very slippery. He decided it would be better if he turned over, sat facing up. At least he could see where he was going. Gingerly pushing himself up, he flipped carefully onto his back.

As he completed the maneuver, he realized what a mistake it was. His feet gave way, and he was sliding fast. Clawing uselessly at the tiles, he craned his neck to see the edge of the roof beyond his feet rushing to meet him, the hungry void beyond.

Blue-black sky went shooting over his head, streaked with white. It was just as if, he thought with a strange pang, he was back playing on the big slide in the park where his mother and grandfather used to take him when he was small, some crisp night before Christmas, coming home from the doctor's. He hadn't thought of that park in years.

The memory triggered another: standing small and half-asleep in pajamas outside the half-closed living room door after another hospital visit back then, a conversation half-caught, half-understood.

His mother's voice: ". . . *know* there's something wrong."

His grandfather, trying to sound reassuring: "Anne. He'll be fine. Children grow at different speeds. You'd never have known, but his father was much the same."

"I just . . . If there's something wrong with him . . . I don't think I could stand to lose them both. I don't . . ."

A harsh breath. A sound of sobbing.

"Sorry, Mum," Alex whispered now as his heels were about to hit the flimsy gutter. He stopped hard. His grandfather had caught him, he thought. But when he twisted his neck to grin up at him, there was no one there.

He lay very still, staring up at the slow clouds, trying to work out what had stopped him, trying to make sure he didn't stop it stopping him. The night seemed oddly silent, then he realized: all he could hear was his own ragged breathing and rapid pulse, hammering in his head.

Gaining a purchase with his feet, he began pushing back, away from the roof edge. Grunting, he worked his way upward, until he saw his savior: a small iron pipe, sticking out between tiles. It had snagged on his rucksack. He looked from it to the roof's edge, not far beyond, began laughing, then stopped himself.

The ladder was close. Carefully, he pushed over to it. Very, very carefully, he turned onto his stomach and lowered one foot then the other onto the top rung, the most beautifully solid thing he had ever stood on.

He took several steps down, then turned to look beneath him. There was the catwalk his grandfather had promised, leading to a section of flat roof. He turned back to see where his grandfather was.

The sight chilled him. The pulsing between his ears froze.

The old man was still far away up there, still on the peak of the roof, a shadow fighting shadows under the pale moon. From one side, he was being attacked by both bald men, knives slashing amid snowflakes. From the other, he was under harder assault from the tall man. He had a cane like his grandad's, and they were fencing savagely. As the wind shifted, the clacking noise came drifting down on the night.

Alex's grandfather was leaping from one attacker to another, coat swirling. Alex saw him raise an arm and twirl it around his head, almost as if he were dancing. Then he realized: he was flinging salt desperately at the air. The smudges of two fliers swarmed around his head, nipping in nastily to sting. Farther along the rooftop, the girl lurked among chimney pots, gesturing in their direction like a conductor.

Alex started back up the ladder.

One of the bald men made a wild thrust. The blade slashed his grandfather behind his knees. One leg buckled. Alex registered the blow as a physical sensation, as if he had been struck himself, punched hard in the chest.

The old man righted himself, kicked out. As he did, the tall man swung his cane hard at his head.

Alex saw his grandfather raise his own stick to parry the blow, too late, saw his head snap back, saw him shaking his head, trying to clear it.

Pushing up the ladder, Alex's foot slipped. His chin crashed against a sharp metal rung. He tasted blood, stood stunned a moment.

The second bald man lunged, stabbing forward. He was met with a foot in the face and sent staggering.

Alex's grandfather was upright again, going hard and fast at the tall man, driving him back. Raising his stick to fend off the old man's blows, he curled into his curious crouch, then leapt high, shooting over Alex's grandfather's head to make a precarious, skidding landing beyond the groggy bald men.

As the old man turned after him, the girl spun in a pirouette. Both fliers came swooping at once, smashing savagely into his head. They stayed close, hovering, blades biting, until he batted them fiercely away with his cane. As he struck each one, the girl's head snapped back like she had been slapped.

The tall man took his chance, jumped again. He swung his cane wildly as he came down.

Alex saw his grandfather spin from the blow.

The tall man's blade arced up at him in a vicious slash.

The old man hung there upright for a second under the moon, as though gathering himself to begin fighting again. Then Alex saw him sag, go limp, saw his foot slide away, saw him fall straight back, saw him pitch backward off the roof, saw him fall away out of sight. Then he couldn't see him anymore.

"Grandad!"

The shadow figures stood gazing down in the direction his grandfather had dropped. Hearing Alex, they snapped around, started moving.

"Grandad?"

His hands were numb on the icy ladder. He stood frozen, staring up at the horrific empty space where his grandfather had been.

They were getting closer, scraping toward him over the treacherous surface. The tall man had already left the others behind. He came crawling at furious speed, cane rattling a cold, evil tattoo on the tiles.

"Grandad."

Alex had no idea what he was supposed to do.

The tall man was closer, this long, lightless shape, moving faster, slithering, coming down on him like The End.

"Grandad."

The tall man lifted a hand. Alex heard his grandfather's words echoing in his head:

"Whatever happened back there just makes me more determined to make sure that he never gets his hands on it."

He flung himself roughly down the ladder.

His eyes burned. He was weeping. He didn't bother wiping the tears away. He didn't want to.

The bleak French roofs were gigantic and strange. The snowy night was vast and dark around him. Now, he realized, he was truly afraid. Truly alone. The tears stung. The pale catwalk blurred before him as he tore along it. When he reached the end, he leapt straight onto the iron railing without thinking, landed like a cat. A flat roof beckoned several feet away across a long black drop. Without breaking his motion, he jumped, landed in a run, sprinted recklessly on.

He flew over massive and mysterious roofs, breath tattered, not glancing back, not thinking where he was heading. Uncaring snow fell, impossibly soft. Then suddenly there was no ground beneath him. He pitched forward, spinning, as the snowy world hushed.

Forward and down into black silence. Falling.

After what seemed a long time, his head hammered something hard that would not move. He saw the moon. His grandfather smiling. His grandfather gone. White lights went off inside his skull, outlined in electric red. It was strikingly pretty. The lights moved off into blackness leaving twin trails, distress flares shooting out over a dark and empty sea. The red-white lines curled and bucked and struck themselves.

The darkness doubled, then doubled again.

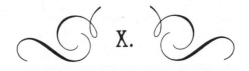

X.

A FISHY ESCAPE

FISH.

That was the first thing he became aware of. A stinging smell of fish.

Alex opened heavy eyes. Nothing but black. But he could smell fish. He let his eyes close and thought about it.

He had the odd sensation of being upside down. Things pressed against his face. Lots of small, hard things. Smelling of fish.

He felt sleepy, despite the pungent smell. It wasn't so bad when you got used to it. He was snoozy, warm, and comfortable. A picture swam lazily into his mind: a tall man in black, all shadow, reaching out.

With a surge of panic, he remembered. He scrabbled blindly in the choking scratchy darkness until his body worked out which way was up. Fighting desperately in that direction, he broke through into cold, sharp air, gulped down burning lungfuls, blinking rapidly, fearfully around in a bright light.

He was in a pale, narrow alleyway. More to the point, he was inside a deep open dumpster, filled to the brim with what looked like the claws of thousands of crabs and lobsters, the bones of countless fish.

He looked up. High above, the roof he had plunged from. How long ago? Pulling out his phone, he saw his hand shaking. A crack ran the length of the screen. He pushed the button. Nothing. Dead.

Dead.

The word sat like a stone in his racing mind.

Snow was still falling. He tried to slow his breathing, calm his nerves. A salt taste on his lips. Tears. His eyes were still sore. He must only have been out for a few minutes, he decided.

He grabbed at his shoulders. The rucksack was there. The toy robot still inside.

His head throbbed. He pressed at a tender spot, lifted trembling fingers away. No blood.

What to do?

He thought again of his grandfather, saw him falling again.

Alex hauled himself out of the dumpster, staggered, stood brushing crabmeat from his clothes. An oyster shell dropped from his shoulder. He blinked dumbly at a small plate screwed to the door.

Cesar & Fanny & Marius:

La haute gastronomie de la mer

He looked around, trying to get his bearings, trying to work out which way his grandfather must have dropped. Keeping close to the wall, he started along the alleyway on watery legs, stopped as his knees buckled beneath him.

He let himself crumple to the cold ground, forcing himself to rest a moment. His head buzzed horribly as the bleakness and weirdness of his situation came into full focus. A sharp shadow play of images repeated in his mind, the tall man's knife swiping up, the old man sagging, falling backward. Hurt. Helpless. Down.

Dead.

Even if that violent knife blow wasn't fatal, there was no way his grandad could have survived falling from the roof. But, then, Alex had survived. Maybe he was lying somewhere around there, injured, needing his help. Maybe he was okay and already looking for him. Maybe, maybe.

He wiped his face on his sleeve, stood. Leaning against the wall, taking deep, shuddering breaths, he stamped his feet to ease the shaking. It didn't help. Tugging the straps of the rucksack tight, he crept along the alley.

Coming out onto a small, quiet street, he could now see the pitched part of the roof they had stood on not long ago, looming dark and high against the moonlight. If he judged correctly, the old man must have fallen in front of the hotel, at the end of this street.

He paused, staring at the dirty white ground between his feet. On the snowy screen, the limp figure dropped endlessly backward. Another kind of sick feeling joined the nausea already clogging his throat. He didn't want to go around there and see. He had to. He took another breath, let it out, padded on.

At the corner, he crouched against the wall and peered around.

Nothing. He had been expecting to see, had been dreading to see, a crowd, an ambulance, police. Instead, it was simply the warm lights of the hotel entrance down there, a bright oasis in the night.

He looked up. The roof edge, the long, sheer drop. He scanned the hotel wall, the shadowy balconies. Nothing.

Maybe he'd been unconscious longer than he'd assumed. Maybe it was already a day later. Maybe the tall man's gang was bigger than he knew. Maybe there had been more of them, waiting down in the street. Maybe they'd had time to clear it all up and bundle his grandfather's body away and—

His grandfather's body.

What could he tell his mother? How would he tell her? The street dissolved in painful shapes of gold and white as fresh tears dazzled him. A sob racked his chest. He caught himself, wiped his eyes, forced his rushing mind to a halt.

He hadn't been out that long. Maybe they had smuggled his grandfather inside the hotel. Or his body. He needed a plan. His mind felt blocked.

He ground his teeth and looked back to the doorway. A taxi pulled up. An elderly couple in evening dress got out and entered the hotel, smiling and nodding to a small group coming out. The tall man. Beckman. The girl. The bald men.

They formed an animated huddle, the tall man pointing this way and that. He turned sharply. For a chilling moment he seemed to point straight at Alex.

Alex ducked back around the corner, sick with fear. When he forced himself to look again, the group had broken up, heading in different directions. He could see the bald men disappearing toward the far end of the street. The tall man turned and stalked back inside the hotel. The girl and Beckman were coming Alex's way fast, scanning the sidewalks.

He ran back the way he had come, passed the alleyway, kept going.

He had a rough plan to circle back to the hotel, get behind them, get inside. But the streets he took refused to lead the way he wanted to go. Soon he had lost his bearings entirely.

He came to a larger, brighter road, still busy. Groups of people, sounding excited and happy. Two street cleaners stood muttering grouchily, waving their hands at the snow. His mind bleached with blank white panic. What to do?

He went on at a run until he spotted a darkened shop doorway and dived in. He stood panting, looking back and searching faces.

No faces he recognized.

He chewed his lip and counted to ninety, then stepped into the street again, still glancing over his shoulder. When he was sure there was no one coming after him, he turned and ran straight into the girl.

Alex froze.

She stood small and alone on the busy pavement, face blank, large eyes burning darkly. They stared at each other as crowds brushed past in a constant stream. Once again, he was struck by the strange familiarity of her face—he felt certain he had seen her before all this, but couldn't think where. Panicking, he began to back away, turning.

"Now, now."

She lifted a finger. Her tone was fussy, her voice surprisingly deep. She spoke quietly, yet the words carried sharp and clear above the street noise. Despite himself, he turned back.

"Look, see?" She was smiling. She held two curious little brass discs, like tiny cymbals, each with a small loop of purple-and-black-striped cloth attached. Slipping them over the thumb and second finger of her right hand, she held them so they caught the light, then snapped them briskly together. The resulting *ting* was sharp but sweet and sounded to Alex as if it were ringing somewhere deep inside his head.

"Listen, now." She tapped an intricate rhythm, the varying rings of the cymbals linking up in a resonating chain between Alex's ears.

"Whatever are you doing out here all alone and lonely, child?" The lulling voice came floating on warm, rippling patterns of rings and tings. She started walking toward him. "Where have you been? It's late. Time to get you home."

Still keeping up the rhythm, she held out her other hand. Each fingernail was alternately painted black and purple. Alex watched his own hand reach to take it. With a reassuring squeeze of his fingers, she started leading him along the street.

As they went, hand in hand, the bell-like chimes washed over Alex like waves in her wake. Staring at the small black head bobbing along in front of him, he felt himself relax. The golden Paris night was vibrating, warm and very beautiful. He tried to remember why he was in Paris and why he was worried, but then he remembered that it didn't matter. Reflecting off the snow, the streetlights were the same color as the shining sound of little brass cymbals, and all the people were busy and happy. Just ahead, a dozen or so young men and women came spilling softly from a cinema and launched into a snowball fight, laughter playing like a melody on the vast shaking beat that filled his mind.

"Not far now, little Alexander," the girl said. "Then you can have a nice long sleepy-bye."

"Not far now," he echoed. He lifted his head to the sky. Beyond the haze of city lights, dim stars winked in blackness. "Not far," he whispered again.

The snowball that hit him was the perfect kind—the kind that's solid enough to fly fast and straight, and yet, when it smacks you in the face, breaks apart in a dusty explosion of frost.

The shock brought Alex back to himself instantly. Staggering and snorting, half of it up his nose, he was vaguely aware of a French girl shouting *"Pardon!"* through giggles off to his left.

Most of his attention, however, was taken up with his sheer horror at what he was doing.

"Oh, that's a shame," the small girl said, pouting a mock-sympathetic frown.

She tightened her grip with alarming strength, little fingers crushing his. For several seconds they stood arm-wrestling like that, until, with a desperate heave, Alex managed to rip free. Then he was moving.

"Run, then, dreary rabbit," she called.

He went dodging between grumbling bodies, barely seeing where he was going. He could sense her not far behind. She ran with ease, holding her coat above her ankles, dodging blackly among pedestrians like a small dancing storm cloud.

The crush of people on the sidewalk made the going slow, and when he saw a narrow alleyway looming ahead, he tore into it. He was halfway along before he realized he had picked a dead end. The way ahead lay blocked by a blank wall twenty feet high.

Overflowing trash cans lined the walls on either side. Alex threw himself down to his left, crawling between bins and foul-smelling plastic bags. Pressing into the dingy dampness, he peered back, trying to lie still and hold his shredded breath.

He saw her framed motionless in the alley's mouth, the bright busy street behind her looking as distant as another world. Slowly, she came walking in his direction, then stopped.

"Little running rabbit?" she called. "Listen now."

Again, she began tapping a splashing, lulling rhythm.

Feeling the sound creep over him, Alex dug his thumbnails into his fingers, fighting to keep his mind clear.

"No?" the girl said after a moment, stowing her cymbals away. "Oh, well. Hide-and-seek. How deeply tedious."

Rummaging inside her coat, she primly set something on the ground Alex couldn't see. A moment later, she had a second something balanced on her palm that he recognized all too well.

"High and low," she said. "Fee, fi, fo."

With a tiny motion of her hand, the flier lifted, disappearing into the shadows across the alley. Meanwhile, the other thing was moving over the ground on the side Alex hid. He heard it before he could see it: a strange, thin, shishing sound, shivering closer.

He shifted carefully among the garbage bags until he had a view. It was both deeply odd and bleakly familiar: a spring-thing much like the Slinky toy he used to play with when he was years younger. Except, instead of walking down stairs pulled by gravity, this one was walking end over end up the middle of the alleyway under its own eerie steam. Between each step, it paused and hung erect, quivering snakelike from side to side in the air. Hunting.

"Come on, bunny." The girl sounded bored. "Out you come. Hoppity-hop. Time for the pot. It's too late for games. Everyone will be here to see you soon. And then we'll have story time." As she spoke, she reached down and pulled something from her boot, held it sharp and ready, and took a few cautious steps into the alleyway.

The spring thing shuddered closer. Alex's racing mind ran empty. He felt rooted in terror. His whole world had become impossible and deathly.

"Sometimes there isn't time to think things all the way through. You just have to accept what's happening and get on and deal with it."

The memory of his grandfather's words came out of nowhere, close and clear. He blinked, shook his head. Deal with it. He started looking around, searching for inspiration.

A movement in the shadows across from him caught his eye. A thin gray cat sat hunched on a heavy wooden crate, watching the spring with the same fearful fascination he felt himself. As the thing took another coiling step forward, the cat backed away, lifting a thick, mangy paw. Instantly, with a whipping hiss, the spring lashed out, stretching across the alley at lightning speed. The crate exploded in vicious fragments, ripped apart.

The girl stretched on tiptoe to see what was happening as the spring gathered itself among the splinters, searching. Alex could see no sign of the cat—then he caught sight of it: high behind him, somehow scaling the wall at the end of the alley, clawing upward in pure fear. Watching with grim envy as its tail disappeared over the top, he noticed that, just behind him, an old metal bin lay empty on its side, lid beside it.

"Your turn next," the girl called.

With a roar half terror and half anger, Alex burst from hiding, grabbing for the bin, trying to lift it. It was heavier than he'd thought. The spring was coming fast, readying itself to lash out. As it did, he managed to haul the bin around to meet it, catch it. He quickly upended it, holding the spring trapped inside the way his mum caught wasps in jars at home.

But this was no wasp. The steel coil was thrashing power-fully. He could feel it whipping inside with a force that set his arms quivering. The bin was beginning to buckle.

The girl was stalking fast up the alley, one arm outstretched, fingers gesturing strangely. Her teeth glinted as she smiled. It was only when he heard its furious buzz that Alex remembered the flier. It came ripping from the shadows, an angry little orange glow. Without thinking, he let go of the bin, rushed to lift its lid as a shield.

At the edge of his vision, he was aware of the spring smash-ing free, but he was focused solely on the machine screaming at his head. The girl was drawing closer, raising her arm. The spring contracted to strike. He had a flashing memory of his grandfather swiping at the fliers on the roof, the girl's head jerking back as he struck them. Donor. Connected. Maybe get one and you can get them all.

Alex swung the lid savagely at the flier, turning so the entire force of his momentum was behind the blow. He didn't quite catch it full on, but he hit it hard, driving it against the alley wall. As it smashed against the brick, its nasty little blade arm was caught outside the lid, severing off with a satisfying snap.

He heard the girl gasp. She dropped, clutching her fore-head. The spring and the flier instantly fell lifeless. Alex took his chance. He saw her reach out weakly as he hurtled past, then he was out in the streets.

He ran a long time, sprinting, then jogging, dodging across roads and around corners until finally he had to stop. Pressed into another doorway he fought for breath, searching faces in all directions. The street was smaller, but still busy.

What to do?

What would his grandfather do? Alex swallowed, tried to concentrate, turned that question over. Thinking about the old man was painfully raw. Finally, an answer swam into focus:

Have yourself something to eat.

He sniffed and laughed. Then he thought. He was freezing, hungry, and exhausted, shivering from more than cold. Food wasn't a bad idea.

He stepped warily out, joining the current of passing strangers. After a while, he spotted a small, crowded café, people lingering at tables in the blushing window.

Conversation buzzed as he entered. A bank of six or seven computers lined the back wall under a neon sign that read CYBERC@FÉ.

A bored-looking teenager with half her hair shaved off and the rest swept into spiky black bangs leaned at the counter, nose in a book, _Le Vicomte de Bragelonne_. Sandwiches glowed in the blue light of a cabinet. Alex scoured his bewildered memory for anything of the French he had learned in school. As the word for tea slipped away, he recalled something his grandfather once declared: _"Basic rule of travel, Alex. Remem-_

ber this and you'll never go wrong: you can't get a decent cup of coffee in Britain. And you can't get a decent cup of tea anywhere else."

"Uh, bonjour," he tried. "Eh, *une café et une* . . . uh."

The teen lifted a pierced eyebrow at his disheveled state. She aimed a sniff in his direction, wrinkled her nose, and sighed before saying in English:

"What kind of coffee?"

"Oh." Alex had never drunk coffee before. He pictured his grandfather. "Just a black coffee, please."

"Sugar?"

Alex nodded. The girl pushed two packets and a wooden stirrer at him.

"Uh, and can I have that, please?" He pointed at an open baguette. "And can I use one of the computers?"

"Five euros for thirty minutes. No point buying a card for any longer, we close in twenty. I'll bring your sandwich over."

He sat at the computer in the farthest corner, stirred in sugar, and tried a sip. Bitter but sweet, the burning drink made his eyes water, then they were watering from something else. The white light reflecting in the steaming surface became a moon pushing through wispy clouds above a high roof.

Alex slumped. He felt his dead phone useless against his trembling thigh. He needed a plan. He stared blankly at the keyboard. All the letters were in the wrong places.

He logged into his email account. Another orchestrated campaign of messages from Kenzie and Co. lined up bold in his inbox. He almost had to admire the dedication. One from David, with an attachment: is your phone broke? phoned your house, your mum told me you're in paris!!! sneaky! old mr pin asked me to send you this sheet for an early xmas present its your favorite . . . quadratic equations!! Hahahaha give me a shout bon voyage.

He read in numb panic, barely taking it in. A message from another life. He flinched as the girl from the counter slid a plate down beside him.

"Enjoy."

He sighed, swallowed, tried to think of a way ahead. Hunting among the keys, he pecked a shaky message to his mother's address:

Mum, you need to come get me.
Grandad's gone. I can't find him.
I think he's dead. I think they killed
him.
Still in Paris. People were after us.
They're after me. I don't know what to do.
I'm alone. I need to hide.
I'll stay here another 15 minutes.
If you get this now, reply. But then I
have to go. Phone's broken.
If you don't answer, I'll hide until
tomorrow.

```
Then I'll come back in the morning and
email you again and you can come and
```

He stopped typing. And what?

He suddenly pictured his mum getting his message: her tablet pinging as she sat watching TV in the soft light of their living room, or reading in bed, or at breakfast tomorrow. Her panic, her face crumbling.

He had always tried to shield her from his troubles, if he could, as far back as he could remember, ever since the time of all his hospital visits. Those were the grieving years, when her sorrow was constant and she would still cry at the smallest things. Spilled milk, misplaced keys. A photograph she thought was lost. She was vulnerable to his vulnerability back then, and so he'd taught himself to avoid adding to her worry, avoid trouble and damage. The same way he had learned to stop asking her and his grandfather about his dad—because he could see the hurt, even though they tried to keep it hidden. *He was an architect. Here are all his books and pens, his drawings and his vinyl records. And there was an accident in a street far away before you were born . . .*

He read over what he had written. More terrible news from another distant street. He deleted the message.

Strangers chatted and laughed around the warm room. The girl by the cash desk stretched and looked at a clock behind her, scowled over the busy tables, then returned to her book. A heavy sense of isolation and desolation settled on him.

If he could hide out tonight, he could get a train for London in the morning. He still had his ticket. Just say his grandfather had sent him home. Make up a reason. Sometimes the old man disappeared for months on his travels without a word, so his mum wouldn't ask much at first. He suddenly realized that, all these years, he'd had no real idea just what it was his grandfather did for a living.

Used to do.

So: he could get home, just say nothing. Then take the toy robot somewhere, somewhere remote and lonely, bury it deep by moonlight where no one would ever find it, and then just keep quiet and . . .

He cut off this line of thought, ashamed to be thinking it. The idea of his grandfather's death had twisted into a hard knot in his chest. If he sent his thoughts too close to it, his entire body started to shake and shut down.

He couldn't just leave. Not without trying to do something. Not without knowing what was going on. If he had to tell his mum anything, at least he could find out the truth first. Besides, he suddenly realized: they knew where his house was. They would surely come after him eventually, looking for the robot. He couldn't risk his mum.

Drumming the table, mind a jittering blank, he forced himself to concentrate, pushing his thoughts forward, through all the bizarreness and horror, through his swarming panic and pain, to find the way ahead. An answer. There had to be one.

He thought briefly about the police but gave it up as he tried picturing what he might say. The unread emails from Kenzie's gang hung in a dull, mocking list before him.

What you gonna do about it?

Alex frowned at them.

What you gonna do about it?

His frown straightened. Sitting forward, he wiped his eyes, took a deep swig of coffee, and started typing:

```
Hi Mum—
Having a great time. Up late!
Going into the country to see Grandad's
friend's house.
Txt you soon.
Love,
A
```

He hit SEND before he had time to change his mind, then clicked into the search box and typed:

```
travel from paris to fontainblue
```

The results page asked:

```
Did you mean travel from Paris to
Fontainebleau?
```

He supposed that he did, clicked that, clicked the first result, and studied the screen. Fishing a pen from his rucksack, he copied timetables and directions onto a napkin between hungry bites of sandwich. He called up a map. He typed:

```
fontainebleau barbizon
```

He looked at more maps, scribbled and sketched more. As he finished, he noticed his hands had stopped shaking. He drained his coffee and left the café.

Then he turned around and went back in.

"Excuse me. Do you know how I get to, uh"—Alex glanced at the napkin in his hand—"the Gare de Lyon?"

"Métro." The girl at the register pointed a long lazy finger. "Line one. There is a station just along the street."

"*Merci.* Thanks."

Alex left again, turned around again, came back in again.

"Do you have any salt?"

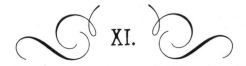

XI.

GOING UNDERGROUND

A GLOBE LAMP glowed across the street, illuminating an elegant iron sign that read METROPOLITAIN.

Alex hurried purposefully down the stairs, then gazed around, at a loss, trying not to look lost. Ticket machines lined the wall. He stared at the buttons and screens in incomprehension.

A boy and girl of about seventeen appeared beside him, leaning into each other, giggling. Alex watched carefully as the boy touched carelessly at buttons, then dropped coins into the slot as they went into an oblivious hanging kiss. When they had gone, he hit the same buttons, fed in some of the coins his grandfather had given him. A pinkish ticket popped out.

Through a turnstile. He squinted at a map on the wall. Down more stairs.

On the platform a few stragglers waited in weary fluorescent light, wending their ways home before the Métro shut down for the night. A train appeared, rattling out from the tunnels. Alex got on, took a seat by the doors. The doors closed. The train bumped off.

The carriage was around a third full. Tired-looking people under harsh gray light. A few empty seats along, the young lovers sat draped around each other, gazing into each other's eyes. Next to them, a young woman in a thin coat with dark rings around her eyes cooed quietly to a burbling baby in a stroller.

Looking at the mother and her tiny child, Alex sensed sadness welling from some place deep inside and turned away, watching the darkness rush past the windows. In the reflections, his grandfather fell endlessly. He pretended to yawn, tried to blink away the burning behind his eyes.

At the next station, a large group of men in soccer shirts boarded. As the train moved off, they stood around the doors in a rowdy huddle, singing a raucous song, loud even above the tunnel's roar.

Two more stations rolled past, looking like deserted fish tanks in the greenish light. At the third, the soccer fans started spilling noisily onto the platform, followed by everyone else in the carriage except Alex.

Looking up to watch them go, he recognized the name of the station on the tiled wall and realized with a pang: it was the station beside the hotel, the one his grandfather had pointed out on a street map a million years ago. The train had carried him back the way he had come.

He half rose, sat back. They would be long gone by now. He would stick to his plan. Get to Harry. Tell him what happened.

Give him the robot. Hope he could tell him what to do next. What was going on.

The line of people trying to get off had come to a muttering, impatient halt. Half the soccer fans were out on the platform, half still inside. Those outside seemed to have decided it would be a tremendous joke to stop their friends getting off. Behind them, two tall men in black coats, hats, and sunglasses stood waiting to board, one carrying an enormous white double bass case.

Inside the carriage, the soccer fans had taken it upon themselves to help the young woman with the baby get her buggy off the train, despite her protests. So far, they had managed to get themselves tangled in the stroller's wheels while they sang a drunken song to the infant. Hoisted between them, the baby sat in his chair like a triumphant little king on his throne, waving a tiny, happy pink fist at the hullabaloo.

Finally, with a lot of pushing and pulling and to an angry hail of advice from the passengers stuck behind them, the fans wrestled the stroller out onto the platform, cheering one another and accepting the thanks of the harried young woman. As the last passengers departed, the two men pushed their way on and sat awkwardly at the far end from Alex, case propped between them. No one else boarded. The train lurched off into the thundering tunnel.

Aside from him and the two men, the car was now empty. Alex's eyes wandered while his mind raced. He looked down at the men with the double bass. They sat with heads bowed sleepily, hats tugged low, coat collars pulled up.

He gazed at the signs and strange advertisements without taking any of them in. He looked at the double bass case. He looked at his own reflection distorting in the rushing window. He looked at the double bass case again.

There. On the curving side, near the bottom. A smear of red. And just above it, sticking out from inside, an edge of gray cloth.

Dove gray. The exact dove gray of his grandfather's coat.

Alex sat frozen. He pulled his eyes from the bloody smear to the men's faces. As he looked, the man closest turned his head. Fresh horror broke over him.

Beneath the hat, the face was unfinished, made of dull, silvery metal.

Life-sizers. The word popped starkly into Alex's head.

The thing sat utterly still, seeming to stare at him. Its companion hadn't moved, remained head bowed, one huge, leather-gloved hand resting on the double bass case. The train's rattling roar rang between Alex's ears, one clattering thought pounding out over and over to the rhythm:

*They're-*hi-*ding-his-body-they're-*hi-*ding-his-body-they're-*hi-*ding-his-body-they're—*

Drenched by an icy wave of fear, he got to his feet.

The things sat motionless.

Feeling weak, he started backing away, stopping only when he got to the end of the carriage.

The things remained immobile.

The rucksack on Alex's back pressed against the door to the

next car. Pulling his eyes from the silver giants, he quickly studied the door, opened it with difficulty, slipped hurriedly through.

The carriage was empty except for a solitary man, slumped asleep. Alex shook his shoulder. A smell of alcohol rose from him.

"Please. Can you help me?"

The man grunted an angry snore.

"Please, I think there's . . . a body." The words jolted him as he spoke them. He felt sick.

The man snorted in his sleep, turned away, breathing louder.

The tunnel howled. Alex turned back. Through the glass door panel he could see the robots just sitting there. The one nearest still faced in his direction. Everything in him told him to flee for the opposite end of the train. He saw his faint reflection, framed in the glass. He looked small and pale. A familiar sense washed through him, the frozen feeling of being trapped forever inside that photograph from his childhood, the helpless little creature.

He pushed out a trembling breath and muttered aloud: "What are you doing, Alex?"

He went back through the door.

The life-sizers didn't move as he reentered. He stood with his back against the door, trying to gather courage, trying to think of something to do. Reaching slowly into his pocket, his fingers closed around the salt packets from the café. He took a tentative step forward.

Nothing happened.

The scream of the train boomed to the same thundering tempo as his heart. Another step. Nothing. Another step. Another.

The closest machine shot to its feet. It stood well over six feet tall, face glinting in the flat light. The sunglasses stared blindly down at him.

He started backing away. The thing stood, seeming to watch him. Then it came at him.

As Alex drew level with the doors in the center of the carriage, the life-sizer whipped out its arm like black lightning. Alex stumbled and fell back more than he actually dodged the blow, but it was enough to carry him just out of its reach. The giant gloved fist swiped viciously over his head, smashing into the steel pole by the doors, buckling the metal, tearing the pole from the ceiling.

Alex scrambled backward along the floor, the robot striding after him. Getting to his feet, he flung himself at the door to the next carriage. It wouldn't budge.

He fumbled desperately, turning just in time to see another vicious blow swinging at his head. As he ducked, the thing's fist smashed through the door's thick safety glass. When it tried to pull back its arm, its heavy coat sleeve snagged on the broken pane. It stood there, momentarily caught, silently trying to yank itself loose.

Alex was trapped, pinned against the door by the struggling machine. It smelled like coins, oil, and sweat. Digging frantically in his pocket, he pulled out two salt packets and ripped them open with his teeth, tasting the salt. Without thinking, he rammed them against the life-sizer's mesh mouth, scraping hard along the grill.

The robot abruptly stopped moving.

Alex pulled himself free, staggered out of reach. Stopped. Still it didn't move.

He hadn't known what the salt might do, but he hadn't expected this. The machine stood motionless, pressed to the door, arm still stuck through the shattered glass. Alex looked back to the other. It sat unmoving, head bowed. He looked back at the thing behind him. Lifeless.

The train rumbled and rattled on its way, unconcerned.

Alex moved tentatively toward the middle of the carriage. His plan now went only as far as getting off alive at the next stop, whatever it was. It couldn't be long now.

He stood by the doors, muttering "Come on," and keeping his eye on the robot seated by the instrument case. A huge, sickening crashing and ripping came from behind him.

The machine at the door had returned to life, and it had gone berserk. It punched furiously at the door, smashing out the glass. As it pulled itself free, its coat sleeve ripped, exposing a girder-like iron arm. It wheeled, came stumbling down the aisle toward Alex, both fists windmilling wildly, flinging blind, lethal punches at the air.

Now, with horror, Alex saw the other come awake, too. It rose abruptly, stood seeming to watch its colleague. Then it strode quickly up the aisle toward Alex.

He was caught in the middle. He searched his pockets furiously for more salt. His fingers closed around two last packets. He pulled his hand out—too quickly, watched in dismay as they slipped from his grasp and sailed feebly across the car, disappearing beneath the seats.

The wild life-sizer was almost upon him. He could actually feel the breeze as its savage arms whirled. Seized by hopeless instinct, he threw himself to the floor. Wrapping his arms around his head, he closed his eyes and waited for the blows to rain down.

Nothing. A second passed. Alex forced one eye open. Then both popped wide.

The mad machine had gone by him, was now bearing down upon its partner. The other life-sizer stood in the aisle, looking calm. As its frenzied twin approached, it took small steps backward, keeping out of reach of the swinging arms, until it was almost at the double bass case again. There, it stopped. When the demented thing came at it now, it raised its arms to ward off the assault, then went into a ferocious counterattack.

Alex pressed himself against the doors, watching the two giants go at each other, trading horrific metal blows. Sparks flew as they flung each other around the carriage, smashing seats and shattering windows with heads, fists, and elbows. But the salt-crazed life-sizer was being pushed steadily back. Back toward Alex.

The train was slowing at last. He could see the lights of a Métro station rolling toward him in painful slow motion. With the battling things almost on him, he wrenched at the doors, stabbing at the button to open. For a second, he felt one huge metal hand tug almost gently at his rucksack. Then he fell onto the platform, scrabbling furiously for cover as they came tumbling out behind him.

The machines stood trading blows in the deserted station. The mad robot held its partner by the wrist, throwing a flurry of punches at its head as it tried to get back onto the train. The train doors closed. With a surge of violence, the other robot broke free, knocking its deranged doppelgänger down.

The train had started moving again. Stalking after it, as the last carriage passed, the robot whipped out an arm, sinking a hand like a hook into the rear of the car, allowing itself to be dragged off behind it.

Crouched behind a bench, Alex caught a final regretful glimpse of the white instrument case sitting in the empty, battered carriage as it rolled into the tunnel. Spread-eagle a few feet away, the crazed robot lay flailing uselessly at the ground, then pushed itself awkwardly to its feet and tottered drunkenly to the platform's edge.

In a thoughtless rush that surprised himself, Alex burst from behind the bench, launching a desperate shoulder charge at its back. It was like running into a brick wall. As he bounced painfully away, the machine whipped around, swinging out wildly. The blow barely connected, and Alex's rucksack took the brunt of it, yet the force still sent him sprawling to the floor. At the same time, it was enough to send the thing rocking off balance. Toppling backward, the machine fell to the tracks with a resounding *clang*.

Crawling to the edge, Alex saw it lying unmoving, face-up, then he flinched back as it hauled itself upright again. It ignored him, lurching crazily off in the direction the train had disappeared, arms whirling.

Alex realized he had been holding his breath. He peered after the life-sizer as it vanished down the tunnel. Faint clanging noises in the humming darkness. Maybe a small spark. Then nothing.

He checked himself over. He still seemed to be in one piece. Massaging his aching shoulder, he weighed the idea of jumping onto the tracks and heading into the tunnel, then dismissed it. Even if he caught up with the double bass case, even if the mad robot wasn't lurking in the darkness ready to pulverize anything that came near it, he would be no use alone.

He had his plan, as far as it went. He had to stick to it. It was all he had.

The platform was cold. He shivered. There were voices sounding above, footsteps hurrying on the stairs. Métro workers. A security camera gazed impassively down on him. Sprinting for the exit, he ducked past two men in uniform before they could stop him. Ignoring their shouts, he ran, up and out, into the rest of the night.

XII.

SOUTH, THEN NORTH BY NORTHWEST

SHORTLY AFTER SIX the following morning, the first train went rolling southward through Paris toward Fontainebleau.

Alex slumped sore and exhausted in an empty carriage. Holding his throbbing head to the cold window, he watched the dreamlike white city slide past in the darkness and fought against the lulling motion, trying to stay awake.

Following his escape from the Métro, he had spent the night stumbling a frightened and wary circuit around the vicinity of the Gare de Lyon, waiting for the station to open and the first trains to begin. Long, dim hours of trudging through grimy snow, sticking to back alleys and side streets, crouching in basement doorways and huddling over mysterious steaming vents, seeking warmth, seeing robots and a tall man and small girl creeping out from every shadow. More than once, he had decided to go to the police after all, or give it up and go home. But here he was still. Getting on with it.

Every part of him ached—the parts he could feel, anyway. His feet were still numb from cold. At least the heat was on. Hunching over the radiator by his seat, he gulped the coffee he had bought in the station and tore halfheartedly at a dry croissant. He was sure he was very hungry, but the emptiness in his stomach had curdled into a sick, acidic ache. Painful, weary life crept gradually back into his limbs.

He fell asleep for a while, and while he slept, he dreamed. He dreamed of his grandfather. He watched that dream spin and fall and drain away like water down a plughole. Black came pouring up, spiraling out, a spreading shadow, thin and tall. This shadow jumped through the world like an alien cricket, filling it with blackness, creaking and clattering. Then the dream of shadows jumped away into shadows. Finally, he dreamed he was weeping. He woke.

Lights winked past outside. Setting his rucksack on the seat beside him, Alex dug down and pulled out the white box containing the robot. Despite the cushion of clothing around it, it was a little crushed from the life-sizer's punch. He got the original old box out of that, relieved to see it intact, then finally the tin toy itself, cold and pristine in his hand. He sat studying it, rocking gently with the train. In the strange surroundings, under the bare light, its eager shambles of a face looked uglier than ever.

"See what you've done?" Alex murmured bleakly. "I should throw you under this train, just let it roll right over you."

The empty eyes stared up.

"What can you tell me?" he whispered. "What do I do?"

The train clacked quietly along, as though trying not to wake anyone. Holding the toy, Alex began nodding toward sleep again. And then he felt it. The same sensation he had experienced in his bedroom. He couldn't turn away from the robot, couldn't shift his eyes from the devouring black holes in its head. But at the edge of his vision, he sensed the carriage around him flickering, changing.

A cold grip settled around his heart, immense loneliness. But something was different. Before, the chill, melancholy sensation had left him feeling sick. This time, after a few seconds, he began to feel he recognized its touch, could almost settle into its somber embrace. His pain drained away.

He sat like that for what felt a long time, until, from far away, he heard the door at the end of the carriage open. He looked up, feeling as though he were lifting his head through treacle.

Three teenagers had entered, swinging along the poles toward him through the flickering black-and-yellow light. The cell phone of one beat out a tinny din of music, sounding small, ridiculous.

Senses hovering above, looking down, he watched them approach, laughing and pointing as he bent disheveled and wet-eyed over his robot. Without understanding their words, he knew they were berating him for playing with toys, knew further that this was only the excuse for what was about to happen.

He actually saw the current between them, the chain of

small exchanges and signs. The dilations of the pupils of their eyes, the quickening pulses at their necks, chemical scent signals, the three of them working themselves up, waiting to see when it would start, who would go first. Two, he saw now, were looking more eagerly to the third, the leader. It was as if he was watching a playback of a scene he had already studied many times before.

Sure enough, this boy was going to take the toy. They took a long time moving through the thick and pulsing air. He was still five feet away, slowly drawing back one hand, preparing to aim a slap.

"I want you to leave me alone and go away," Alex distantly heard himself say. Faintly, like a stir of a breeze, he felt the words go from him, moving.

Full horror and grief dawned across this other boy's face. He stumbled softly backward, crumbling against his friends, who took an age turning their faces down to him in confusion. He collapsed gently, choking, clawing at his throat, gasping small noises. Alex sat watching through the vibrating light, distantly heard the others shouting, shaking the suffocating boy. His eyes were bulging, desperate, rolling back, getting lost.

"No! *Stop!*"

This voice was loud. Alex realized it was his own. His mind came shooting back to him as though carried on the end of a cosmic elastic band that had been stretched too tight, then let go. The rush made him feel sick. Pain came flooding back into his head and shoulder.

Retching, the boy on the floor stumbled up, staggering quickly away without looking back. The other two stared at Alex, then at each other. They hurried away after their friend.

Alex sat panting, head in hands. Cold tin pressed against his pounding temple. He pulled back, looked at the robot, looked away. Packing it up, he stowed the toy deep in his rucksack.

His hands trembled badly. Leaning back, he gazed at the murky landscape slipping past outside. His reflection stared gravely back from the phantom world of the window. He tried to work out what it was thinking.

BEFORE LONG, THE train pulled into a small, plain white station, FONTAINEBLEAU AVON, glowing ghostly in the early dark. It was not quite seven o'clock. A few scattered people haunted the gloomy platform, bundled in scarves and hats against the weather.

Alex spotted a guard busying himself with pamphlets at a rack inside, a small man with a bushy gray mustache and spidery eyebrows. He approached him, clearing his throat.

"Uh . . . *pardonnez-moi.*"

The guard turned, frowning and yawning.

"*Il ya un* . . . uhm. Do you speak English?"

The guard's frown deepened. He shook his head.

"I need to get to Barbizon. Barbizon?"

"Barbizon." The guard nodded.

"Is there . . . *il ya un autobus?*"

The guard raised his eyebrows. "Ah!" he said. *"Non."* He showed Alex his wristwatch, tapped it, shook his head, and shrugged. Lifting an armful of tattered leaflets, he headed off toward his ticket booth.

Alex shrugged after him. As he turned back idly to the display, his gaze stuck on a brochure in English: "Walking Tours of Fontainebleau."

It opened out into a rough map of the area, which he compared against a quick line diagram he had sketched in the Internet café. There was Barbizon, highlighted vaguely northwest. It didn't look too far. He studied the brochure a little more and tucked it into his pocket, then headed out into the black winter morning, back into the cold.

The snow had stopped falling but lay thick. Leaving the station, he passed through the lights of a slowly waking town, then struck out along a dim deserted main road, soon swallowed on either side by tangled trees as it plunged into a vast forest, silent and dark.

An hour and a half later, he was still tramping through these woods. Snow came and went intermittently. The wedge of sky above bled slowly from navy blue into purple then slate gray. Otherwise the view was unchanging. Ahead, nothing but endless white road cutting bleakly between dense and jaggy black trees. Behind, more of the same.

His legs felt leaden. His body felt too hot and painfully cold. From time to time, he tensed as a solitary car swished past, headlights staining the snow, blurry drivers staring out at the puzzling figure he cut by the roadside in the pale morning.

He heard a soft crashing among the trees and almost jumped out of his skin. Dropping into a crouch, he desperately scoured the misty inner landscape for movement, tired eyes straining. The seventh or eighth time it happened, he finally saw it was only snow falling, dropping in drifts from black branches.

At long last, he came to an intersection he hoped he recognized from the map. Another bare road cut across the one he stood on and led off left, through more trees. After a while, he came out into a landscape of farmland, flat under a low, featureless white sky. Far to his right, a small plane buzzed over a distant field, a smudgy speck in the air. Snow came on again, thin flakes stinging his cheek.

His stomach gave another long, gassy gurgle. He had bought a bar of chocolate with raisins at the station in Paris but had been unable to face it and fished for it now in the side pocket of his rucksack where he'd slipped it. He froze as his fingers brushed something unexpected. Something cold and jagged.

Cautiously, he set the bag down, stepped back, and stood regarding it. Taking a breath, he dived at it, grabbed inside as fast as he could, and pulled his hand back out.

The robot he held was very small, khaki green, around three inches tall, and utterly lifeless. Lolling loose, its head was a flattish circle, like a shallow saucer, with a sharp spike protruding from the center. Two big eyes and a happy, grinning mouth were painted above and below the spike. Its thin little body had been bent in two until it had almost snapped.

A jittery kaleidoscope of thoughts tumbled around Alex's head. He flashed on an image of the life-sizers fighting in the underground train: one had tried to reach him, tugging at his rucksack by the door . . . Planting this? He shivered as his body remembered the other big robot's wild punch smashing into his rucksack . . . Crushing it? Killing it?

He laughed, a hysterical chuckle of triumph, kicking his feet in the snow in a little dance of celebration.

Fascinated, he held the machine close, turning it, studying the rough welding, the minute joints of its limp limbs, the talented yet somehow childish cartoon painting of the face. There was a tiny hairline crack where it had been dented. He ran a finger over it, and moisture glistened. Condensation, he thought, then his stomach turned as he remembered: *pieces of people*. With an involuntary shudder of revulsion, he dropped the robot.

It landed headfirst on his foot, and, as it struck and bounced off, its head snapped to another angle. With a sudden *whirr*, its arms started spasming. It sat up in the snow, broken body hanging at an awkward slant. But fully active.

"Oh, that's great, Alex," he said to himself. "Oh, well done. That was brilliant."

The tiny robot's head was lifting, rotating. It reminded him of something. As soon as he thought it, the answer came. Satellite dish.

He spun, suddenly desperate, searching for a sign of anyone or anything following. There was nothing. Only the snowy road, the trees, the flat fields, the little plane whirring in the stony sky.

He lifted his foot, thinking of stamping the robot into the ground, when it jumped nimbly at his leg, beginning to climb his trousers, clambering behind him, spindly arms working fast.

For the next minute, anyone passing would have seen a boy engaged in a curious, awkward kind of dance by the roadside, bending, spinning, and twisting, seemingly punching himself about the body. Finally, he caught it, stood holding it squirming, trying to think what to do. Stamp it. Bury it.

Stepping into the ditch by the road, he began kicking a hole in the snow while the robot thrashed weakly in his hand. The plane sounded louder, a high whine. Glancing up, Alex thought it was perhaps some trick of the frozen landscape, distorting, flattening, and amplifying sound. It didn't look any nearer. He tried to focus on it and felt his eyes sliding cross-eyed.

Blinking, he looked again. The buzzing was louder, angry. Sickeningly familiar. It wasn't a small plane on the horizon at all. It was something much smaller, and much, much closer.

As he watched, the vibrating black smudge split in two. A pair of growing dots lined up side by side. Their mosquito-like buzz was furious. Two fliers. Shooting straight for him.

Alex flung himself down to the ditch as the angry whine swooped at him in stereo. When he lifted his head, they were on the other side, climbing, turning, coming again.

The only cover lay back among the trees. Scrambling up, he

launched himself desperately along the road. There was snow in his mouth. The struggling robot went flashing up and down in his grip as his hands pumped air. He heard the whirr, very close, threw himself down, feeling the flier's touch in his hair.

He'd made it halfway. The black trees waited ahead. The fliers were arcing high behind with a hungry hum. Seized by a thought that had been chewing at him since the train, he lurched up, digging in his rucksack. Pulling out the boxes, he threw them aside and turned, brandishing the tin toy robot at the sky.

He stood wielding it as though it were an ancient and mighty torch in his fist. He held the heart of everything, all the strangeness, violence, and mystery. The fortune-telling machine Marvastro had prophesized *power*. Well, here it was. Alex stood tall, channeling all his thought, all his will into the weird old toy, silently commanding the fliers to explode, to fall burning from the air.

Exactly nothing happened.

He was surprised to find he had time to feel stupid. Then the flying things came whining fast. Diving down, he felt one slice his ear. Lifting his head, he left a red stain on the snow. Staggering up, he ran, a robot in each hand now.

Torn breath rattled his chest. His exhausted legs slid and stumbled. He looked back. Something slashed his face, knocking him down again.

Breath slammed out of him. The flying thing bore in,

drilling savagely at his neck. Gasping, Alex rolled away, flinging himself over in the snow. He got to his feet. It hovered in front of him. Too late, he remembered the other. A *shish* whipped the back of his head, sending him to his knees.

Almost at the trees.

He went into a swaying run as the fliers regrouped. Their buzzing scream reached a frenzied pitch as Alex launched himself desperately forward, falling into the trees at last, hurling himself deeper into a wiry tangle of undergrowth, branches scratching at his eyes.

With difficulty, he turned and looked back. One of the fliers hovered jerkily out there, just beyond the trees. The other had come into the woods, droning among the thin trunks, holding its vicious little arms ready, the hook, the blade.

The machine was moving slowly, searching for him. As quietly as he could, Alex stowed the old toy robot back in his rucksack. As he shifted to rebalance, his hand closed around something solid on the ground: a broken branch, half-buried in frozen snow. He shoved the struggling dish-headed robot into his pocket and zipped it shut. Tugging at the branch, he began working it loose.

The flier was almost upon him. Alex shot up, swinging the branch like a baseball bat. The machine ducked, but not fast enough. He sent it smashing against a tree. It hit hard and fell to the forest floor. Before it could take off again, Alex had both hands around it.

The flier slashed frantically at him. He tried to dash it against the tree, against the ground, but the pull of the propeller on its head was too strong. It was all he could do to keep hold.

The other flier, on guard outside the trees, was buzzing furiously, jerking angrily up and down. The landscape beyond it was empty, as white and peaceful as a dull Christmas card. Far off along the hazy road, Alex could see a large truck, moving slowly toward him, orange lights flashing front and rear.

He slowly forced the flier down, holding it against the ground, leaning his weight on it, hoping this would at least stop it from cutting his hands so much. His arms were numb from cold and effort. He clung on desperately.

The truck was getting near. He could hear its steady rumble over the fliers' livid buzzing. Alex gazed out at it with distant longing. It offered confirmation that a normal world still existed, even if he was no longer part of it. A fine spray came off the back of the vehicle. A calm part of his mind observed: they're out plowing the roads, putting down salt to melt the snow.

The flier strained mightily in his stinging hands. The robot in his pocket tickled his stomach miserably.

They're putting salt down.

Alex burst from the trees, taking the waiting flier by surprise. He tore across the snow toward the truck, almost level with him now, dimly aware of the machine behind climbing high again. The one in his grip was making a bloody, sticky mess of his hands, but he held tight.

Hitting the road, he almost fell as he bent to scoop up some of the grit the truck was trailing. He rubbed the stuff hard into the nasty little machine in his hand. Instantly, it stopped struggling. Gathering up more, he dropped a handful into his pocket, grabbed the robot in there, and rubbed it around in it.

He took off after the slow-rolling truck, bringing the robot out of his pocket and ramming it together with the flier. They wriggled lazily but made no effort to get free. Drawing level with the plow, he threw them hard, watched them curve over the side, plopping down into its vast load of salt.

Alex stumbled to a halt, stood doubled over, retching after breath, watching the truck rumble off into the forest. Then he fell as the other flier smashed into his head.

Rolling onto his back on the road, half-dazed, he saw the thing rise high above him, then turn, jackknifing into a plummeting kamikaze dive, flashing down in a screaming streak.

"Not yet," he said.

He forced himself to lie still, watching it come.

"Not yet."

It was close enough now he could see its arms were raised, held before it like a superhero in an old comic book, blade and hook coming straight for his eyes.

"Right."

With the little machine less than three feet above, Alex violently scooped up two handfuls of salt-laced snow, heaving them into the air. The two piles exploded in a messy cloud around the robot.

A shower of gritty frost rained down on his face. Something heavier fell onto his chest. Rubbing his eyes, Alex lifted his head to see the little flier sitting stunned and dejected on top of him.

Getting to his feet, he carried it to the trees, threw it as far in as he could. His hands were a mass of bloody scratches. He bent and packed snow around them, holding them under until he couldn't stand it.

He upended his rucksack, emptying everything to the ground, searching for any more surprises. Nothing. He recovered the discarded boxes and packed the old robot away. Sitting on a fallen tree, waiting for his heart to stop racing, he munched the chocolate bar, suddenly ravenous. He watched the day around him. The changing French light. Then he stood, brushed the worst of the mess from his clothes, and headed on along the road.

XIII.

DUNROAMIN'

ENTERING BARBIZON HEIGHTENED Alex's sense of having wandered far from reality. A small, curious collection of stone buildings, the place seemed to have been dropped at the edge of the forest from another age, a Hansel and Gretel landscape, gingerbread houses iced with snow.

There were few people around. The town gave an impression of being shut for winter. He slunk warily along narrow streets, asked fruitlessly at a café, a bakery, and an art gallery with nothing on display. No one knew of a house called Dunroamin'.

The cold had seeped into his bones, numbing panic, grief, and fear to a dim hum. He had moved beyond exhaustion, walked mechanically, as though someone had stuck a key in him and wound him up.

Finally, a dignified old woman walking a fuzzy white dog nodded, pointed, and gave vague instructions in English. The dog yapped incessantly at Alex's ankles. The woman stared at his stained clothes, scratched hands. With a brisk good-bye, she strode on, little dog snarling and straining at its leash.

A road lined with hedges led out of the village. The low slanting sun sent Alex's shadow stretching bleakly before him on the snow. Every so often, he passed an iron gate. He counted four, stopped at the fifth, out along an isolated stretch. A plaque was screwed to the gatepost.

DUNROAMIN'

A chain with a well-worn wooden handle hung alongside. Reaching out, Alex hesitated, drew back. He looked farther along the road. It curved out of sight. Stepping back from the gate, he let his shadow lead him on around the corner.

There were no more houses, nothing but a tree-lined road with empty fields on either side sloping up to crests where the great black-green forest began again. He walked until he had counted twelve trees on his left, then stopped, stepping off the road.

Glancing cautiously around, he knelt at the tree and dug in the snow with his stinging hands. Propping his rucksack against the trunk, he took the robot out of its boxes. Rummaging deeper, he found a crumpled plastic bag, wrapped the toy inside, tying it tight. Setting it in the hole, he filled it in, patting the snow carefully smooth. Finally, he gathered more snow, scattered it loosely on top. Standing, he put the empty boxes back in his rucksack and considered his work. No obvious disturbance.

Twelve trees. Just to be sure, he walked around the trunk to the side farthest from the road, took out his house keys, and scratched a small *A* into the bark. He paused, looking at the keys with a sudden pang. He wondered when he would see his own front door again.

He started back, then stopped, suddenly painfully uncertain about leaving the robot, but equally uneasy about taking it into that house without knowing what waited. The whole landscape seemed pregnant with threat. The fliers had come from somewhere.

He considered his trail of footprints in the snow, a lonely, single, perfect set—leading straight to where he'd buried the toy. He couldn't see much he could do about it. A thought occurred. Stepping back into the road, he headed for the next tree, walked down and around that, then back into the road and on, doing the same thing for the next five trees.

"Okay," he told himself aloud. "Come on."

On his way back, he dutifully circled around the eleven other trees he had passed, glad no one was around to see him.

At Dunroamin', he yanked the bell chain. Nothing seemed to happen. The gate squealed as he pushed it open. A thin path twisted through dense, high bushes, bringing him out at a large house. It was a long stone building with lead glass windows, one story for the most part, save for a squat, three-floor tower above the front door, a Swiss-style construction of white plaster and dark wooden beams.

His feet crunched on the doorstep. Looking down, his skin prickled as he realized he stood on the remains of a thick line of salt. The urge to run overtook him. But even as he turned to go, he knew he couldn't. He could barely move his legs. And run where? His entire plan took him as far as this door. Beyond this, he had nothing. This was it. Taking a breath, he tried rehearsing what he would say.

His grandfather. Stabbed. Fell. And.

Another chain hung by the door. He pulled it, and chimes sounded deep inside the house. Nothing else. He reached for it again.

"Stand out where I can see you."

The voice came from above. Alex stood back, squinting up. A window in the tower was slightly open. The black barrel of a shotgun pointed down at him.

"Mr. Morecambe?" Alex called.

Silence. The gun wagged.

"Who are you?"

"I'm Alex . . . I was coming to see you with my grandfather, about the robot, but . . ." His voice caught. "He's dead." He swallowed hard, looked at the ground, blinking tightly.

When he looked back up, the gun was gone.

"Mr. Morecambe?"

He heard a rattle of bolts at the door and the scrape of keys in several locks. Finally, it opened.

A tubby man in his late fifties with a florid, flushed face and slicked-back black hair shot with white stood before him, wearing black dress trousers, a white shirt, and a green bowtie that looked to be cutting into his neck. He stared at Alex, hand opening and closing on the shotgun.

"Mr. Morecambe?"

"Call me Harry. Please." He had a faint accent Alex couldn't place. "Come in."

Morecambe stepped out and looked around as Alex entered, then, with much scraping and rattling, quickly locked and barred the door again.

They stood in a pale lemon hallway, regarding each other awkwardly. A staircase curved up into the small tower. On a cabinet, two antique mechanical musketeers held their swords poised either side of a vase holding a spray of winter flowers.

"Your grandfather's—?" Morecambe began, then stopped. He patted Alex's shoulder. "You look half-frozen. As if you had been in a war. Let's get you something hot to drink."

Frowning grimly, Morecambe led him into a large, dim kitchen. Pulling a chair out from a bare wooden table, he gestured for Alex to sit by the fire crackling beside a black iron stove. Alex did, thankfully, feeling weariness wash over him completely.

Morecambe leaned his shotgun in the corner, between the door to the back garden and another closed door. He opened a cupboard, closed it, opened another.

"Here we are. You look famished. I'll make you something."
He busied himself at the counter, his back to Alex. "Tell me
what's happened."

Morecambe listened without interrupting. Alex told him
everything—everything except the part about the boys on the
train, the way he had made the boy choke, the odd sensation
he had felt with the robot. Something stopped him there, some
vaguely shameful, secret feeling. By the time he had finished,
gulping down the last of his coffee and thin cheese sandwich,
the afternoon was growing dark outside. He flexed his fingers
and winced, studying the slashes on his hands, waiting for
whatever would come now.

"My God," Morecambe finally muttered. He sat bowed, rubbing his forehead, eyes shielded by his hand.

"I don't know what to do," Alex prodded, after they had sat
in silence several moments. The meager meal seemed only to
increase his exhaustion. He slumped forward, staring at the
table. "I just know Grandad wanted me to get to you." The
wind picked up, moaning mournfully in the eaves of the house.

"You saw him . . . die?" Morecambe said.

Alex opened his mouth. Nothing came out. He nodded
weakly, turning his palms up in helpless confirmation.

"He said you could check if the robot was definitely what
he thought it was," he finally managed. "I don't know what
he planned after that. What I should do now. There's so
much I don't understand. These people, those _things_. The

Tall Man, I call him. The girl. Do you know who they are?"

Morecambe regarded Alex in the faint light. Firelight danced in his eyes.

"He hasn't told you anything, has he?" he said after a long pause. "No, well, he can be like that. Your grandfather. A most infuriating man."

Alex glared up at him, instantly liking him less. Tears nipped briefly at his eyes, putting a swaying gray screen between them.

"Part of his charm, you might say," Morecambe hurried on placatingly, looking away. "Now, what can I tell you? This Tall Man of yours. Well. He and your grandfather go back a long way, you know. The girl, too. You didn't know? A long way. Longer than you might imagine. Right back to the beginning. And now, here we are, close to the end."

Morecambe rose, gathering up cups and plates, and carried them to the sink, filling it with frothing water.

"Yes, there is much you should know," he said over his shoulder. "About your grandfather and his history. After all, it's your history, too. You can't know your future if you don't know your past. And you have to look to your future now. Your grandfather would have wanted that for you. But first—you have it?"

"Huh?" Lost trying to follow the man's conversation, Alex blinked dumbly up at him.

"You have the Loewy robot?" Morecambe clarified.

"Yes. Well, no."

Morecambe turned sharply. "No?"

"Not actually with me. I've hidden it, not far away. After those things attacked me, I thought maybe they might be near. They might have worked out I was heading here."

"Yes, I see. Admirable. Good thinking. We should retrieve the toy now and think about getting out of here, just in case. Then we can decide on our next step. So. Shall we fetch it?"

Alex rubbed regretfully at his hands and hauled himself up, using the table for support. His legs felt feeble and his mind crawled with questions. But Morecambe seemed excited, impatient, and Alex had a sudden anxiety himself about getting the robot back safely in his possession.

"Yeah." He nodded. "Let's go."

It had started snowing again, thick new flakes falling on a thin crust of frost that had formed since the earlier fall. The ground crumped under their feet as they walked in silence. In the fading light, the road looked lonelier, more sinister, the trees sharp and black. Morecambe carried his shotgun in one hand. Alex noted that his footprints from earlier were already covered.

Around the corner, he counted eleven trees, then stopped in shock. At the base of the next tree, the snow was very disturbed, piled up around a small deep hole.

He flung himself down, digging. Nothing. He scrambled around the trunk. There was the *A*.

He heard a crow bark, sounding almost as if it were laughing. Morecambe looked on aghast. There was no need to say it. Alex said it anyway:

"It's gone."

XIV.

SOMETHING IN THE DARK

HURRYING BACK IN the last failing light, Alex could hear Morecambe cursing and fretting under his breath. He struggled to keep up with the man, who seemed unconcerned about leaving him behind.

A new sensation gnawed Alex's stomach. The early evening was bitterly cold, but he was sweating, a sick, sticky, hot-cold sweat. The thought of having lost the robot, never seeing it again, never touching it again, played over and over in his mind, a loop he couldn't break out of. A feeling of fevered pain. A new kind of fear. Snow nipped his eyes. The gathering darkness pressed in.

At the gate, Morecambe slowed, approaching the looming house cautiously, increasingly nervous. He turned from side to side, gun flicking desperately this way and that. Once inside, he scrambled at the locks and slumped against the door. Then he straightened in alarm. Without turning on the lights, he strode urgently past Alex, toward the kitchen.

A single lamp glowed weakly, making the gloom around it even darker. Morecambe stood in the shadowy corner looking back and forth from the back door to the closed doorway beside it. Sweat glistened greasily on his forehead.

"It must have been him," he said, speaking to himself. His hands worked wetly at the shotgun. Pulling at the bowtie around his neck, he seemed equally scared and excited.

"Stupid boy," he said, voice suddenly sharp. "What were you thinking? Burying it in the snow? You think this is a child's game? A treasure hunt? I could . . . We could have had it to ourselves."

"What?" Alex felt stung. He had never been so tired, but on the far edge of his fatigue, something was dimly nagging at him, if he only had the energy to focus on it. Morecambe's actions threw him. In all the effort it had taken to get here, he hadn't tried to imagine what Harry might be like. But he would never have pictured this. The man had a perplexing coldness. Alex's grief over his grandfather was hot, constant, but the old man's friend had barely flinched at the news. He was far more concerned about the tin robot. Then again, Alex knew the toy was part of something bigger. Maybe Morecambe had his reasons.

"Yeah, okay. I'm sorry. I shouldn't have left it out there. I didn't know what—" Alex sagged, legs failing. He collapsed onto a chair. "I don't feel well. I don't know what I'm supposed to do. I don't know what's happening."

"No," Morecambe rubbed his nose itchily with the back of his wrist. "You don't. Well, you'll see soon enough. He'll be here soon, I suppose."

"Shouldn't we go?" Alex said, half rising. "Shouldn't we get out of here?"

"No." Morecambe raised the gun, almost pointing it at Alex. "Stupid boy. You stay. We stay."

Confused, angry in a weary way, Alex bent forward, putting his forehead to the table. He felt dreadful. Various pools of pain and fear ran together, spreading to ache in his joints. It was fully dark outside now.

"He told me a little," Alex said, without lifting his head. "Grandad. Well, he started to. About the golem. In Prague."

"Oh yes?" Morecambe peered dimly from across the room. "And what did he tell you?"

"Well, nothing much. He started telling me about the guy who made it, the golem, I mean. That was about it. I really think we should get out of here."

He said the last part almost reluctantly. He wanted to talk about the toy robot, even if he didn't know what he was talking about. He felt sure Morecambe had more to tell him. And the idea of waiting and seeing it again, even in the tall man's hands, even after everything . . . He realized with shame it felt strangely good. Maybe he and Morecambe could get it back. They had the gun.

"No," Morecambe said. "We wait. So now. Did your grandfather tell you how the golem was given life?" He leaned intently across the table.

"Uh, no. I mean, magic, wasn't it? It's just a story."

Morecambe straightened, tutting a disgusted noise.

"Tch. Magic. Stories. Typical. He is a child, your grand-father . . . Sorry. I should say *was*, shouldn't I? A silly man, everything a game, an adventure. He left you unprepared. Unaware. He didn't tell you about the name of God?"

"What? No . . . the *what*?"

"The name of God. This is how the master Rabbi Loew gave his golem life, by using the holy and awesome seventy-two-part name."

Alex blinked stupidly at him. Morecambe hissed another impatient sound. The dim lamp buzzed in the ever-darkening kitchen. Vague snow flurried at the window, white streaks fleeting against black.

"Tchhhh. The seventy-two-part name of God," Morecambe repeated. "A secret name. The true name."

"God's . . . name?" Alex ventured, trying to follow. "I thought he was just called, you know, God."

"This is pointless talking with you," Morecambe spat.

"Yeah, okay. God's got a secret name, great. So what is it? Barry?"

"You," Morecambe hissed, "are blind and deaf and don't even know it. The most powerful name. The name revealed to Moses at the burning bush! The name used to part the Red Sea! Were

I to try and say the seventy-two-part name, you would see me destroyed before you. Struck down. Consumed by fire. But for those who have studied truly and wisely, who have prepared themselves in body and mind—to them, all power. The power to create with a word! To destroy with a wor—"

He stopped abruptly, turning his head, listening hard.

"What—" Alex began.

Morecambe hushed him furiously.

The lamp buzzed in the silence.

"There!" Morecambe whispered. "Did you hear?"

Alex shook his head.

"Ach."

Morecambe's hands fretted at his gun. He suddenly raised it to Alex again, wide eyes wild in the weak light.

"You must have heard that!"

"I didn't hear anything!" Alex whispered. The shadows seemed to move. Thoughts of the secret name of God, of being consumed by fire, swam around the room. Another thought struck him, bubbling up out of his exhaustion.

"Why would the tall man come back here? I mean, if he's got it . . ."

"Ach." Morecambe glanced fearfully at the unlit corridor leading out of the kitchen. He shook his gun at Alex. "Stay here, you."

"No!" Alex looked at the murk beyond the doorway, suddenly terrified at what was out there. "Don't go."

"Shhh," Morecambe spat. Gun before him, he started stalking warily toward the corridor, walking out of the light. He paused at the threshold, looked back at Alex, nervously licking his lips, a pale face floating in the gloom. Then he turned and went on, swallowed utterly by darkness.

Silence. The lamp buzzed.

Alex strained to squint after him. All he saw was the empty black hole of the corridor.

The lamp buzzed. Seconds crawled past, one after the other. The devouring black doorway loomed on the edge of the room like an open grave. He couldn't move.

The lamp buzzed.

Then: a loud, flat bang.

A scuffle and scrape.

Silence. New, sharper silence. Long, desolate seconds of it.

A faint, despairing groan.

The lamp buzzed.

A slow, dragging shuffle and scrape.

This shuffling dragged slowly closer. Alex gaped in horror at the gaping black corridor. Something began to resolve there in the gloom, slowly taking pale shape, shambling nearer.

Eventually, the shape became Morecambe, dragging his feet, staggering weakly out of the darkness, clutching oddly at himself with one hand. The other reached out to Alex, groping terribly for help in the empty air.

Morecambe's eyes bulged, staring horribly at Alex without

seeing him. His mouth opened and closed noiselessly. A few steps into the kitchen, he pitched forward, collapsed face-first to the floor, lay unmoving in the half-light.

Alex sat rooted to the spot. It was all he could do to lift his gaze from Morecambe's prone body back to the corridor.

Nothing there but black silence.

The lamp buzzed.

Then: a small stirring in the black.

Blinking, Alex could now faintly see a small, dim amber-colored spot. A tiny orangey glow, hovering silently down there in the dark, floating a little above eye level. It seemed to stare at him.

It moved oddly. It vanished. It came back, burning brighter, nearer.

Alex sat paralyzed, unable to think or move or feel anything beyond fear as he watched the little glow bobbing toward him. There and then not there, and then there again, winking in and out of existence.

Closer it came, closer again.

At the point where he felt he couldn't take it any longer, a voice spoke from the darkness.

"Sorry, Alex."

A tall gray figure stepped from the corridor into the light, disheveled but elegant. He carried the shotgun loosely balanced in the crook of one arm. A battered cane hung from his other hand. A cigarette burned between his lips, glowing as he puffed at it.

"I seem to have started smoking again."

"Grandad!" Alex cried.

He felt all the sickness and fear drain out of him as he pushed his chair back and jumped to his feet. And then he must have fainted, because he didn't feel anything else.

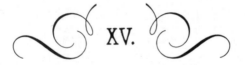

XV.

A CATCH-UP
AND SCRAMBLED EGGS

A SOUND OF voices from another room woke him.

Alex found himself on a bed in a darkened room, a blanket over him. A weak angle of light leaked in through the doorway. Throwing back the covers, he saw his scratched hands had been cleaned and dressed. He followed the light, down a curving staircase, along a corridor, back into the now brightly lit kitchen.

His grandfather stood by the stove in his shirtsleeves, stirring a huge pan of scrambled eggs.

"Ah!" he said, looking up, a dusty bruise on his forehead. "Perfect. Just in time."

Alex blinked dumbly, trying to make sense of the scene. Behind his grandfather, Morecambe sat morosely at the table, head in hands. Alex's rucksack lay open on a chair. A few things from inside were spread on the table around the robot's bright, empty old box.

"I—" Alex began. He broke off as the door in the corner opened, making him start back in fright.

A man he had never seen emerged, gazing down at something in his hand. He was around his grandfather's age, thickset, with short gray-blond hair. Looking up, he smiled at Alex, one eye screwed around a jeweler's eyeglass.

"Evenin', son," this stranger chirped in a Cockney accent. "Gawd," he continued, turning to Alex's grandfather and nodding at Alex, "lookit the size of 'im. Not seen you since you were a nipper, Alex. Tiny-wee you was. Knee-'igh to a baby grass'opper."

Alex said nothing, staring at what he held.

The robot.

"What," Alex tried. "Who—"

Gripping Alex gently by the shoulders, his grandfather steered him to the table. The unknown man pulled out a chair and sat beside him.

"First things first," Alex's grandfather said. "What you need is some scrambled eggs." He paused, considering. "Or should that be 'are some scrambled eggs'? Harry?"

"Beats me," the man replied, bending to squint through his eyeglass at the robot. He pulled a small lamp at his elbow closer. "Grammar was never my strong suit."

"Alex," his grandfather said, "meet my good friend Harry Morecambe, whose beautiful home this is."

The man removed his eyeglass and held out a big hand. Alex shook it in distant bewilderment.

"Lovely to see you again, son," Harry said. "Though you won't remember the last time." He smiled and stretched to Alex's things on the table. "But this takes me back." He tapped the photograph of Alex's mum and dad, lying on top of the pile.

"No watercress." Alex's grandfather sighed as he placed plates of eggs and toast before them. "But needs must." He sat, rubbed his hands together, and started eating with gusto.

"Quite superb," he mumbled happily through his mouthful. "Y'know, I can never get my eggs like this back home. I don't know what it is. Maybe the butter. Or maybe it's just the eggs? What do they feed French chickens, Harry?"

"Ach." The man Alex had previously known as Morecambe muttered in bleak exasperation and slumped forward, putting his forehead to the table.

"But I thought," Alex began, then stopped, trying to work out what he had thought. His grandfather leaned over and placed a fork in his hand.

"Eat something," the old man said gently but firmly. "Probably don't have much time."

Alex had been following everything his grandfather did in a trance, amazed to see him doing anything. Now, though, he snapped out of it as he remembered how frustrating the old man could be. Scowling, he huffily scooped up some eggs and began a petulant display of chewing. After half a second, however, he realized his grandfather was right: these eggs were wonderful, and eating them was indeed the most important thing in the world right now.

"Should've made double helpings," his grandfather said when they had almost done. He mopped a last buttery corner of toast around his plate with sad satisfaction before pushing it away. "Ah, well."

"Less is more," the man Alex now knew to be Harry Morecambe said, still scrutinizing the toy.

"In architecture, yes. In other areas of design, often, if not always," Alex's grandfather said, dabbing his mouth with a napkin. "When it comes to a good plateful of scrambled eggs, though, I think you'll find there are definite camps of opinion."

The other man gently banged his forehead on the table.

"Now," Alex's grandfather said. "Questions."

Alex grabbed the first he could get hold of. "*Who*," he said, pointing his toast at the mysterious man who wasn't Harry, "is *that*?"

"Ah," his grandfather said. "Alex, this is Colonel the Baron von Sudenfeld. Known to his friends, of which there are few, as Willy."

The man glared up at Alex. "Charmed," he muttered with a queasy sarcastic smile. He lowered his head to the table again.

"You remember, when we were talking about the robot before?" Alex's grandfather went on. "I told you Loewy had made three copies, and two were in the hands of collectors? Well, Old Willy the Colonel the Baron here is one of them. Always been a solitary soul, has Willy, but lately it would seem he's thrown in with, eh, you know, the fellow who has been causing us so much trouble."

"I thought he was Harry."

"Yes, well, that's through no fault of your own, Alex. You find Harry's house, you find a man in it, he tells you he's Harry, and what are you supposed to think? Although—and no offense here, Willy."

"Oh, but none taken, I'm sure," von Sudenfeld muttered without lifting his head.

"But I would like to think you would have begun to realize before too long that he's not exactly the splendid sort of fellow I would have as one of my very closest friends."

"Aw, shucks." Harry beamed.

"Yeah," Alex said. "I had wondered. He's not very nice."

"Don't mind me," von Sudenfeld said. "Just you all go right along with your conversations as though I'm not even here."

"I think you've been let off lightly as it is," Alex's grandfather snapped back, glowering. The old man turned to Alex with a smile, leaning in conspiratorially. "Piece of advice, Alex. Always be wary of a man who chooses to wear a bow tie. If there's only one thing I can teach you in life, let it be that. Now, you see that door there?" He nodded to the corner. "Leads to the cellar. Where, actually, among other things, there are some rather fine wines, I seem to remember, Harry. Don't suppose you fancy a quick little glass of something?"

"Thought you'd never ask," Harry said, disappearing eagerly.

"That's where Harry was," Alex's grandfather went on. "Tied to a chair down there, gagged."

Alex nodded numbly. Something cold and hot and urgent welled inside him.

"I thought you'd died! I saw you fall!"

The old man leaned quickly over, put an arm around his shoulder.

"Here, now. It's okay. I'm okay, I'm here. See?" He squeezed Alex tight. "This is me. Still kicking."

"But I saw you fall . . ."

"Oh yes," the old man said, letting go. "I fell all right, went skidding down the roof. Knocked out for a second, I think. Came to just as I was coming to the edge and managed to catch hold. So there I was— Ah, thanks, Harry," he said as Harry reappeared, handing him a large glass of red wine.

"Mmm. Oh, very passable, Harry, well done. So, there I was, hanging there, thinking about the thing to do, when I felt this tugging at my legs. Life-sizers. Two of them, standing on the balcony below, one on the other's shoulders. Well, it got hold of me, pulled me away from the roof—I thought we were all going to go toppling to the street. But they got me down, then gave me a quick punch—bloodied my nose, actually."

He pulled at his red-smeared shirt collar.

"Shirt's ruined. Next thing I know, I'm waking bundled up inside what turns out to be the case for a double bass. I can feel myself being dragged along, then we stop and I'm dropped. I get ready to spring out and have at them when they open it— but nothing happens. Just some curious noises.

"They had some damned fiendish lock on the case, so I couldn't get it open at first, but I managed to budge the lid enough to peek out. They'd taken me off along some lonely part of the Métro line, an abandoned tunnel. And what do I see but two life-sizers, fighting each other. One seemed to have gone haywire, but it was still putting up a decent effort."

"But that was me!" Alex interrupted. He quickly relayed his adventures since he had seen his grandfather last.

"My word," the old man murmured at length, tapping a finger at his lip. "Good show, Alex. You've done yourself proud. And me."

"They don't fall far from the tree," Harry chipped in, beaming, then stopped abruptly. He exchanged a serious glance with Alex's grandfather, then bent back to the robot, tapping softly at its chest with a tiny screwdriver.

"Anyway," the old man continued, "the other machine finished off the damaged one soon enough. By that time, I had just about managed to wrestle myself out of the case, and it was coming at me, but it didn't have much fight left. Probably running out of juice. They need, ah, charging up, every now and then.

"But as we're fighting, we're joined by the villain of the piece and his two shaven-headed goons. There are hidden entrances from the Métro leading into the Catacombs, the old burial tunnels under Paris, and I suspect our friend has set up a lair down there where he planned to invite me to join him for some uninterrupted interrogation about where I might have hidden our robot. He has rather a dramatic bent, all very _Phantom of the Opera_. So, as you can probably imagine, there was some escaping and chasing, all the usual rigmarole. I kept them busy for a few hours, until I finally managed to give them the slip. Then I headed down here.

"Which reminds me," the old man went on. "I mean, well done avoiding capture and making your way here, Alex—but you could have saved yourself a lot of time and trouble if you'd just taken a taxi. I mean, that's what I did. Bit of an extravagance, but, oh, I think the situation warrants it. I have accounts with a couple of the better Paris companies. Nice cars, clean and warm. Didn't I give you a card?"

"No," Alex said.

"Oh. I meant to. Are you _sure_ I didn't?"

"You didn't," Alex fumed.

"Oh. Oh, well, maybe turned out for the best," the old man hurried on, seeing the look on Alex's face. "Who knows where I'd have wound up if you hadn't managed to get salt into that life-sizer, eh? Not sure I could have handled two.

"Anyway, I arrived here this morning, but something didn't feel right. So I camped out in the trees at the top of the hill, watching Harry's place until I knew what was what. Beckman had read Harry's note about coming here, and they would have been keen to get Harry out of the way, even if they hadn't guessed you were heading this way. I have a feeling they were still busy searching for you in Paris, actually; that's why they used the life-sizers to try and take me to their hideout.

"Sure enough, I soon saw them, Beckman, the girl, and Old Willy von here, moving around the house with a gun. Next thing I know, Beckman and the girl just went racing off. That had me a little baffled, but I think I've worked it out. That damaged robot you found on you, that was a tracker, fairly dumb little thing, but effective. When you set it off, they went chasing after it. But if it's wallowing around in a load of salt now, the signal will be going crazy, so they'll probably be quite a while tracking it down.

"Meanwhile," the old man went on, "just as I'm about to come down to the house, I see *you* turning up. I wanted to get to you while you were burying the robot, but I was trying to make sure I wasn't spotted. I'd seen the girl sending fliers out in various directions to patrol the area, and you were too quick. Suddenly you're inside the house with Willy and his shotgun, so I held off. By the way, what was all that walking in circles around the trees business?"

"My footprints led straight to where I'd buried it," Alex said, a little embarrassed. "I thought if I did that, it would put off anybody who was following."

"Mmmm," his grandfather considered, nodding. "False trail, eh? Well, yes, it might have worked. I left something similar in Paris, hoping to keep them tied up for a while. Although, when laying a false trail, it pays to bear in mind to not make it look like it's been left by someone who has suddenly become a lunatic. Tends to rouse suspicion. But, as a general point, good thinking. Although, as it happened, I didn't need any trail, because I'd seen you burying it. *Et voilà.*"

He pointed to the robot in Harry's hand.

"So, Harry, what's the verdict?"

Harry put the robot and screwdriver down by the lamp, removed his eyepiece, and sat back, gazing at the toy standing in its halo of white light.

"Well, lessee," he said, clearing his throat. "I am 'ereby pleased to report I 'ave successfully developed my prints and conducted my preliminary study."

"Harry here is exactly the astonishingly useful kind of chap who would buy a secondhand X-ray machine from his local vet and keep it with a darkroom set up in his cellar," Alex's grandfather said. "And he also has something of a flair for the dramatic himself. For Pete's sake, man, don't keep us in suspense. Is it or isn't it?"

Harry took a sip of wine, savoring the moment. "That's it," he said quietly. "That's it, all right."

"Splendid," said Alex's grandfather after a pause, slapping his hands. "Of course, we always knew it, but pays to be certain. Who knows how many other copies might have been made over the years. And so?"

"Yeah," Harry said, tapping the robot's head. "It's in there."

"Well, well," the old man said, rubbing his chin. "There we have it."

Alex looked from his grandfather to Harry and back.

"What? What's in there?"

"The holy and awesome seventy-two-part name," von Sudenfeld groaned, without raising his head from the table. "The true name of God."

XVI.

WHAT'S INSIDE A ROBOT

IN THE CELLAR, a sharp memory of chemicals and electricity hung on the air. The red safety light Harry had been using while processing his film was still on, a bare bulb on a wire, carving everything out in livid crimson and black, except for a stark, glowing white lightbox mounted on one wall. Two ghostly black prints were clipped to it.

"Let's have a look, then," Alex's grandfather said, striding to make a closer inspection. "Uh-huh. And there you are," he muttered.

"If I'd 'ad more time, I could've got us a clearer look inside," Harry said, setting down his wineglass and shotgun and starting to shuffle together a mess of notes on a workbench. Beside it, a chair stood pulled out, the cut remains of a rope lying around it on the stone floor. "It's fiddly tryin' to work out the right radiation levels for a clear image. But it gives you an idea."

"This is wonderful work, Harry," Alex's grandfather said. He touched a finger to one of the prints, tracing a line.

Alex joined him, peering up at the X-rays. They showed the tin robot's unmistakable skeletal white phantom, photographed once from the front and once from the side against a world of black, leering its savage smile.

Alex was puzzled. In the torso of the thing, where he would have expected its clockwork mechanism, there floated instead a translucent gray shape, a rough rectangle that took up most of the toy's insides, surrounded by a brighter, whiter cloud. Bending closer, he could faintly discern small, dark lines running across it.

"Extraordinary," his grandfather murmured.

"Right," Alex said, stepping back. "You need to tell me what's going on."

"Later, Alex. We should probably think about getting out of here—"

"Oh, no," Alex cut him off. "You tell me what's going on. Right now."

"But, Alex, my dear chap—"

Alex pulled out his phone, taking care to cover the cracked screen. "Or I could call Mum, and you can tell her. After, you know, I've told her how my holiday's been going."

"Really, Alex." His grandfather stuck out his bottom lip. "No need for that, old man."

"*He* has been going on about this name of God thing all night." Alex pointed at von Sudenfeld, who had moved to take his place at the screen. His face shone deathly white as he stared at the spectral pictures. "What's he talking about? What *is* that in there?"

Alex's grandfather looked at Harry as though for help. Harry shrugged, raised both hands palms up, sipped some wine.

"Yes, thank you, Harry. Okay. Name of God." The old man glowered darkly at von Sudenfeld. "Let's see: I told you about the golem. Well, there are various versions of that story, various explanations of how exactly Rabbi Loew brought it to life. And one of them is that he used the name of— Well, really, it's just a magic word. Like *abracadabra*."

"Ha!" von Sudenfeld snorted.

"Honestly, Willy, you're on thin ice," Alex's grandfather snapped. He turned back to Alex. "These holy men and mystics, like Loew, they had come up with all these secret names for God. They just made them up, basically, like a kind of code. They took different letters from here and there in various paragraphs in their Bibles, stuck them together, and came up with these nonsense words, these names."

Von Sudenfeld sighed. But he didn't say anything.

"But there are legends," Alex's grandfather went on, "that the true name of God was actually revealed to a chosen few great scholars. These names were all supposed to have power. But this true name was supposed to unleash the most terrible power of all. Some people say that Moses—y'know, the baby in the basket chap—he'd been told this secret name while he was having his chat with the burning bush. You know that story?"

Alex nodded. "Kind of." He strained his memory. Picture book images came flickering back, pages from childhood, a man with a staff in a lonely place. "He was a shepherd, out with his flock, when he saw the bush on fire. But, yeah, I remember: even though it was burning, it wasn't being *burned* by the fire. And when he went to look closer, he heard a voice from the bush. Eh, God talking to him. He told him he was going to make him the leader who would lead his people to safety."

His grandfather nodded. "Close enough. So—"

"So, what is it?" Alex interrupted.

"How's that?"

"God's secret name, what is it?"

"Yes. Well. The idea was you had to study and meditate on the name for a long, long time before you could begin to understand it or even try to pronounce it. It's got, what, two hundred and sixteen letters or so in it; it's unpronounceable. Gobbledegook. But the story was you had to treat it with care and respect, not just invoke it willy-nilly. Because, if you made a mistake trying to say it, or if you weren't in the right state of what these self-styled great sages would call *spiritual purity*, you'd be struck down dead."

He paused, then leaned over Alex and said: *"Boogie-boogie-boogie,"* widening his eyes and wiggling his fingers in the vibrating red light. "Superstitious twaddle, of course, but it made them look good."

"Okay." Alex frowned. "I've got it. But what does he mean the name's in there?" He pointed at the X-rays. "What's in there?"

"Well, there are versions of the story. But in the one we're talking about, to give the golem life, Loew was supposed to have carved this all-powerful name out onto a small clay tablet, and then put this tablet into the golem's mouth—like a magic battery—and, hey, presto."

Alex turned back to the prints, struggling to put it together. "And that tablet—it's inside our robot? That's it?" He reached to touch the translucent shape shown inside the toy.

"Looks like," his grandfather said. "You see, the golem stories all ended rather badly. Everything went to plan for a while, but eventually Loew couldn't control it. The creature grew bigger and bigger, stronger and stronger, until it finally just went mad, out of control. A monster loose in the countryside. Torn-up buildings. Killings. The old story: the Sorcerer's Apprentice, Frankenstein's monster, HAL in *2001: A Space Odyssey*, and on and on—the magic gets out of hand, the creation becomes uncontrollable and almost destroys the creator, you know?"

Alex nodded. "Well, *Frankenstein*, I know that. And *Terminator*. That's about machines taking over and—"

"So, anyway, finally he had to deactivate it and return it back to being just a lifeless clay statue. And he did that, more or less, by taking the tablet back out of its mouth again. Pretty handy, eh?"

At Alex's side, von Sudenfeld had reached to touch the picture, too. He began making a small, quiet cooing sound, almost a sickly purr. Alex shivered.

"But how did it wind up in there?" Alex asked, stepping away.

"Well," his grandfather said, "the idea is that, after it went mad and he removed the tablet, Rabbi Loew hid the golem's body, in case it was ever needed again. If it was, they'd be able to restore it to life, you see. But, to do that, they'd need the tablet to pop back into its mouth. And so the tablet was hidden, too, but separately, just to be safe. It was secretly passed down through generations of people in Prague, until finally it came to our old friend, the toymaker Mr. Loewy. Who, as you might have worked out, was a vague descendant of the original rabbi.

"Now," the old man went on. "Loewy came up with an ingenious way of hiding the tablet, the best hiding place of all: in plain sight. He made our little robot here, and he popped it inside. A kind of an in-joke about the original golem, you could say. Then he made copies—he was supposed to have made three, but I suspect he might have made more that have been lost—and he put them all on display in his shop. He'd never sell the real one, of course. He would have kept it safe, then passed it on to the next person, who would have kept it safe after him. But then the war came along, and everything was scattered and lost. But: that original robot was different from the others in one other key respect. Right, Harry?"

"Oh, er, right." Harry had taken the gun and stood halfway up the stairs, peering into the kitchen, on guard. "Yeah. The other toy robots, well, that's just what they was: toy robots. Clockwork, y'know, wind-up toys. But this one, see, its key ain't to wind it up. Its key's to *unlock* it. Loewy, 'e was right clever with 'is 'ands, and 'e came up with this devilish locking mechanism. See, 'e was a watchmaker an' all, so you can imagine: 'undreds of intricate little coils and springs, all wrapped around the tablet in there, keeping it 'eld, cushioned tight. See?"

Harry pointed to the X-rays. Alex stepped forward, looking closer at the white cloud surrounding the shape of the clay tablet. It seemed composed of countless hairlike threads.

"But there's a catch," Harry went on. "Try to open it *without* the key, and those coils will tighten around the tablet and destroy it, crush it to dust. I've looked at it every way, but I can't figure a way to open it safely."

"The tablet is just clay," Alex's grandfather pitched in, "and very old and fragile by now. Which I suspect is where you come in, eh, Willy?"

"Eh? What?" von Sudenfeld grunted, turning back from the screen. He kept his gaze lowered.

"Well." Alex's grandfather fixed him with a friendly stare. "Our friend who's so desperate to get his hands on the robot here, he has a very tight-knit little group and doesn't generally invite anyone to join without good reason."

"I don't know what you mean." Von Sudenfeld's voice sounded gritty.

"No? Well, I've been thinking. You already had your own Loewy robot, but of course it turned out to be only one of the copies. And just as well, as, from the photographs I've seen, you busted it open trying to get inside. But a collector like yourself, you'd have learned the full story soon enough. Now, someone like you, with the resources you have at your disposal, if a chap like that were to turn his mind to finding something, chances are he could have it found. Not the robot, of course, because we have it, although I'm sure you've had people of your own searching for it. But the key."

Von Sudenfeld said nothing. A nerve started twitching under one eye.

"The key," Alex's grandfather repeated. "You've found it, haven't you, old man?" He kept his eyes on von Sudenfeld's face. "Why else would our friend take you under his wing? Only thing that puzzles me," Alex's grandfather pressed on, "is what you think you're going to get out of it."

"He has promised me to share the power!" von Sudenfeld suddenly snapped. "He will teach me. We will all share together! Go on together! Rule together!"

"And you believe him?" Alex's grandfather grinned, but he sounded sad, pitying. "What on earth makes you think he'll keep his word?"

"Ah, but this is it," von Sudenfeld rasped. "He cannot lie. He has been studying, preparing himself, purifying himself physically and spiritually for the procedure. You see? He *cannot* lie! He cannot risk the stain."

"Purifying himself?" Alex's grandfather laughed. "Never mind telling you lies—they've been trying to *kill* us! Now, that's not very spiritual, is it?"

"Pah," von Sudenfeld spat. "You don't count. You are out to destroy the name of God; you are enemies. Killing you would be justified."

"And there we have it." The old man beamed at Alex. "The fundamental lunacy of the people we're dealing with.

"Question is"—he turned back to von Sudenfeld—"if you *did* happen to have the key, where might you keep it, hmm? I think we can be pretty sure you haven't already given it to him—because, as much as you've told us about how *holy and pure* your friend is these days, I reckon you're still suspicious enough not to just hand it over to him until the last possible minute, when you know for certain he's not simply going to take it and get rid of you. But, at the same time, you'd want it close, where you can lay your hands on it quickly when the time comes, eh?"

Von Sudenfeld backed away as Alex's grandfather moved toward him, while Harry casually but not-so-casually stepped down from the stairs on his other side. For a moment the three stood in silence, von Sudenfeld's eyes darting from face to face, until, with a squawk, he ducked his head and the others fell on him.

A flailing arm hit the hanging bulb, setting it swinging crazily. In the lurching red light, Alex could make out only shuddering fragments as the men struggled, all shadows, backs, and elbows: a glimpse of Harry trying to hold von Sudenfeld's arm; the tubby man suddenly wrenching it free, seeming to slap himself in the mouth.

At this, Alex's grandfather and Harry stepped away. Von Sudenfeld stood panting, disheveled but curiously triumphant. There was something different about him. It took Alex a few seconds to work it out. His hair had somehow been pushed far back up his scalp, perched oddly above a large expanse of pale forehead.

"That's torn it," Harry said, catching the light, stopping it swinging.

"Still," Alex's grandfather said wearily, "neatly done."

"What?" Alex asked. "What did he do?"

"Do you mind, Willy?" the old man said. Von Sudenfeld recoiled as Alex's grandfather reached gently for his head, lifting off what was now clearly a toupee. A large piece of white tape hung loosely from the lining. He set the wig back in place, patting it down.

"Had the key taped under there," Alex's grandfather said. "And now he's swallowed it."

"That really is a beautiful syrup, Willy," Harry said with genuine admiration. "I'd never 'ave guessed. That's a lovely piece of work."

"What do we do now?" Alex said.

"Well," his grandfather replied, heading toward the stairs, "we don't need to get the tablet out of the robot to destroy it. But I think we should take Old Willy here along with us, anyway. See if nature takes its course."

"Huh?" Alex said.

Harry raised his eyebrows at him.

"Oh, right," Alex said after a moment. "Yuck."

They followed the old man up to the kitchen, Harry gesturing for von Sudenfeld to go first.

"I say, Harry." Alex's grandfather drained his wineglass and smacked his lips. "You wouldn't happen to have a spot of dessert around, would you? I have a sudden hankering for some . . . tiramisu maybe?"

"Nothin' in," Harry said apologetically. "I got 'ere in a bit of an 'urry"—he nodded at von Sudenfeld—"and then things got kind of busy."

"Oh. Yes. Of course." Alex's grandfather glanced down, then looked up hopefully. "Maybe some biscuits and cheese?"

Harry shook his head.

"Oh, well." The old man patted his stomach. "We can pick something up on the way." He glanced at his wristwatch, stood calculating. "We really should get out of here. They'll be back here soon, all of them."

"What did you mean, destroy it?" Alex said. He felt a pang in his own stomach that had nothing to do with hunger.

"Hmmm? Well, yes. That's the general idea. For a while, I thought we might get away with just hiding the tablet again . . . But no. The man who is after it has decided, of course, that he's going to raise the golem, and he'll be granted all kinds of magical powers as a result. Unlimited wealth, endless dominion, eternal life, and all of that. No, the tablet has to be destroyed, I'm afraid."

"But—" Alex, to his own surprise, started to protest, almost stammering. He stopped himself. "I thought that you said you would destroy it just by trying to open the robot? Why didn't you just do that?"

"You're right," the old man replied. "Opening the robot without the key would result in the tablet being crushed. But, according to the version of the story we're dealing with, to really put an end to it, it must be destroyed the right way. If we just smashed the toy open and broke the tablet that way, it would mean that someone could still create *another* tablet for the golem. Quite a tricky business doing that, but you can be sure that he would have a go at it. He can't create another tablet while this one still exists, y'see. There can only be one empowered for the golem at any time. And if we destroy the original tablet and we do it the *right* way, according to ritual, then that's it: the golem can never be revived, game over, and all home in time for tea."

"So that's what we're going to do?" Alex said, unable to hide his dismay.

"That's what we're going to do," his grandfather said, studying him. "Ah, tell me, Alex. What else was Willy here saying while the two of you were alone?"

Alex stood staring down at his folded arms, then fixed his grandfather with a direct stare.

"It's funny, actually." He heard the sudden bitterness in his voice and leaned into it. "He was telling me about *you*. He was telling me about you and *the man* and *the girl*. The *tall* man. The man who's been after this tablet and trying to *kill* us. With his, you know, gang of oddballs and their, you know, *killer robots*."

Alex's grandfather glanced at von Sudenfeld, who refused

to meet his gaze. Harry coughed uncomfortably.

"Was he, now?" the old man said. "Go on, then. What did he tell you?"

"Oh, he was talking about your past. He told me how you and this man have a *long history* together. He told me you go *way* back."

"Did he." The old man's voice was steely, deadly, as he stared at von Sudenfeld. "Did he really. My, my. He really is quite the conversationalist with a gun in his hands. And?"

"And . . ." Alex slumped. "Nothing. That was as far as it went. Still, it's more than you've told me, isn't it?" He sat heavily and looked away.

The old man rubbed at his forehead. "Okay, Alex. Yes, there are maybe . . . one or two . . . things I haven't told you. I'm not going to apologize. I'll only ask you to believe that I have had the best reasons. I've been trying to protect you, keep protecting you, when perhaps it's too late to protect you by keeping you in the dark.

"But, Alex"—he dropped to one knee and locked eyes with him, urgently searching his gaze—"the only question that matters is: do you trust me?"

Alex, caught by the intensity of the old man's stare, felt his throat catch. He nodded.

"Of course I do. You know I do."

"Good man." His grandfather sagged. "Well, I'll make you a deal. Trust me a little longer. Let's get on with the matter at hand, and then I'll tell you all about it. Well—most of it, anyway. There's quite a lot, I suppose. And I suppose, if it came to it, I'd rather you heard it from me than from the likes of this." He nodded contemptuously at von Sudenfeld, before turning back to Alex.

"Deal?"

"Deal." Alex nodded. "So long as you keep it."

"Oh, I always keep deals. Nearly always." The old man stood. "Now. Do you have fresh clothes, Alex? I'm going to get myself changed, and I think you should take the opportunity, too. They'll be here soon, and then there won't be time for pleasantries."

"I'll keep a look out," Harry said. "I've a couple of things I can rig up to give 'em a nice welcome this time." He nodded at von Sudenfeld. "Meantime, you can get started on these dishes."

"Oh, that's the thing about scrambled eggs." Alex's grandfather frowned. "Lovely, but you have to pay the price in messy pots. Although I hear the new nonstick fellows are rather miraculous."

"But do we really have to destroy it?" Alex said disconsolately. "I thought you said it was . . . just a story."

"It is, Alex," his grandfather said, heading from the kitchen. "It's all just a story. And we're going to be the ones who write an end to it."

XVII.

A VIEW FROM A HILL

THE ATTACK CAME with the dawn, just as the first frail rumors of light began spreading across the blue-black sky in ominous trails of red.

The tall man came first, a stalking shadow on the snow, all angles in the half-light. He moved carefully, approaching the house with caution.

At the front door, he paused, bent leaning on his cane to scrutinize the fresh salt on the step. With almost fussy care, he brushed it away, scraping it with one shiny boot into a tidy mound he covered with a red silk handkerchief, weighing down each corner with a shiny black pebble. Next, he moved from window to window, scooping salt from ledges with gloved hands.

Stepping back, slapping his hands together to shake off the remaining grains, he regarded the house. He stood a full minute, head cocked, looking, listening. Thin clouds of breath rose and faded in the bitter morning. Pulling off one glove to reveal a long, pale hand, he put two fingers to his lips and whistled a piercing note.

They came from the bare black bushes in curiously formal procession. The girl led, two fliers at her shoulders, followed by little Beckman, his glasses lenses catching the first red in the sky. Next the bald men, wearing woolen watch caps against the cold. Behind them, two life-sizers and a dozen or so more fliers in dim formation.

Around their feet, a vague parade of smaller robots trundled and stumbled over the snow, maybe thirty, bright little robot cars and robot trains and robot rocket ships, tiny space bulldozers with robot drivers. Little things on legs and wheels and caterpillar tracks, things that walked and climbed and rolled, things that looked and hunted and tracked and hid, things that picked and drilled. Things that could sting and slash and wound and worse.

The tall man flicked his cane. One of the life-sizers strode forward, put huge hands to the front door, and began to push. After a few seconds it stepped back, stood as if considering the problem, then unleashed a single, savage swipe at the main lock.

As soon as it touched the metal plate around the keyhole, the machine man stopped moving, rooted to the spot. Anyone close enough would have heard the electric current thrumming through it. Anyone close enough would have gradually smelled an acrid, burning scent on the biting morning air.

The tall man shouted brusque instructions. The bald men

ran off into the bushes, one of them rubbing at his head. Wisps of smoke rose from the life-sizer's coat sleeve. The tall man, the girl, Beckman, and all the other robots moved back, forming a silent semicircle around the motionless machine, watching as it started to smolder.

Presently, the men returned, each bearing a large branch freshly snapped from a tree. Standing on either side of the door, they braced themselves against the wall and used the branches to pry the life-sizer away. Finally, with a great heave, the big machine toppled backward, straight as a felled tree, landing faceup, arm still outstretched.

The tall man ignored it. Stepping back, he ran his eyes along the house's facade, pointed a finger. The girl stepped forward. With a turn of her head, she sent a flier darting to the nearest window. Within a few inches of the frame, a sharp blue flash exploded around it. The flying thing fell, showering sparks.

The girl's gasp and the curse the man let out could be heard for some distance.

Alex's grandfather hummed happily and lowered his binoculars.

"Excellent work, Harry. You really are a devious soul when you put your mind to it."

"Coming from you, I'll take that as a compliment." Harry grinned. "Wait'll they get inside, though; that's when the fun really starts. Shame we won't be around to see it. But I'm rather 'opin' they'll 'ave a crack at that top window before we go. I've left it open just a little. Might be a bit obvious, mind."

"You really are like children, you know?" von Sudenfeld grumbled behind them. "Pathetic, stupid, silly children."

"Ah yes," Alex's grandfather replied, raising the binoculars again. "But we've got all the best toys now, haven't we? Now, shut your mouth, Willy, there's a good fellow."

They stood on the ridge of a hill at the edge of the forest, around half a mile from the house, looking back down over the frosted fields. Harry's car nestled among the thin trees behind them, a smooth black shape against the greater darkness of the woods. Alex's grandfather had changed into an immaculate three-piece suit and coat almost exactly like the one he had been wearing before, except perhaps an infinitesimally lighter shade of gray, now topped with a bowler hat the same color.

"Shepherds take warning," the old man murmured, raking his binoculars across the frozen landscape. The world spread out before them in tones of white, blue, and gray and a red now tinged with gold. He drew in a great breath, let it out in a misty, satisfied sigh.

"Amazing air. Astonishing light. Eh, Alex?"

Alex, watching through another set of binoculars, didn't respond. He was fascinated by what the bald men were doing.

They were working at the fallen life-sizer. One knelt by the thing, removed its singed hat, and began unscrewing a plate in its head. The other man had produced from a black case a clear plastic bag, filled with a dark, thick liquid. It reminded Alex vaguely of something.

The kneeling man opened the plate. His colleague now had

a transparent tube leading down from the bag he held. They fed it into the robot's head. Liquid began oozing thickly down the tube. Alex realized with a shudder why the bag looked familiar—he'd seen doctors and nurses using them often enough in the medical dramas his mother watched on TV. He had the terrible sensation it was blood running slowly into the machine.

Satisfied this drip-line was secure, the kneeling man was digging around inside the case. He came out with an oversized woolen purse. Snapping open the catch, he pulled out a fistful of something dark. Producing a cigarette lighter, he held a flame under it until it started to smoke, then began sprinkling it into the panel in the robot's head, patting it around the tube.

"What," Alex said, "is *that*?"

"Hmm?" his grandfather replied. He moved his binoculars until he saw what had caught Alex's attention.

"Oh. Hair, probably. Nasty business. You should never burn hair, Alex. The most terrible smell you will ever smell. Or, well, one of them, anyway," he added, as the kneeling man brought out a squat jar, pulled on a thin rubber glove, unscrewed the lid, and began scooping out a thick, sticky handful of its obscure contents, pushing the gloopy stuff into the robot. "Gads."

"*What* is . . . ?" Alex began.

"Now"—his grandfather cleared his throat—"never mind all that. Keep an eye on the top window; this should be good."

Alex directed his binoculars as instructed. After a blurry few seconds trying to focus, he saw four fliers hovering at a cautious distance outside the tower window. One held what looked like a rusty nail balanced across its hook and scalpel arms. With a jerk, it pitched it forward. Nothing happened. The nail hit the glass, bounced off the frame, fell to the ground.

Below, the tall man stood watching. Behind him, the little girl also stood with her neck craned, staring up at the fliers with great concentration. Beckman and the small army of little robots crowded behind her.

The tall man motioned with his hand. The girl blinked. The fliers moved in.

The window was slightly ajar. White curtains pressed against the glass from inside. Working as one, the four little robots took up a fluttering formation along the bottom of the frame and got their hooks into it, beginning to tug the window farther open. They were clearly encountering resistance. The machines strained, heaving, until, with a suddenness and force that sent two of them shooting backward several feet through the air, the window sprang open.

A huge white torrent came pouring out, falling straight onto the people and robots below.

"Salt?" Alex asked.

"Certainly is," chirped Harry. "Nice big load of fleur de sel. Oldest trick in the book, but, well, old 'uns are good 'uns."

Down at the house, they were scattering out of the way but weren't all fast enough. The tall man's hat and shoulders were coated white. The two fliers that had still been pulling at the window were engulfed and fell to the ground. The little girl clutched painfully at her forehead.

"She feels it," Alex said.

"Ah. Yes," his grandfather replied.

"When you said you didn't like to kill them—what happens to her if you kill one she's controlling?"

"Well." The old man lowered his binoculars and considered. "I suppose it would maybe feel something like having a hand cut off. Or a finger, anyway, depending what it was. Except, you would still have all your fingers and your hands. But you would have felt it going. That shock, that severance. That loss. You know?"

Alex thought about it. "Kind of. Is that why you don't like killing them?"

"Oh, no," his grandfather said. "I'm not worried about the people *using* them. No, it's the machines—if you can use salt on them, it breaks that connection. It's a shield. But they still have some energy left in them: they're no longer plugged in, but it's like . . . a battery, running down. It doesn't last long. But for that little while, when they're not being controlled, it's maybe like they're . . . released. Dumb as they are, it's their one taste of autonomy. I mean, they probably don't feel anything, but . . . who knows? I just started wondering what it must be like for them. Freedom, life. Confusing probably. I know it is for me." He lifted his binoculars again.

After a second staring at the old man, Alex did likewise. Several of the smaller robots were spinning wildly or wandering stupidly around. As the last salt leaked out, the window slammed itself shut.

"How long do you reckon it'll take them to realize they're trying to break in to an empty house?" Alex's grandfather asked.

"Well, they should be kept fairly busy once they get through that door," Harry said. "But, yeah, we should probably think about gettin' movin'."

The tall man was issuing orders. The bald men seemed to have finished repairing the damaged life-sizer. They put its hat back in place, then left it and began clearing away as much salt as they could. After a few seconds, the machine lowered its outstretched arm, sat upright, then clambered stiffly to its feet and strode to join its companion. The two life-sizers stood silently facing each other for a moment, then turned as one, disappearing into the bushes at a rapid march.

The girl was still rubbing her head with one hand. With the other, she clutched to her chest the flier that had been burned by the window, like any small girl soothing a doll. The two fliers that had avoided the salt hovered protectively around her.

Beckman, a hand to one temple, ran in ever-widening circles, trying to round up the smaller robots. Little machines were staggering madly all over the garden. The two life-sizers reappeared, carrying between them an ornate iron lamppost, clearly ripped from the ground. Without pausing, they began battering at the door.

On the path behind them, the robots that hadn't been touched by salt ranked up in position, like cars in a Formula One race. Nasty arrays of blades and needles began to snap out from those at the front. The life-sizers kept ramming the door.

The faint, flat sound of metal hitting wood carried bleakly on the crisp morning air to the hill.

"That won't 'old long." Harry sighed, squinting sadly through binoculars at his door. "Lovely paintwork that was, an' all."

"No," Alex's grandfather said. "Looks like they're getting serious. So. We all ready for the off, then? Alex?"

Alex didn't reply. He was mesmerized. He had his binoculars trained on the tall man, standing motionless at the center of all the activity.

The light was bad, and the focus wasn't very sharp. The figure blurred and lurched in the lens. All the same, dim as it was, this was his first real look at the man who had been pursuing them. As he watched, he removed his hat. A man who looked to be somewhere in his forties, pushing back black hair.

The same nameless, intensely strange feeling he had experienced when he'd stared into the face of the little girl crept over Alex's scalp.

With a distant crack, the door broke open. The man replaced his hat, moving out of Alex's sights. He swung the binoculars after him but found only swarming empty air. He lowered the glasses and stood staring down toward the house without seeing it.

The man was a stranger. He didn't recognize him.

And yet he felt as though he had been looking at his face all his life.

XVIII.

THE GODDESS AND
THE MACHINE

"THEY DON'T MAKE 'em like this anymore," Harry sung out happily from behind the wheel for the third time.

"They didn't make them like this back then!" Alex's grandfather shouted back for the third time from the other front seat. Cold wind poured in through the slightly open window beside him.

The morning was still dark. The roads were empty. Harry drove at ferocious speed. The forest had whipped by in a tangled haze and lay far behind. Now the car was climbing a bare gravel road that wound up into high, dismal gray hills.

Alex sat sunk in silence in the seat behind Harry, caught between trying to shake off the feeling he had experienced while looking at the tall man, and trying hard to work out just what it was he had felt.

The man's face hung in his mind's eye: a distant blur, unknown, familiar, turning, and melting away whenever he tried to bring it into focus.

Gazing at the desolate landscape rolling past, he had the odd sense of the world unfolding, revealing itself to him in incomprehensible patterns. Picked out in the bleak light, everything seemed new. Or, rather, he had a new feeling for just how old everything was out there. His shoulder ached from his run-in with the life-sizer. His mind buzzed with tiredness and confusion. He felt he had moved closer than ever to his grandfather, only to discover a chasm of secrets between them.

But he knew that went both ways. He still hadn't told anyone about how he had almost hurt the boy on the train. He thought of Kenzie on the bus, the anguish on his face. He thought of the toy robot, the darkness behind its eyes.

Glancing up, he caught his own eyes staring back from the rearview mirror. He had a brief, very vivid flash of the dark eyes of the moon-faced girl burning at him in the Paris street.

Something started flickering out on the edge of his thinking.

The hum of the road changed tone as they shifted gears. His grandfather turned to say something to Harry. Alex felt his mind accelerating with the car. The old man's profile hung there before him, shadowed against the wintry morning light. He thought of the tall man, shuddering close but distant in his binocular lens, shadowy, half turned away.

He traced a hand over his own face, the line of his nose, chin, jaw.

A strong resemblance, Beckman had said.

He and your grandfather go back a long way, von Sudenfeld had said. *Right back to the beginning.*

217

You know, you look very much like your father did when he was your age? his grandfather had said, many times.

A man somewhere in his forties.

His rucksack sat between his knees. He held one hand inside, thumb rubbing unconsciously over the robot in its box. He let it go, stuck his hand deeper, searching blindly until his fingers touched what he was grasping after. He pulled out the photograph of his mum and dad until his father's blurry image was visible, and he sat staring down at the ghostly figure.

A vague, tall man.

Black hair pushed back.

Turned away.

He lifted the picture all the way out, held it close, angling it in the dim, moving light.

And, like that, all at once, with a high lonely road turning beneath him and a chill prickling along his spine, his world shifted once more. Things falling into their place. The thought at the back of his mind stepped forward from the shadows into bright, sharp focus. It frightened him. It sent cracks splintering across what was left of his picture of the way things worked. It made no sense. Yet it suddenly made perfect sense of his grandfather's determination to keep the truth from him, all the veiled allusions he had picked up in conversations around him.

He knew who this tall man was—

His thoughts were interrupted by a long, painful burp at his elbow. Von Sudenfeld sat beside him, bent forward, hand over his eyes, emitting groans and deep gassy sounds that unsettled

Alex immensely. Looking up from the photograph, he now saw Harry's eyes, watching him closely in the mirror, frowning. He had the irrational sensation his thoughts lay written plainly on his face.

"What kind of car is this, anyway?" Alex asked, for something to say, as he hurriedly slipped the photograph away. The shining black vehicle was long and low, all curves, a mix of rocket ship and cartoon shark.

"What kind of car is this?" Harry repeated, incredulous, smiling now. He turned to Alex's grandfather. "What 'ave you been teachin' the lad?"

He shouted back to Alex: "Citroën DS nineteen, son. The Goddess! Most beautiful car ever built. This 'ere's my second. Bought 'er new in 1961. Now, see, I *did* 'ave another one before, from '57, but, eh, that got trashed, thanks to 'Is Nibs 'ere."

"Now, no need to get into that," Alex's grandfather said, face turned to the window. "It was a long time ago."

The road curved through a tight hairpin bend as they climbed higher. Alex glanced out. The edge of a steep drop trembled a few feet away. Down below, he could now see the pale, snaking line of the road behind them.

"How you doing there, Willy?" Alex's grandfather said, turning in his seat. "Looking a little peaky. That's what you get for eating *keys*, man. Don't get carsick; Harry here would never forgive you."

"Why don't you just let me go?" von Sudenfeld moaned. "Just stop and let me out."

"Now, now." Alex's grandfather tutted. "That'd never do. Couldn't do that to you, old man, abandon you out here all on your lonesome."

"Ach." Von Sudenfeld doubled over farther, hugging his stomach, emitting a steady series of soft belches.

"Why *do* we need to bring him?" Alex asked. "He's creeping me out."

"Well, for one thing," his grandfather replied, "I'm still rather hoping that key might make its reappearance soon. As I said, we don't *need* to get the tablet out of the robot to destroy it; we can get rid of them both together. But I had rather hoped we might be able to keep the toy intact. He is a beauty. And it would be nice to see that lock working. And, for another reason, I don't particularly want Willy left behind to tell anyone everything we've been saying."

"Well, it's not like we've been saying much," Alex muttered. "I still don't even know where we're going."

"Oh, well, Willy knows that, don't you, old man?"

"Ach," von Sudenfeld grumbled.

"Come on, join in. Why don't you tell Alex here where we're off to?"

Von Sudenfeld rocked backward and forward, clutching his belly. He spoke without opening his eyes: "We are going to Prague."

"The wonderful city of Prague. And why are we going there?" Alex's grandfather prompted.

"Because that is where we—where *you* are going to destroy the name of God." He burped and groaned again.

"There you go." Alex's grandfather grinned happily at him.

"So we need to be in Prague to destroy the tablet?" Alex asked.

"That's it. Y'see, both the golem and the tablet were formed from the same clay on the same day—fresh mud scooped from the banks of the Vltava River. It runs through the heart of the city. The way to properly destroy the tablet is to return it to the Vltava, chuck it back into the river: '. . . *once more to that whence it came,*' to quote a rough translation from the old recipe book."

"Throw it in the river? That's it?"

"That's it. No fuss, no hocus-pocus. And it's nice to have an excuse to go to Prague. Just the most enchanting city. There's a little place just off the Old Town Square; they do these most incredible dumpling things. I mean, you really won't believe it."

"But shouldn't we . . . tie him up or something?" Alex nodded at von Sudenfeld.

"*Tie him up?* Good lord, Alex. We're not barbarians. We don't go around just tying people up, like that lot did to Harry. Well, not unless we have to. Anyway, there's not much danger of Willy wandering off. For one thing, he knows what'll happen to him if he tries. And, for another, much as he *says* he wants us to let him go—he really doesn't. He'd much rather stay close to the robot."

Turning to von Sudenfeld, he shouted cheerily, as though speaking to a slightly deaf retiree, "You like to stay close to the robot, don't you?"

"Feh," von Sudenfeld said.

The old man leaned forward and began rooting through the glove box.

"You must have some driving sweets stashed away in here somewhere, Harry, I know you. Ah." He turned back, triumphantly holding out a crumpled white paper bag. Alex shook his head. Von Sudenfeld didn't acknowledge him at all.

"Don't mind if I do," Harry said, when the bag swung around to him. "Though, should probably warn you, I 'ave no idea when I bought those. Or what they are. They might've been lying in there for years."

"Sweets last forever," Alex's grandfather said, popping a colorless ball into his mouth and rolling it around. "Mmm, bit fuzzy. But still."

More bare road rolled by unchanging as they climbed the rocky hillside. Alex sat back and closed his eyes, trying to test his secret thoughts while the old man babbled brightly on.

His new idea gave him no comfort. In fact, the opposite. But it sat immobile, solid, and clear as a diamond in his mind as he tried to stop thinking it. He pictured the tall man once more. It couldn't be. Could it? It was. He knew.

This would mean going back over it all, reexamining everything that had happened. Everything his grandfather and his mum had ever told him. They didn't want him to know. He had to tread carefully.

His mum. He hadn't thought. That was a whole other . . .

"Awfully drab road this," Alex's grandfather said. "Depressing landscape all round. Who's for a singsong? Got to keep our spirits up. Does everybody know 'The Back of the Bus, They Cannae Sing'? We could make it 'The Back of the Car . . .' Hold up. What's this?"

He sat bolt upright, craning to look out the window on Harry's side. Sensing his sudden unease, Alex snapped out of his reverie and followed his gaze down.

Far below, a single set of headlights was traveling at speed on the road behind them.

"Pull over, Harry." Alex's grandfather was out of the car before it had stopped. Striding around the hood to the edge of the road, he peered through his binoculars. After a moment, he handed them to Harry, leaning out of his window.

"Renault 16 TS. 1971, looks like," Harry said after studying the road for a moment. "That's 'em all right. Not a bad motor."

"Can they catch us?" Alex's grandfather said.

"Well, depends who's driving," Harry replied, grinning. "If it were *you*, I'd say maybe. If it were me—no chance."

The old man swung back into the car. "Good man. Well, let's see you, then."

Alex felt himself pressed back as they shot forward, traveling at an even more alarming speed than before.

As they tore around another hairpin bend, the edge of the road swung in toward him and disappeared briefly from sight beneath his window. They were suspended over the steep drop as the tires fought to grip the loose surface. His stomach turned, but he was glad to note that the headlights had already disappeared out of sight below. He leaned forward, alert.

The road ahead straightened into a long stretch. The landscape was gray in the weak morning light. There was little to see except the gravel track, the dusty ground, clusters of rocks, the odd bare tree, patches of snow, all blending into one colorless smear as they rocketed along.

They were silent, save for the odd grunt from Harry as he worked the brake and gears, and the occasional bubbling moan from von Sudenfeld, who now looked as gray as the world around them. Rough road popped beneath their racing wheels.

After a while, Alex's grandfather gave a short, dissatisfied hum. He twisted to look through the rear window. He sat forward again. He drummed the dashboard. He leaned to peer into his side mirror. He looked to the back window again. Finally, he turned to Harry.

"Don't like the look of this much."

"No," Harry replied, not taking his eyes from the shuddering road. "Me neither. 'Aven't the foggiest what it is, though."

Alex turned awkwardly to look behind them. Initially, all he could see was empty road falling away fast. Then he caught a glimpse of something. Some long, low, shaking dark shape far behind. He screwed up his eyes, trying to stare harder. He couldn't make out what it was. But it was gaining rapidly.

His grandfather had now turned right around, kneeling backward on the front seat with binoculars to his eyes.

"Hmmm." He lowered the glasses. "Now, there's something I've never seen before." He turned to Harry. "Can you see this?"

"Just about. Sad to say."

"Probably an idea to put a step on it, Harry, old chap."

"If you say so." The car groaned in complaint.

Alex's grandfather lifted his binoculars again.

"That's really quite impressive," he muttered. "Never seen the like, I must say."

He tapped Alex on the elbow, offering the binoculars.

At first, all he could see was a jerking vista of rushing gray. He took the glasses away, got a fix on the black shape, tried again, frowning as though it were a mystery picture in a puzzle book. The enigmatic object shuddered in the lens as he shifted the focus. All of a sudden, he saw what it was.

A life-sizer. Lying flat on its back and shooting headfirst toward them like a missile, traveling low over the road at unimaginable speed.

He gaped at it, baffled but hypnotized. The machine, still wearing its hat and coat, was somehow hovering two or three inches above the road. Eventually, Alex saw there was something beneath it—or, rather, lots of small somethings. Straining, he began to make out details as it drew nearer. It was lying on top of a dozen or so smaller robots, gathered in groups to support it at the shoulders, hips, and heels. He vaguely made out the tips of tiny rocket ships, the wheels of little robot cars, the snouts of racing train-like things. As the assemblage came tearing down the road, some of the little machines were giving off happy red sparks.

He turned openmouthed to his grandfather.

"Rather exciting, eh?" the old man said.

The car screamed around another tight turn in the ever-climbing road. Alex looked back. The life-sizer was almost upon them—and then it was.

He gawped out his window in terror as the machine rolled up alongside. Blind eyes stared blankly up at him. Then the robot began to move ahead, drawing level with the front of the car. There, it slowed slightly, until it exactly matched their speed.

For a while, the life-sizer raced along beside them, doing nothing more than keeping pace, sitting between them and the edge of the road. Eventually, it turned its head slightly toward the car. Slowly, it raised one arm. Then it let fly, whipping a massive, savage fist at the front wheel.

Harry cursed as the car lurched sideways. He somehow found more speed. Alex stared as the life-sizer went sliding backward beneath him, out of sight. A few seconds later, the black hat began nosing back into view.

"Here it comes again!" Alex shouted.

"I see it," Harry said, swinging hard left, trying to shunt the machine toward the edge of the road. It dropped briefly back again, then came streaking forward. Drawing level, the life-sizer began showering the front wheel with a prodigious series of punches, its arm a blur.

Harry swore as the car swayed under the incessant pounding. He slammed on the brakes so suddenly, Alex felt his spine was about to be snapped by his seat belt. The life-sizer shot ahead several feet, screeched to a halt, then reversed, shrieking back at them. Harry threw the car forward again, rocketing past it.

"Any chance we can run it over the edge?" Alex's grandfather said.

"Fifty-fifty we'd go with it," Harry shouted. "'Ang on."

The machine was level once more. It unleashed another rapid series of blows. The car rocked, then spun right around, out of control. For a long, terrible instant as Harry wrestled the steering wheel, they were traveling backward along the edge of the road.

"Bloody Nora," Harry grumbled, wrenching them around again. "'Scuse my French, Alex."

"Well, there's not much I can do from in here." Alex's grandfather sighed, unclipping his seat belt and opening his door.

"Grandad!" Alex shouted.

The old man's legs disappeared from view as he hauled himself up and out, onto the roof. One shiny boot reappeared, kicking the door closed behind him.

Alex blinked numbly after him. The car shuddered again.

He bent and began fumbling frantically through his rucksack. Von Sudenfeld was making desperate retching sounds now, as though trying to be sick.

Alex found what he was searching for: a full glass salt-cellar his grandfather had pushed on him before leaving Harry's house, *just in case.* Unbuckling his seat belt, he wound down his window, grabbed the doorframe, and pulled himself halfway through, leaning out as far as he could.

As he hung out there, balanced precariously on the vibrating door, the long, sheer drop racing a few feet away, the shocking realization of what he was doing suddenly hit him. Then it was blown away by the stinging blast of freezing air and grit howling into his face. The life-sizer's legs trembled just below him.

Gripping tighter, he stretched farther out, planning to scatter salt over the machine, then drew back. It was useless: the speed they were traveling, the wind would blow it away before it got anywhere near the robot.

The life-sizer continued hammering the front wheel, by now seriously mangled. Black smoke poured out around it.

"Unscrew the lid," a voice shouted in his ear, over the wind's deafening roar.

Alex twisted to look. Has grandfather's head hung above him against the gray sky. The old man was lying spread-eagle on the car's roof, whipped by the wind. Alex wondered stupidly how his bowler hat stayed on.

"What?" Alex hollered.

"Don't try to pour it out. Take the lid off," his grandfather shouted back. "Then chuck the whole thing. Like a grenade. Try for its mouth."

Quickly pulling himself back inside the car, Alex did as instructed, swung out again. Taking careful aim, he threw the glass as hard as he could.

It bounced off the life-sizer's silvery cheek without doing any damage, but when it hit the road, it shattered. The three small robots beneath its left shoulder were caught in the explosion of salt and glass and fell instantly away, shooting stupidly off over the edge of the road.

The life-sizer lurched down to one side, its unsupported shoulder scraping the ground, sending up a shower of sparks, vivid white against the black smoke in the morning gloom. The big robot slowed as the smaller machines beneath it raced to regroup, redistributing its weight between them.

"Just the ticket," Alex's grandfather shouted.

His head disappeared from view. Then immediately returned.

"By the way, you should never hang out of a car window like that," he shouted at Alex. "Awfully dangerous."

He vanished again. Then Alex froze in horror as he reappeared, traveling through the air above him, cane held high, leaping from the roof of the speeding car.

Landing in a crouch on the big robot's chest, he brought his cane down violently, driving it like a stake through the machine's grill-like mouth. Standing there, leaning hard on the cane, he twisted the silver tip viciously inside the struggling life-sizer's head.

Alex heard the sound of throwing up behind him. Von Sudenfeld must be bringing up the key, he suddenly realized. But he didn't turn, transfixed by the sight of his grandfather racing along the road on the robot, like an old man riding a huge, monstrously bizarre motorized scooter. From time to time he leapt lightly as the machine tried to swipe him off, but the life-sizer was clearly weakening, slowing, dropping back.

"Blummy Moses!" Harry cried out. "Alex!"

Alex turned.

Von Sudenfeld, still bent over, was being sick. But even as he threw up, he was grinning, a weak, evil smile. With one more convulsive retch, something long and blue dropped out of his mouth.

Alex looked on in revulsion and confusion. Threads of drool dripped from the man's mouth to his lap, where shone a small puddle of watery sick. Tiny footprints now led away from it, up the back of the seat in front. And on top of the seatback, still covered in a sheen of vomit, stood a small, smooth blue robot, slowly unfolding spindly arms that ended in serious needle-points.

As Alex stared, the little thing jumped onto Harry's shoulder, then started clambering rapidly up his head.

The road went into another sharp turn. Harry battled to

steer around it. The vicious little machine was hauling itself through his hair, jabbing at his scalp, moving toward his face.

Alex shot into the front, grabbing at the thing just as it seemed poised to take out Harry's eyes. He got one hand around it, repulsed to find it still slippery and warm from von Sudenfeld's sick. It sliced maniacally at him as he struggled to get his window open enough to fling it out.

"Alex!" Harry shouted, pulling furiously at the wheel. "The tablet!"

Alex looked up, too late. In the back, von Sudenfeld had his rucksack. He already had the door open. Turning with a leering grin, he jumped out of the moving car like a parachutist, disappearing straight over the edge of the road.

Alex scrambled to the rear seat, braced himself in the door to leap after him. He lurched backward as Harry fought another curve. The road hurtled inches beneath his feet in a lethal gray blur. The drop beyond looked deadly now. He tensed himself to jump.

The blue robot stabbed down hard between his thumb and forefinger, setting his hand spasming open. As he dropped it, the thing immediately pounced for Harry again, needles knifing. Alex hung torn in the doorway for a second, then launched himself into the front seat, catching the machine with both hands, wrestling it away as Harry finally brought the car to a long, careening halt.

He stared dumbly at Alex. Alex stared dumbly back. Then

he let out a cry as the robot in his hand stabbed him again.

Flinging open the door, he rushed to the edge of the road and threw it as far as he could. It went sailing down, dashing off a rock, spinning out of sight. Farther off down there, he could make out von Sudenfeld, still in one piece, descending the long, steep slope toward the road below in reckless jumps and staggers. Alex started frantically to follow, until Harry's big hand grabbed his arm and pulled him back.

"Even if you didn't break your neck, you'd never catch 'im now, son."

"But—" Alex started. He stopped. Harry was right. The slope at this point was almost vertical.

As they watched, the headlights of the dark car that had been chasing them reappeared around a distant bend below. A high, unhinged sound carried up on the sudden quiet: von Sudenfeld shrieking with joy. In the dull blue morning, the white cardboard box that held the toy robot seemed to glow in his hand.

"Am I right in thinking 'e actually brought that thing up? I mean . . . from 'is stomach?" Harry asked quietly.

"I think so." Alex nodded.

They stood watching the final leg of von Sudenfeld's descent in silence. The car had drawn to a halt beneath him.

"That's disgusting," Harry said after a while.

Alex nodded again.

The waiting car's back door opened. A small figure emerged,

looking up in their direction, her pale face bright in the dim light. The wind picked up.

Alex slumped and sat. Back along the road, he dimly noticed his rucksack, discarded a few feet down the slope. Familiar items lay scattered in the dirt around it. He should slide down and gather it all up, he thought. But he didn't move. He didn't particularly feel like moving again. His head throbbed from trying to process far too many things.

What looked like a piece of white card came tumbling gently toward him, caught by the fading breeze. He trapped it with his foot, picked it up, and turned it over. The photograph. His mum and dad, forever at their party. His dad forever just out of focus. The morning was growing steadily lighter, but the light was cold, blue.

"What you got there?" Harry said, bending to see. "Ah, yeah."

"Harry?" Alex said.

"Yeah, son?"

Alex gestured vaguely at the car far below. "That girl. The tall man. Do you know who they are?"

"Uh." Harry suddenly became absorbed in studying the dust between his feet. "Ah, well, see . . ."

"It's okay. You don't have to tell me if you don't want. I'm getting used to it."

Harry sighed. He went back to gazing down the hillside. After a moment he spoke.

"No, lissen, Alex, you're right. None of this is fair on you.

But, see, you need to remember, your grandad, 'e 'as 'is reasons, son. 'E really is tryin' to do right by you. Me an' 'im, we go back a long, long way, an' I'd trust 'im with me life. In fact, I 'ave done, more times than I want to remember." He snorted a sudden laugh. "'Ere, did 'e ever tell you 'bout the time we were robbin' the Louvre, right, and . . ."

Harry coughed as Alex stared at him.

"Eh, no. No, 'e wouldn't 'ave. I prolly shouldn't . . . uh. It was a long while back, anyway. An' there was a good reason for that, an' all. To begin with. Though 'e kind of got into the whole art thief thing for a while. It was just a fad. It was the sixties, you know. But, anyway . . . I'm not much good at talkin', Alex. What I'm tryin' to say is, you should give 'im the benefit of the doubt, son. Trust 'im. 'E's been tryin' to shelter you and your mum from a lot. But, no, you're right, it's not really fair. I've told 'im as much. But then, see, it's not really my place to tell you. One thing I've learned, Alex, is to never get involved in people's family business—"

He broke off abruptly, wincing as though he had said too much. Alex took a breath, held it in, blew it out. Time to push.

"Harry?"

"Uh-huh?"

"You used to know my dad?"

"Uh . . . yes, son. I did."

"What was he like?"

"Well . . . Blimey. 'E was a bit like you. I liked 'im a lot."

"He was tall, wasn't he?" Alex turned, squinted up at him.

He gestured with the photo. "About as tall as that tall man down there. About as tall as my grandad. They're about the same height, aren't they?"

Harry frowned, looking off down the hill. His eyes widened. He stared down at Alex as if seeing him for the first time. "Oh, Gawdammit," he muttered, after a long pause. He screwed his eyes shut. Alex sensed him struggling to make a decision, fighting himself.

"Look, Alex," he finally said. "Things . . . things is complicated. There's things . . . It's up to your grandad to tell you what you need to know. But I'll tell you one thing. Rather, I'll show you something."

He dug into his pocket, pulled out a large and worn black wallet, began rifling the contents.

"'Ere we go."

He held out a small black-and-white photograph, creased at one corner.

Taking it, Alex saw a picture of two people. One, he instantly recognized: his grandfather, only younger than he had ever seen him. Perhaps twenty years younger, in his early fifties or so, his hair dark, but already heavily peppered with silvery flecks.

He stood grinning, wearing what looked like a smart army uniform. In one hand, he held a cap with a shining peak. The other hand clasped the shoulder of a thin little boy who stood proudly beside him, maybe about six years old, smiling at the camera with a cheeky face. They posed cockily together in a ruined, chewed-up landscape, standing on a mound of pale rubble. The phantom wrecks of burnt-out buildings hung in the grainy air behind them, wrecked facades, broken windows. It looked cold and smoky there.

"Wow," Alex whispered. "This is the only photograph I've ever seen of him. He always said he hates getting his picture taken. Where's this from? Who's that boy?"

Harry let out a sad-sounding sigh. "That's me, son. That's not long after we first met. London. Just after the war. I was orphaned, y'know. Living in the bombsites, bit of a toe-rag. 'E found me and kind of took me under 'is wing."

Alex looked at Harry, looked at the picture. He felt his battered brain buckling.

"But . . . Hang on. It can't . . ." He looked at Harry again, thinking furiously. "How old are you, Harry?"

"I'm seventy-nine, son." Adding, to himself, "'Ow did that 'appen?"

Harry watched him staring at the photograph a few more seconds, then lifted it gently, tucking it carefully back inside his wallet.

"But that doesn't make any sense," Alex stumbled, gesturing uselessly after the picture. "You two are about the same age today."

"There you go," Harry said. "Uh-oh, speak of the devil. Shtum, now."

Alex's grandfather came wandering casually around the curve, cane at a jaunty angle over his shoulder.

"Hallo!" He nodded down over the edge of the road. "Saw

old Willy leaping his way down there. Who'd've thought he had it in him? Look at him go! Like a mountain goat."

"That's not all 'e 'ad in 'im," Harry muttered.

"Eh?" Alex's grandfather said.

"The robot," Harry said. "'E's got it."

"Oh. Ah. I see. That's not so good, is it, Alex? Alex? Are you okay?"

Alex stood staring at him, trying to make himself see his grandfather as though he had never seen him before, furiously turning over the question of how old he looked.

The old man joined them gazing down at the road below.

"Maybe we should've tied him up at that." Alex's grandfather pushed back his hat and scratched his head. "Ah, well. Can't be helped."

Alex looked down. He could just make out von Sudenfeld and the tall man in animated conversation. It seemed as if the girl waved cheerily up to them. Then the distant sound of a door closing sounded flatly across the morning. The car turned and sped off, back the way it had come.

"That's it, then," he murmured in a monotone.

"Hmmm? How's that?" his grandfather said.

"Well, that's it, isn't it?" Alex said, bleakly regarding the picture of his father in his hand. "He's got the robot, he's got the tablet, he's got the key. He's got it all. It's finished. We've lost. They've won."

"Oh, pshaw," the old man said. "Chin up. Don't be such a defeatist."

"But what can we do?"

"Well, we'll, y'know, just take the robot back."

"And how do you plan to catch them?" Alex said, gesturing at the empty road below, then toward their car, where Harry knelt examining the wrecked wheel.

"Oh, Harry'll patch up something to get us moving, won't you, old chap?"

"Er, maybe," Harry called back. "Great thing about this car is it can limp along on three wheels. What they call"—he cleared his throat—"*hydropneumatic suspension.*"

"We'll never catch up," Alex said.

"Oh, well, we don't want to *catch up* with them so much," his grandfather said, tapping his cane at his shoe to dislodge some dirt. "We want to get *ahead* of them."

"How do you mean?"

"Well, you're right—he's got the robot and the key and all that. But we know where he's going with it, don't we?"

Alex tucked the photograph inside his jacket and gazed blankly at him. Despite the cheer he tried to force into his voice, the old man looked very grim as he stared out over the low world.

"The golem, Alex. They're off to see the golem. All we have to do is get there first."

His face darkened.

"We'll have to get a plane. I don't like planes."

XIX.

A PROWL THROUGH PRAGUE

THE OLD MAN spent the flight staring fixedly at the back of the seat in front of him, muttering occasionally like a mantra under his breath:

"I don't like planes."

Alex sat by the window. Nothing but clouds. The whole world hidden.

The memory of Harry's impossible photograph had joined the unreliable gallery of images in his mind, swaying in the fog alongside his glimpse of the tall man's face, his vivid impression of the girl's. One second he was certain what he'd seen. The next he doubted he remembered it clearly at all.

He pulled out the picture of his parents, wrinkled now.

If this tall man was his father—

As soon as he thought it, he flinched away from the idea again. Yet it was the only thing that made sense, if anything made any sense anymore. The resemblance he'd registered almost as a physical sensation. His grandfather's determination to keep the tall man's identity hidden. He glanced to his side, struck by the queasy notion the old man could overhear his thoughts. He put the photo away.

His dad had died before he was born. An accident. A car in Germany. He was on a job. His grandfather had been visiting him there. That was what he'd always been told, what he'd always accepted. He'd had lots of other questions—a million, all boiling down to one, *what was he like?*—but he realized he'd been waiting for the right time to ask, and the time had never quite come.

A million new questions buzzed now. If this tall man was his father . . . why had he never come for him? Why had he gone away? Why had they told him he was dead? He stopped on that one, unconsciously rubbing his finger hard back and forth against his lips.

Did his mum know he was alive? No. She couldn't. There was no way. Her grief, her pain all those years was unmistakable, unmistakably real. Even as a little boy he'd understood it. It was with her still, a dim scar that would never fully fade. She wouldn't want it to. What would this do to her?

His grandfather had kept them both in the dark, then. To shelter them, Harry had said. Alex knew about that, about keeping quiet to keep the trouble away. *Pieces of people . . . voodoo . . . golem . . . name of God.*

Strange and desperate schemes. Violent . . . horrific . . . evil. He considered that word. What was he like? Was that his answer? Had he discovered his dad was alive only to discover he was a monster? What kind of cruel miracle was that? Then he thought again of his mum's sadness. Her love. There had to be more. Some reason he might have gone away from them to do these things. A purpose. Maybe if they could talk—the very notion stunned him as he thought it: *maybe they could talk*. Maybe there was some mistake, some misunderstanding. Something else. Something missing. There was so much his grandfather hadn't told him.

His grandfather. He was at the center of it all. He knew all about this dark and wild hidden world. What else was he hiding? How to ask him? He strained to picture Harry's photo again. He'd been trying to tell him something.

The only question that matters is: do you trust me? the old man had asked. Did he? Did he even know him?

The plane rocked. The cabin filled with gasps. They seemed to plummet, bouncing hard on the air. Alex grabbed unconsciously for his grandfather's hand, felt the old man's grip tighten around his wrist. For an instant, they clung to each other like that, looking into each other's eyes, high above the earth.

His grandfather's grip relaxed as the pilot's voice droned placidly about turbulence over the intercom.

"I really don't like planes," he said, with a grin of relief.

Memories flashed in fragments. The shadowy figure leaping, weird machines slashing. Knives and blood. His grandfather falling.

Alex squeezed his arm. And how could he ever doubt him?

"We'll be okay," he said. He turned back to the thickening clouds.

RAIN HAMMERED AROUND them as they touched down in Prague in the early evening. Alex watched it whipping in black sheets across the runway as they taxied to a halt. His grandfather shook Harry awake, impatient to get off.

In the busy concourse they gathered around their meager luggage, agreeing on a hasty strategy. Harry would check them in to a hotel, then "'ave a sniff around, phone some people, see if there's been any trace," before rejoining them.

"'Ere, son," he said, nudging Alex and pointing across the hall to a small kiosk. "Reckon you could run over and grab me a coffee before we go?" He dropped coins into Alex's palm.

"Harry." Alex's grandfather sighed. "We *are* in a bit of a hurry—"

"I," Harry said, with a meaningful look, "am parched."

The old man frowned. "All right, Alex, off you go, quick as you can. Nothing for me, thank you.

"Coffee, Harry?" The old man sighed as Alex trotted off. "Now? Really? *Airport* coffee?"

"Lissen," Harry cut him off urgently. "You know what 'e thinks, don't you?"

"Eh?"

"Alex." Harry jerked a thumb in the direction of the kiosk. "I think 'e thinks it's 'is dad."

"What? Not following you, old bean. Alex thinks what's his dad?"

"'*Im*. Ol' Springy Shoes. The lad thinks 'e's '*is father*."

Alex's grandfather stepped back as though he had been slapped. "His fa—" He stared off in silence before trying again.

"He can't . . . I mean, why ever would he think that? He knows his fath—" He cleared his throat and blinked. "He knows his father is dead. Harry, what makes you say that? Are you sure?"

"Well, 'e 'asn't come right out and said so. But, yeah. Things 'e asked me, things 'e said, or tried to say. The way 'e's been starin' at that photo of 'is mum and dad 'e carries around. I'm sure. 'Aven't you noticed?"

"Well, no, I mean . . . I've never been much good at that kind of thing, Harry."

"Yeah. Well. At the risk of teachin' you 'ow to suck eggs, you should prolly consider that it's just possible the lad's mind is a little messed up by all this palaver. I'm speakin' as one who knows. I still remember 'avin' to fight my first ghosts and tin machines around the age of ten. I'm used to all this now, but 'e's not. 'E's all over the place. You're goin' to 'ave to say something. And maybe tellin' the lad the truth wouldn't be such a bad idea."

"Hah. Never been much good at that, either." The old man

laughed bleakly and stared off to where Alex stood waiting to be served, looking small between the adults in the line.

"No," he said decisively. He straightened his shoulders, shook his head, banishing the thought. "No. You just *can't* be right, Harry. He's always known about his dad. You must be picking this up all wrong. Alex knows his father is *gone*. He *knows* that. As for the rest . . . I never wanted him involved, but I've always planned on telling him something someday. About his dad, too. You know that. But *later*, not now."

He turned back to Harry, voice unsteady, "He's not ready. *I'm* not ready yet. I mean, Harry . . . he might think I'm some kind of . . . *monster*. He might think *he's* some kind of monster."

Harry sighed, patting his shoulder. "I can't tell you what to do or when to do it. I know that by now. But I can tell you: whenever the time comes, whatever you do, you'll do the right thing."

"Hah," the old man said, watching Alex hurrying back toward them. "Suppose we'll see, eh?"

AN HOUR AFTER they'd parted ways with Harry, Alex found himself struggling to keep up with his grandfather as he went striding over the cobblestones of the Old Town Square.

A strange, tall building dominated the skyline. Spotlights lit it from below with hard white light that threw sharp black shadows over its huge facade. A pair of spiky twin towers rose on either side, weird gothic horns, like stone rocket ships from another age, straining for the heavens. It seemed an ominous portent. *Dracula's castle*, Alex thought, then pushed the thought down.

The rain had stopped. Beneath a lowering black sky, the square bustled brightly with tourists, sellers, and street performers. A Christmas market had been set up. Dozens of small wooden huts were laid out, glowing red and green, selling hats and scarves, candles and wooden toys, sausages and candy, and mulled wine that scented the air with cinnamon.

A giant Christmas tree towered over them, around eighty feet tall, wreathed in a blazing multitude of lights. A choir sang carols beneath it. People held out phones in gloved hands, taking pictures of themselves looking happy. Huge decorative lights flickered, vanishing and springing back to life in the skeletal shapes of leaping reindeer and shooting stars.

The whole place thrummed with excitement and good humor, like a Christmas card come to life. But his grandfather ignored it all, even the food, cutting a path through the crowds with brusquely muttered "Pardon"s and "'Scuse me"s. Beyond this, he was curiously quiet, saying little to Alex, lost in thought. In one hand he clutched his cane. In the other, a Gladstone retrieved from Harry's house, much like the bag he had abandoned in Paris.

Soon they were on a long, tree-lined street leading away from the square, winding roughly north and west. The night was getting toward freezing. A fine, frosty mist clung to every-thing. Streetlamps floated feebly in bitter fog. People moved along like echoes of shadows.

Alex labored to keep pace. A sickly feeling crawled around his stomach. He felt like he had when he thought he had lost the robot before. Trying to remember what its presence felt like, he felt only its absence. The idea that it was gone resounded in his mind. That, and getting it back.

The crowds thinned. The Old Town seemed to grow older around them as they walked. Finally, Alex's grandfather stopped in the frail light beneath a lamppost and raised his cane:

"Here we are."

The building he pointed to wasn't very big, but it loomed strikingly stark in the fading evening.

A bare construction of mushroomy gray stone, all crude angles, it looked like something that had grown out of the ground rather than been built, like something that had always been there. Backlit by lamps in the street behind, it seemed almost to emit a smoky glow.

A jumbled single-story outcrop clustered like a skirt around the main edifice: one large, brute rectangle, topped by a dark, high triangular roof, a jagged, barnlike structure of brick and tile that reached to a height of about five floors. A few small dark windows were the only decoration.

"That's it?" Alex asked.

"That's it. The Altneuschul. The Old New Synagogue."

"I thought it would be . . . grander."

"It is grand," his grandfather said, "just in a different way."

"And the golem. Its body. It's really in there?"

"Up in the attic. That's where Rabbi Loew stowed it all those years ago," the old man said, adding, after a pause: "if you believe the story."

"So what do we do?"

His grandfather glanced around. A few dim figures moved along the pavements. He looked at his wristwatch.

"Well, I think the thing to do now is a spot of lurking," he said, his breath adding to the mist. "You stay here. I'm going to walk around the place, have a look-see, take up a position on the other side. Be careful. You see any sign of them, come get me. I'll be around exactly this spot over on the other side, okay?"

"Okay."

"Good man. If there's nothing doing, I'll come and get you. Stamp your feet; it'll keep you warm."

Alex watched his grandfather hurry away into the shining murk. He sank back into the shadows. It began raining again, suddenly, enormously, like someone throwing the switch on a vast shower system in the heavens. Falling water hissed around him, sounding silver and black. He was soon soaked through. His trousers stuck coldly to the pain in his legs. Time went by. How long had his grandfather been gone?

Every now and then, footsteps. People would appear, shades hurrying in the downpour, and he would tense anxiously. But no one stopped.

The raw chill of the paving stones seeped into his aching feet. He stamped. It did nothing. Time ebbed by in a measure-less lump. The rain thinned to a drizzle. It left him feeling even colder.

The voice made him jump:

"How we doing?"

His grandfather stood over him, water dripping from his hat. He held two steaming plastic cups, proffering one.

"Get yourself around this."

Alex accepted it thankfully. Coffee. Hot. Sweet. His grand-father produced a small flask that glinted silver, splashed a healthy measure of something into his own cup.

"Just a nip. I'd offer you a little, Alex, but that wouldn't be very responsible of me."

They stood gulping their drinks, Alex loving the warm cup in his cold hands, the glowing sensation as hot coffee ran down his throat.

"I picked up a paper," his grandfather said. He gestured vaguely at the dripping dark city. "There are flood warnings everywhere. Lots of rain and melting snow. Snows, then melts, then snows and melts and snows again. The river's running very high, close to breaking its banks."

He drained his cup with a satisfied sigh.

"So. That's the weather report. I take it there's been no sign?"

"Nothing."

"Excellent. Well, street seems fairly empty now. I'd say we

could advance from lurking to Stage Two of our plan. This way, please."

He led around the old building, down shallow stairs into a smaller, grayer alleyway behind. Checking to make sure they were unobserved, he dropped his Gladstone, crouched, and began digging inside.

"Keep a look out."

Alex glanced nervously around as his grandfather busied himself over his bag. The old man stood and turned to him again. Beneath his bowler hat, he now wore a thin black eye mask.

"What's that supposed to be?" Alex asked. He felt dimly like laughing, but not much, and so he just blinked.

"What's it look like? It's my mask." The old man held out his hand, offering Alex another exactly the same. "And this is yours."

"I'm not wearing that."

"Yes, you are. This is mask business."

"It's stupid."

"It's no such thing. It's rather dashing, if I do say so myself. 'Everything profound loves a mask,' or something like that."

"But you just look exactly the same."

"Ah, but you're just saying that because you saw me putting it on," his grandfather said, thrusting the strip of black cloth at him. "If you didn't *know* this was me, you'd never recognize me in a million years. No, believe me, this is time-tested, the perfect disguise."

"But—" Alex began, then stopped, giving it up as another lost cause. Sighing, he tied the mask around his head, then stood there, his feelings of uncertainty, anxiety, and fear shifting slightly, to allow room for the sense of looking ridiculous.

His grandfather bent to the bag again. This time he came up with a knotted rope, a nasty-looking three-headed hook at one end.

"Now," the old man said, "over here."

They slunk along the side of the building, past a dark doorway, until they reached an angle in the wall.

"See that window?"

Alex looked up. A dark, round hole loomed about thirteen feet above.

"Now, look just to the right."

Alex followed his grandfather's pointing finger. Beside the window, he could just make out a thin, rusted iron bar set roughly into the concrete. Above it, there was another, and then another and another, leading up the wall toward the shadowy roof, like rungs of a ladder.

"That's the way up to the attic," his grandfather said. "Story is those steps used to come all the way down to the ground, but they took the lower rungs away when they put the golem up there. Stop any nosey parkers climbing up to visit him."

He unfurled his rope and, with a grunt, hurled the grappling hook upward. It caught on the first try, snagging the second rung above. He tugged the rope hard then stepped back, satisfied, slapping his hands together.

"Now. How are we at climbing ropes? This might be a two-person job, Alex, and Harry isn't quite as nimble as he used to be."

"Right," Alex said. "Just so I know? The idea is we climb up there and break into the attic. Into the attic where the insane clay monster from God lives. That's what we're doing."

"Well, not so much *break in*. I'm rather hoping not to have to break anything." From a pocket, his grandfather fished out his pouch of lock-picks and waggled it. "But, essentially—yes." He nodded, eyes glittering behind the mask.

"Just thought I'd check," Alex muttered. "And then what?"

"Still working on that. Right. I'll go first. Keep a look out."

Taking hold of the rope, he jumped and put both feet against the wall, then began hauling his way easily up, an increasingly vague figure scaling the side of the building. Alex heard soft clangs as his grandfather's feet found the iron rungs above.

His voice sailed down in a hissing stage whisper:

"Forgot to say, before you come up, could you tie the rope around the handles of my bag?"

Alex did that. He stood staring at the line of the rope hanging against the white wall. He looked around. Back along that misty street, people were buying Christmas presents and singing songs under twinkling lights, eating hot chestnuts and laughing, and never once thinking about clay monsters or how life can turn inside out without warning. He had never eaten a chestnut. He closed his eyes. He felt stupid and scared and lost and more than a little excited. He opened his eyes, gripped the rope, and climbed.

It was harder going than his grandfather had made it appear. His biceps were trembling by the time he made the first rung. Despite the cold, he felt sweat trickling down his back. He pulled himself up until his feet found the bottom step but couldn't go much farther. The old man was perched only a few rungs above. Alex stood with his face to the back of his grandfather's legs.

"Keep watching out. Pretty fiddly lock this. But I suspect not as tricky as that one was. See?"

Alex strained up. The old man was pointing out an old blackened gouge in the attic doorframe by his elbow. Embedded in the wood, the remains of a scratched metal plate shone coldly.

"Probably what's left of Benjamin Loewy's original lock. The Nazis broke in during the war, y'see, trying to find the golem. I remember, those beasts, they—" He broke off and looked down at Alex through the crook of his arm. "Well, there was a story about all that, anyway. Oh, by the way: it goes without saying you should never really go around breaking into places of worship."

He turned and grumbled over the lock a few seconds more. Then:

"Bingo."

Alex watched his feet step up, saw his legs disappear into

the building. He followed. The ladder ended at a small, arched doorway. As he was about to climb through, his grandfather's head popped back out from inside.

"Cuckoo," the old man said. "Now. Rope?"

"Huh?"

His grandfather nodded downward.

"Doesn't really do to leave it hanging on the ladder, old bean. Bit of a giveaway."

"Oh. Yeah."

Alex clambered back down, bent to grab the hook and work it loose. As he started to pull the rope up, he almost fell, unprepared for the weight of the Gladstone tied to the end.

"Might find the bag's a bit heavy," his grandfather called.

Alex grunted in response, concentrating on hauling himself back up with his free hand, palm growing slick with sweat on the rungs. As he reached the top, his grandfather took him by the wrist, pulling him up into the attic.

He sat blinking at the darkness as his grandfather leaned out, briskly hauling in the rope and the bag. The attic smelled musty, like a mixture of paper, spice, and ancient damp. The faint street light reached in for a foot around him. Beyond that, solid black.

"What kind of knot is that? What are they teaching you these days, anyway?" the old man muttered as he untied the bag. Quickly winding the rope into a small loop, he stowed it away, then turned to Alex, holding out a flashlight.

"Grab hold of this, would you? Going to be pitch-black when I close this door."

And when he did, it was.

They sat silently in utter darkness. His grandfather spoke.

"Ah, so now would be the time to turn the flashlight on, Alex."

"Oh. Right. Hang on, I can't find the . . ."

"Give it here."

"I'm trying to, but I can't see you . . . there."

"*Oww!* That was nearly my eye!"

"Sorry, hang on . . . right, there, take it."

Alex winced in the sudden glare. The old man held the light briefly beneath his chin, the blinding beam streaming up into his masked face so it hung illuminated, suddenly weird, brutish, and evil-looking in the darkness.

"*Bwoooah-har-har!* Here you go."

He handed it back. Alex held it pointed at him.

"Excellent. Now, can you shine it away from my eyes and over at the door? I need to lock it again."

Kneeling, Alex shifted his weight anxiously as his grandfather worked with his picks.

"That's us," he said presently. "All locked in safe and sound. May I have that again, please?"

Taking the flashlight, he sent the beam exploring around them. Disturbed dust motes danced shining in its path. He shone it upward, crawling over the steep, sloping insides of the high roof. Alex saw pale beams and rafters, long shadows swaying. Awkward wooden columns reached up and branched out like barren, malformed trees, strung thick with derelict cobwebs. He glimpsed a higher balcony section above, shelves up there.

The circle of light came down to run over the floor. Almost the entire space was strangely carpeted with paper, ripped and torn pages covered in writing he couldn't read: single pages, entire sections of ragged and rotting books, tattered scrolls, abandoned letters.

"What's all that?" he whispered.

"Just what it looks like. Old books. Or what's left of them. Mostly holy books, bibles, but other documents as well."

"What are they doing up here?"

"Not a lot. Now: look."

The light stretched to the far end of the attic. There was even more paper there, piled in high mounds against the gable wall.

"Okay. Uh . . . what am I looking at?"

"The golem, Alex. That's it. Over there. Hidden beneath the paper."

The old beams supporting the roof moaned quietly as wind hit the building. The rain had grown heavier, battering harshly on the ancient tiles. Alex looked from the pale heaps of torn paper to his grandfather and back again, mouth dry.

"So," he managed. "What do we do?"

"Well." Shadows leapt upward as the old man shone the light down on his wristwatch. "Not a lot to do now but wait. They could be here any minute. Then again, they might not come tonight at all. But I rather suspect they will. I suppose we should hide. And then: we wait."

"But." Alex glanced back to the now dark corner. It seemed that the darkness had a different quality there. Denser, somehow. Colder.

"It's really over there? The golem? It's real?"

"Well—"

"No. Don't say, 'So the story goes.' Tell me. Is it real?"

The old man sighed. "Look. Alex. The first thing to do is find ourselves a nice comfortable spot to hide."

"Can I look? Can I see it?"

"Probably not a good idea to begin disturbing the scene. They'll be on guard. We don't want them to know anybody has been here before them. They'll dig it out soon enough; you'll see it then. Come on."

Shadows shifted and paper rustled as he waded farther into the attic, shining the flashlight at their feet. In the center of the space, he stopped, stood flicking the beam around.

To the left, rickety shelves had been erected between the wooden columns that supported the roof. They held more books, badly worn old volumes arranged in toppling piles. The old man stepped over and shone his flashlight through the makeshift bookcase, illuminating a small triangular corridor-like space formed behind by the steep slope of the roof.

He directed the light back along the shelves. They ended a few feet short of the doorway they had entered. He stood considering, running the flashlight back and forth from the mound of paper at one end to the door at the other, finally aiming it directly at the shelves again, holding it there for a long time. He nodded.

"In there should do it," he said. "Come on."

Crouching, they worked their way behind the shelves, almost as far as the end of the room with the ominous paper pile. There, the old man stopped and sat, dust flying around him in the light. Setting down his bag, he motioned for Alex to sit.

"Okay, it's time to turn the flashlight off, Alex. Don't want to risk giving ourselves away. And it doesn't pay to waste the batteries when we don't know how long we're likely to be up here. So. It's going to get dark. All right?"

"Okay."

"Good man."

Alex saw his grandfather's head bow in thought. He heard the switch click. Blackness fell like a hammer.

He tried closing and opening his eyes. He couldn't tell the difference. After a while, he wasn't even sure whether his eyes were open or shut. He lifted his fingertips gently to check, flinching when they touched the cloth mask he had forgotten he was wearing.

They sat without speaking, listening to the rain. Aside from the icy lash of the downpour and the wind driving it, the silence was solid. Minutes crept by. Alex began almost to doubt that his grandfather was still there, beside him. His limbs ached in his damp clothes, but not as much as his mind ached from the blare of his thoughts, chasing one another in a carousel of half-formed suspicions, frustrated questions.

He started at a sudden sound. His own voice, decisive in the dark.

"Grandad."

"Uh-huh?" The old man's voice floated out of the blackness. *"Who are you?"*

XX.

THE OLD SCHOOL IN THE DARK

THE WIND HOWLED sadly outside. Old roof beams creaked.

"Well," said Alex's grandfather after a long silence. "'Who are you?' That's a rum question, I must say. Are you okay, Alex? I know we've not had much chance to talk in all this excitement—"

"Yeah, well." Alex could hear his voice shaking, a mixture of trepidation, determination, and faint anger. He forced on, speaking to the darkness. "We've got a chance now. While we're sitting here. I'm sick of being kept in the dark."

"No pun intended, eh?" The old man laughed bleakly.

Alex ignored him. "We made a deal. You promised."

"Ah. Yes. I suppose I did. Okay, then. Eh." He cleared his throat. "Who am I? Well, first and last thing you have to remember, Alex, is, I'm your grandad, same as always. Always will be . . ."

He trailed off, clearly reluctant to continue.

"Hah. Not really quite sure where to begin, old chap. Maybe

this would work better if you ask me what you want to know."

Alex took a breath. How to proceed. *Is he my dad?* The question thrummed loudest in his head. But when he opened his mouth, the words wouldn't form.

"The golem first," he finally said. "Is it real?"

"Alex. I've said this before. Sometimes, you just find yourself in the middle of something, and the only thing to do is get on with it. Situations arise, you act accordingly. And that's where we are."

"But, I mean, do you believe—?" Alex started.

His grandfather cut him off. "Sometimes it doesn't matter what you believe or don't believe, old chap. It's other people and their beliefs that land you in trouble." He took a deep breath, puffed it out in exasperation. "Okay, look. Put it this way. In the world you've been living in, the world most people live in, the world I'd *like* to live in, the golem isn't real, no. It's just a good story. And that's the way we've got to keep it."

"But . . ." Alex stopped, trying to gather his thoughts. "But I've felt it." He spoke quietly, as though making a confession he didn't want heard.

"Okay." The old man sat silent for a beat. A weary sigh. "You've felt what?"

"The— Well, I dunno. Like my homework, I was telling you, my English essay, right? The one I didn't finish, then it was finished. And then, on the bus—"

"The bus?"

Alex told him now. Words came pouring out in a rush. In the close darkness, he felt he was unburdening himself of secrets, glad to be rid of them. He spoke about the strange, flickering sensation he had experienced sometimes with the robot. About his run-in with Kenzie Mitchell on the bus, a lifetime ago. About the fear on the other boy's face. About the boys on the train from Paris. About how one had almost choked to death before him. Because of him.

He heard himself talking faster, tried to keep up with himself, tried to plan ahead for the question he wanted to ask most of all. He was getting lost. "It's like, sometimes . . . the robot, or the tablet, it's doing what I tell it. Making what I want to happen happen. Finishing my work for me. Protecting me. Von Sudenfeld, he said there was power . . . the name of . . . And it's as if I'm not really there anymore. Or I'm still there but watching myself from somewhere else. But I don't know how it works. I don't know how to *do* it. I tried once. When the fliers were attacking me in that field, I tried to use it, to make them stop. But nothing happened. I don't know what's happening; I don't understand any of this."

He trailed off, staring at the dark. A solid silence settled.

"I wonder," the old man finally said. "Loewy, the toymaker, I always think, hid the tablet in the toy as a kind of in-joke. The robot as a representation of the golem, you know. The golem itself was a shell; the real power is in the tablet—or rather, the tablet is the conduit for that power. Maybe the toy has become a kind of golem. Maybe it always was. Loewy had studied his family history; he would have been versed in the procedures. There actually were some vague stories that he could make the toy move, that he would put on secret shows . . . Well, I don't know how any of that works, really. I don't want to know.

"But, you see, Alex, the thing about the golem is that it was rather stupid. I mean, even at its best—before it went mad and started killing. It was supposed to have access to all these great powers and knowledge: invisibility, the ability to raise the dead, all sorts. But in itself, it was dumb as a rock. You had to know how to use it. You had to tell it *exactly* what you wanted it to do before it would do it. And you'd have to be very, *very* specific to make sure it did it exactly the way you wanted. Very clear instructions."

Alex nodded. "Garbage in, garbage out," he said.

"Eh?"

"It's a thing they say about computers; we did it in school. You have to feed the correct information in to get the correct information out. You have to know what you're asking."

"Yes, that's the idea. A golem's essential nature is to serve. That's what it was created for. It's hungry for work. It looks for work and for a master to give it work, give it instruction. Maybe you could say that it's been yearning for a master all those years while it was lost, and maybe you've made a kind of connection with it. Or it's made a connection with you is maybe more like it. And maybe much worse."

His grandfather paused, as though struck by a notion.

"Alex, while you had the toy, you didn't *give* it anything?"

"Huh?" Alex was baffled anew.

"Put anything in there. In with the tablet. Anything of *you*. Hair maybe, or fingernails or blood, or—no, course you didn't. I mean, why would you? Alex?"

Alex sat silent.

"Alex," the old man repeated. "You didn't."

"I . . . I didn't mean to. I cut my thumb. It was really bleeding. Some might have got inside. Just a little. Uh. Is that bad?"

Darkness hung heavy between them.

"Suffering cats," the old man muttered. "It's probably not great, Alex, no. The people who dabble in this—they use *themselves*. Bits of their own bodies. Like in the robots you've seen—hair, skin . . . other things. It basically boils down to a rather horrible mixture of science and engineering and . . . what you might call black magic, for want of a better term. There's a lot of boiling involved, actually. Blood is considered the most potent element of the lot. Now, there was no blood used in the creation of the golem. But that's not to say that directly exposing the tablet to blood won't have some effect. It's bringing together two things that aren't supposed to be brought together. Two powers. And if it's *your* blood . . ."

He stopped abruptly. Then:

"Ah, so tell me, Alex," he continued. "That feeling you've described, that power. The things that happened. Did you enjoy it?"

"No," Alex murmured slowly. "No, it . . . scared me; I felt

sick—*alone* is the only way I can describe it. Just suddenly really lonely. The first times, anyway."

"The first times?"

"The last time it happened, on the train, didn't feel as bad. Well, not until I saw that boy was . . . being hurt. I didn't like it, but it was like I was getting used to it. And . . ."

"Yes?"

"I want it *back*." He was talking faster again. "I need it back. I need to *learn* . . . The robot, or the tablet . . . I mean, if I learn how to use it, we could do things. Couldn't we? Good things. Protect people . . . Maybe that's why *he* wants it . . . But it's *mine* now, isn't it? I mean, you gave it to me . . . It's *mine*."

Alex stopped himself. His voice had a savage heat he didn't recognize. He hung his head, thankful now no one could see him.

"Listen to me carefully, Alex." The old man's words carried softly in the lightless room. "That feeling you described, when you've felt that power—that sense of being alone. That's what lies down at the end of that road. Just more of that. Nothing else. Nothing good. Remember, in all the stories, the golem went mad. All it ever brought was destruction."

Another heavy pause. Alex heard a noise he identified as his grandfather unscrewing his flask and taking a swig.

"I should never have started any of this, Alex," the old man continued. "All this madness, I've been trying to keep it away from you. Then, once you were caught up in it, I thought maybe if we could just batter through it quickly enough, you could just get back to normal again."

"Back to *normal?*" Alex spluttered. In the pitch-blackness, he gestured uselessly at the fact that they were sitting in an ancient attic in the middle of Europe, waiting to prevent a medieval monster from being resurrected. "After *this?*"

"Ha, yes. Well. To be honest, I've been caught up in this so long that maybe my idea of normal isn't quite as sharp as it could be. Who wants to be normal, anyway, eh?"

He gave another hollow laugh. Another sigh.

"I should never have sent you the toy, Alex. I'm sorry. That was a mistake. I tried to get it to the river and end all this the first day I laid hands on it, but they cut me off. I put it in the mail only as a last resort, because I was in a hurry, and because I was in danger, and because I needed to get it away, and it really was the safest place I could think to hide it. I thought, if I could get it to you, he'd never find it."

He fell silent again.

"Okay. The tall man," Alex prodded, seeing an entry. "The girl. Von Sudenfeld said you went back a long way."

"Yes." The old man sounded more reluctant than ever. Another deep breath. "Okay. The tall man. The truth of it is, Alex, we, that is, he and I, a long time ago, yes, we used to . . . I mean, you could say that we used to . . ."

"*Grandad.* Spit it out!"

"We used to work together. In this kind of affair. Investigating the lost things. The other sides of things. The things behind things. Stories, secrets, and superstitions. Myths and magic and general mumbo jumbo. You know. Looking for the truth."

"So . . . more than just the golem?"

"Hmmm? Oh, yes. The search for the tablet has taken up quite a lot of time, all told. But there were lots of other things. Let's see." There came a sound as though he was scratching his neck. "Ah, the Spear of Destiny, Excalibur, and old missus in the water there. The Tree of Life. Nessie. The Grail, of course. Fair amount of time wasted on that one over the years. The Grand Rat. A henge or two. And then, ah . . . well, some stickier bits and pieces. Witchy business, that kind of thing. All nonsense, of course."

He cleared his throat again, hummed an intricate little tune to himself.

"But who is he?" Alex pushed. "And the girl?"

"Her." The old man sounded irritated, bitter. "I mean, just don't even bother about her. She's—his daughter. Okay? Hideous creature. Hideous family. Forget about her."

"Why won't you just tell me who he is?" Alex felt a stinging at his eyes, blinked it away.

"Look. Alex. I have told you: it doesn't matter. He's just who he is."

"What's his name?"

"*It doesn't matter.*"

"Yeah, well, if *it doesn't matter*, why don't you just tell me?"

"Alex, for—" his grandfather snapped in exasperation. "Right. Okay. Well, he's had different names. Jack. There you go. People called him Jack for a while. Back when he was doing a lot of that jumping trick. You could call him Jack. Happy with that? Honestly, the Tall Man is as good a name as any other. Forget him. Forget her. They're my problem. Not yours."

"But I . . ." Alex swallowed hard. It lay on him heavy as a boulder now. In the silence, in the pitch-black room, it seemed as though they were testing the moment. He sensed they had moved to the edge of something, and that the old man was reluctant to go on. Every word now was like stepping farther onto the surface of a frozen lake, watching for the fractures to appear beneath them.

"Okay." Alex pressed on, stepping carefully. "Once? When I saw him? I didn't get a good look at his face, but I almost felt like . . . I knew him. Recognized him. And, the girl, the same—"

"You do not know him," his grandfather interrupted very sharply, then caught himself. He continued in a softer, less certain tone. "Listen, Alex. He's— We were . . . friends. Once. The best of friends. Close. For years. But then we had a falling-out. I came to realize we had very different reasons for doing what we were doing. You see? Seeking out all these things. I was never looking for power. Just for the *story*, just for the fun of looking and finding out. Well, so I thought, anyway. But for him, I realized, it was only ever about power. And then power to get more power."

The old man's voice was sad, distant. He paused. Outside, the wind whistled wintry, vast. "When I understood that, I went away from him. I stopped. I tried to find my way back. Back to life. But he didn't stop. Seeking out these old things, lost things, putting them together. Relics, objects, books, words, creatures, plants . . . Like pieces from different jigsaws. And the picture that's waiting to be revealed is a mess, a new Dark Age, an age without an end. Eternal life, essentially. That's his true obsession. That's what he promises the girl and their little circle. Life everlasting. With him in charge, of course. The golem would be a very, very big piece for him to control. Big enough for them to come out into the open and drag the rest of the world into their madness."

Alex frowned, concentrating hard. "But, you said the golem went crazy. It went insane. So he must know that, too."

"But that's the problem with people like this." The old man sighed. "They go on and on about *belief*, then ignore the parts of the story that don't quite fit in with their own plans or desires. It won't happen to him, that's what he believes. He's the one who can control it. He's quite insane himself by now. And quite brilliant. That's the saddest part. You've seen what he can cook up. Those machines, the way he can control them, send them out, teach others to control them. In terms of technology, what he's learned is way ahead. Or way *behind* is a better way to put it. And it's better to stay there.

"But the golem is of a different order to anything he's ever gotten close to. Those machines of his, there are secrets and powers at work there, yes, but, really, those are just toys, party tricks. They control them by expending themselves—like, imagine a ball: a ball won't move unless you throw it or kick it, unless you transfer energy from you into it. See? *They use themselves*, and it takes effort.

"But this is different. The golem itself is very powerful, but that's not the half of it. Like I said, the creature is only a conduit to another power, one I can hardly begin to understand. He's studied this in far greater depth. What powers the golem is a *force of life itself*, an independent thing. The essential spark that comes from . . . somewhere else. And then goes back there. Or goes somewhere else again. Controlling the golem would be a step toward him accessing that—the life force itself. The golem exists only to serve its master, and given time, he could try and make the creature explain. It would only be a matter of him working out the right questions to ask in the right order. Reverse engineering.

"Then he could bypass the old rituals and create more of them, an army. But that's not the worst of it. This is power that should not be in *anyone's* hands. If it were revealed, it would show humanity everything it believes, everything we thought we had worked out, is wrong. People would lose their minds . . .

"Alex, listen." Alex flinched as his grandfather grabbed his arm. "If you only hear one thing I'm saying, hear this. The reason I went away from him in the first place was when I

realized he was . . . that other people were getting hurt. *Killed.*
Lots. For us . . . for him to keep doing what he was doing. This
is who we're dealing with, Alex. Remember that. A man who
has gotten himself very deep into some very bad places, doing
some very bad things. And who doesn't even want to come out
anymore. Just go deeper.

"So I set myself to stopping him. I've spent a lot of time
doing that. Anytime he and the girl try to open some strange
door, I try to make sure it stays closed and nothing gets out.
Nothing gets through. In a way, I'm still trying to help them—
like by getting rid of the tablet now. That ends all that. No
more golem. No more name of God. All of this is very old stuff
and very mean stuff, Alex. Stuff that takes the life from you.
And takes you out of life. It's voodoo for another, darker time,
not for today.

"Not for you," the old man added quietly, more to himself,
letting go of his arm.

Alex sat near hypnotized. "But don't you want . . . don't you
believe . . . ?"

"I *believe*," his grandfather cut him off, "in nice biscuits and
strong cheddar and good wine. I believe in making a few good
friends and watching old films. I believe in fish and chips and
snow and salt. Sugar and coffee and tea and books. I believe
in good design. Music, good songs. Not the stuff you listen to.
I believe in the rain in your hair and the sun on your face. I
believe your mother is lovely and that Carl isn't so bad, and

that they will both be pleased to see you back home in one piece in time to open your Christmas presents. I believe in the wind in the trees on quiet afternoons. Shadows and colors. I believe in lots of things, Alex. Millions. A lifetime's worth, and more. And most of all, I believe that eternity can look after itself. Because it has no interest in looking after us."

He sounded angry. The flashlight clicked on. Alex blinked, dazzled in the sudden glare, feeling exposed.

"Course, now, it doesn't really matter what I believe. Or don't." His grandfather's voice came out of the blinding white light, his face gradually resolving before Alex's eyes. He didn't look angry.

"You'll be able to work out what you believe perfectly well by yourself," he went on. "I have no doubt about that. To be honest, I don't care much what anybody believes anymore, just so long as they don't try to tell me about it. You said it best yourself not long ago: all of this is nonsense. But no matter what either of us thinks about anything, we're in the middle of it here, and whatever's going to happen will happen. Then it's only up to us to choose how to react. You know: act accordingly."

The old man smiled and patted Alex on the shoulder: "Clear as mud?"

Settling back, he rummaged in his coat, producing a small paper bag of black-and-white-striped candies wrapped in clear plastic. They glowed brightly as he directed the light onto them.

"Humbug?"

Alex distractedly lifted one of the proffered peppermints to his mouth, then, as his grandfather shook the bag at him, dropped a few more into his pocket. He sat sucking for a second, the solid sweetness the only thing he could hang on to.

Exhausted from trying to follow him through the strangeness of everything he had said, he felt like the old man had told him a lot, yet hadn't told him anything. And still he had failed to quite ask the one question he had wanted to ask above all. He couldn't tell whether it was because he lacked the energy, or the courage. Or because his grandfather had somehow steered him away from asking, like a conjuror misdirecting his eye. He decided to try along a different tack.

"Grandad?" he mumbled, rolling the word out around the candy.

"Hmmm? What else now?"

"How old are you?"

The old man turned sharply.

"That's a rather rude question, young man." He regarded Alex suspiciously, narrowing his eyes behind the mask. "Why do you ask?"

Alex opened his mouth, but no words came. He felt seized by a feeling new yet familiar: a distant, chill, electric shiver bubbling in his veins. Eyes wide in the light, he turned to his grandfather.

"Mmmm. I know," the old man said. "Pretty good humbugs."

"Turn the light off."

"Eh?"

"Now. They're coming."

His grandfather stared questioningly at him. He clicked the switch. A cosmos of black fell on them again.

"Did you hear something?" the old man hissed urgently.

"No. I can . . . *feel* it. The robot. The tablet. It's close."

"Are you—" His grandfather broke off. "*Shhhh.*"

They heard a dull thunk outside, below. And then another, not quite so dull, nor quite so far below.

XXI.

SEVEN TIMES AROUND

THE ATTIC DOOR rattled. Then silence.

Alex strained to hear.

Slow, heavy clanging on the iron rungs.

A sudden slam as something pounded the door.

Another crashing blow. The sound of thick old wood splintering.

"Barbarians," his grandfather muttered.

A third smash and the door burst open. Framed in the archway, Alex could see the silhouette of a life-sizer's hat, head, and shoulders. The hazy light in the street beyond had a silvery quality. Rain had turned to snow, huge flakes whirling down fast. With much clunking, the shadowy machine disappeared awkwardly downward, out of sight.

Alex sensed his grandfather tensing.

From below, there came another sound he recognized: a metallic, juddering creak. A new silhouette appeared. The tall man, landing atop the ladder having leapt straight from the ground. Alex shrank back, then, helplessly drawn, leaned forward, fascinated by the figure.

He pulled his long frame through the doorway, then crouched, reaching back down. Feet were sounding on the ladder. Light flared around him. He turned and straightened, like a thing unfolding itself. An old-fashioned oil lamp blazed in his hands, sending shadows scurrying.

Alex shrank back. The dusty shelves before him held hundreds of torn and damaged old books and scrolls, but there were enough small gaps that he could just about see through. He only hoped they couldn't see through from the other side.

The man stood motionless, holding up the lamp, regarding the attic with careful suspicion. He seemed almost to be sniffing the air. Barely daring to breathe, Alex was conscious only of his heart thumping, the feeling it had swollen into his throat.

The man turned back to the doorway. Leaning out into the flurrying night, he rapped his cane briskly on the top rung.

Clang. Clang. Clang.

As he turned and came striding deeper into the room, the ladder echoed with more feet. The girl.

His daughter.

His . . . sister?

Little Beckman followed. All three wore long black coats that reached their ankles.

Beckman knelt in the doorway, grappling with a large bag

handed up from below. As he heaved it in, Alex felt the eerie, shivering sensation inside him quicken. A small commotion sailed up from the street. Von Sudenfeld's voice, protesting loudly—"I demand"—abruptly muffled.

The tall man hung his head and sighed. He strode back to the doorway, handing Beckman the lantern as he passed.

"Let him up," he called down.

While more feet came clattering, Beckman and the girl removed their coats, revealing long white gowns beneath. The costumes had large, monkish hoods they tugged over their heads.

Von Sudenfeld's round face appeared in the doorway. Before he could climb in, the tall man stepped forward and placed one shiny black boot on his shoulder, pushing him slightly back down. In the lamplight, the complex assembly of metal straps and springs glinted around his heels.

"You do not say one word. You do not move from where I put you."

"Yes, yes, I—"

The tall man pressed down.

"One more word."

Von Sudenfeld opened his mouth to respond, then stopped. Frowning, he nodded.

"So." The tall man turned and strode back, tossing his coat in a pile with the others. His gown was immaculate, very white in the lamplight. Removing his hat, he threw it casually onto his

coat and ran a hand through his hair, thick black shot through
with delicate silver strands, swept back from a high forehead.

Staring at his face, Alex felt the recognition tighten in his
bones. His grandfather's words echoed desolately in his mind.
People were getting hurt. Killed. Lots.

The man's features disappeared as he pulled the cowl of
his robe over his head. He turned back to von Sudenfeld, still
hovering in the doorway, and pointed to one side with his cane.

"There."

He turned back, pausing to pat the little girl's hooded head.
Beckman held the lamp high.

"Now, then," the tall man said, and led the three of them
forward.

Old pages rustled like dry leaves on the floor as they
approached the mound at the end of the attic. The tall man
lifted one hand. Beckman and the girl stopped as he took the
last steps alone. When he reached the moldering paper pile, he
raised his cane, pushed it gently deep inside. Withdrawing it,
he selected a lower spot and probed again. This time, it struck
something with a hollow knock.

He took a deep breath, let it out.

"And so."

He leaned forward, began brushing paper away.

Alex pulled his eyes from him with difficulty, turned to his
grandfather. The lamplight streaming through the bookshelves
played in bars across the old man's masked face.

Alex mouthed words without speaking: *What—do—we—do?*

His grandfather shook his head and mouthed back: *Wait*.

The tall man had started to uncover something. A large box of plain grayish wood gradually emerged, around nine feet long by four feet wide by four feet high. Moving to one end, he nodded to Beckman, who handed the girl the lamp and took up position at the other.

"Now."

They lifted the enormous casket with surprising ease, as if it were empty, and carried it into the center of the attic. Setting it carefully down, the tall man reached through an invisible slit in his gown into a pocket beneath and produced a small, circular object. He beckoned for the girl to lift the lamp higher. Fully transfixed, Alex could see he held something that looked like an old watch. A single needle on the dial caught the light as it danced around. A compass.

The tall man set it down on the casket, watching closely. When the needle had stopped quivering, he lifted his end of the box again, shifting it slightly, aligning it exactly in the direction of the pointer. He stood regarding the arrangement a few seconds more, then, satisfied, deftly returned the compass to his pocket.

He bent to the casket, placing one cheek to the rough wood, stretching out long arms as if embracing it. His pale hands ran caressingly over the surface. Straightening, he gestured to

Beckman, who produced a small claw hammer from his bag. Taking it, the man leaned over one precise spot. There came a small, horrible squeaking as he began wrenching a nail from the lid.

Beckman moved to stand at his side. He held a glass jar. When the nail popped free, the tall man dropped it carefully into the receptacle, then bent to the next nail. Then the next. Then the next again. Alex stopped counting after thirty.

No one spoke. The wind moaned mournfully. Nails squealed in protest as they were pulled from the wood.

Finally, he had them all out. Beckman screwed the lid on his jar and stowed it away with the hammer in his bag, then went to stand at his end of the coffin, placing his hands on either side of the lid. In the depths of his hood, Alex could see the bright yellow scarf the little man wore. The knot at his throat bobbed up and down. Beckman was swallowing rapidly.

The tall man gave a nod. They lifted off the lid.

A small cloud of dust rose from the casket, tiny particles glittering in the lamplight. Alex stretched his neck, but from the angle he was sitting he couldn't see inside. He didn't risk moving.

The tall man and Beckman stood the lid almost tenderly against the wall at the gable end. Rejoining the girl, all three retreated several paces.

The tall man bent to his daughter, murmured in her ear. Handing him the lamp, she stepped forward alone, taking position at the foot of the casket on the right-hand side. Her hood moved as she nodded to herself. Then she stepped forward, beginning to softly chant words that were meaningless to Alex, speaking in a high, trilling monotone.

She walked slowly, taking deliberate, carefully measured paces as she went around the coffin, singing out her steady stream of sounds. As she walked, she lifted her arms. The robe's sleeves fell back. Her arms were bare. With a shudder, Alex saw that both were entirely covered with scars and scratches, a mass of wounds running from wrists to elbows.

She completed one full circle, kept going. Her words hung in the air, seemed to link up in a chain of sound behind her, strange, intertwining sets of syllables. After a while, the chanting had a weird, lulling effect. Twice she went around the casket. Three times. Five.

Upon completion of her seventh circuit, she stopped, stepped back.

Silence settled on the attic again. The three hooded figures stood still. In the shadows by the door, Alex saw von Sudenfeld lift a hand to his mouth and bite down on it. The silence seemed to grow deeper.

The interior of the coffin suddenly started to glow, pouring out a fiery red light that emitted no heat. Strange, quiet flames licked six feet into the air.

The tall man motioned with his hand. Beckman walked to the foot of the silently flaming box, stood on the left side. His hooded face was in shadow. Fire danced in his glasses lenses. He began walking and chanting, circling seven times left to right.

When he stopped and stepped back, the red light changed. A small sound suddenly broke in on the silence, like a distant downpour of heavy rain. The flames turned blue, then gray, then disappeared. Gouts of pale yellowish steam billowed from the box.

The tall man strode into the clouds to stand on the right-hand side.

As he began his first circuit, the girl crouched to the bag. She produced the white cardboard box, took the smaller, older toy box from inside. Then the robot itself. Reaching inside her hood, she pulled out a tiny silver key, worn on a purple ribbon around her neck.

Completely absorbed in the ceremony, his tingling senses singing sharply at the nearness of the robot, Alex started violently as his grandfather nudged him. Looking up, he saw the old man was grimacing and holding his nose, wafting his other hand just beneath.

The tall man was walking very slowly, singing mystifying words in a loud, sonorous voice, disappearing in and out of the mist pouring from the casket.

Alex's grandfather put his mouth to his ear, an urgent whisper:

"Getting close. Going to have to make our move. Timing is everything. Now, listen carefully. When I tell you, quietly as you can, move back to the end of these shelves. Get as near to the door as possible without being seen. Then be ready to move. And be ready to catch."

"Catch?"

"Our toy robot. We have surprise on our side. They're too wrapped up in what they're doing to even be thinking about anybody else. So, when we're ready, I'm going to jump out and grab it. Then I'll toss it over to you. And then, you know, you just scoot down the ladder and, eh, run away. Fast as you can."

Alex blinked at him. "Grab it and run away? That's the big plan?"

The old man pulled at his lip and shrugged. "Best I can come up with."

"We won't get three feet!"

"Well, you never know. Stranger things have happened. Now, when you're ready—wait . . . Hang on."

He broke off, listening hard.

The tall man was chanting louder, more insistently. Halfway through his seven slow circles, his rising singsong had taken on a blissful, rapturous tone. Behind him, at his heels, a faint, thin line of white light was now shining up from the floorboards, tracing out the path he walked, steadily brighter.

"Something's wrong," Alex's grandfather muttered. "Something's not right."

He sat listening and watching a moment longer. His face darkened.

"No, no. Something's wrong," he said again. "Ah, stay here, Alex, there's a good chap."

Before Alex could stop him, his grandfather was on his feet. Striding boldly out from behind the shelves, he stepped into the center of the attic, in full view of everyone.

XXII.

WHITE LIGHT

BECKMAN AND THE GIRL were staring mesmerized at the tall man inside his ever-growing circle of light, blind to anything else. Von Sudenfeld was the first to notice Alex's grandfather. He gave a strangled squawk of alarm from his position by the door. At the sound, Beckman spun, fumbling at his robe, and leveled a small gun at the old man. The girl quickly reached out, pulling down his arm.

"But," Beckman whined.

The girl shook her head.

The tall man ignored them all. The wall of light around him and the coffin was waist-high, growing taller, pulsating.

Alex's grandfather stood on the edge of it, just beyond the head of the casket. A beating, silvery light strobed his mask.

"You need to stop," he called urgently.

The tall man kept walking and singing. Completing a circuit, he was now coming toward Alex's grandfather, only inches away from him inside his glowing arena. The same height and build, they stood with the light between them like reflections on either side of a weird mirror lens. As their eyes met, the tall man's chanting grew faster. He sounded ecstatic, triumphant. Behind the shelves, Alex winced as he caught another glimpse of the face in the hood, running with sweat, set in a delirious grimace. An ugly face to see.

The tall man completed his fifth circle around the golem's coffin.

The wall of light stretched up, bent in to meet itself, forming a shape like a bell jar over him and the casket. Its pulsing quickened, the light fading to a dim milky glow, then blazing blinding white, until the man inside seemed only a disintegrating shadow. A noise started up, a sound like wind whistling around the distant chimneys of a very old, very dark city on a very dark, very stormy night.

"Listen to me," Alex's grandfather was shouting. "Forget everything else. You need to *stop*. Something's *wrong*. D'you hear? *Something's wrong.*"

Still chanting, the fraying figure in the light began his seventh circle.

Alex's grandfather spun to the girl.

"I'm not lying. Listen. Please now. You have to stop him. For his own good. Look."

He pointed to the base of the cocoon of light. The intense white was broken in places by small, thin black lines, reaching up like infected veins from under the floorboards. Alex saw they were wriggling, branching toward one another, trying to link up.

The girl folded her arms. She smiled. "Too late."

Alex's grandfather turned desperately again. "Stop!" He swung his cane hard, uselessly, at the light. Without a sound, he was thrown instantly, violently back, landing hard in a heap among the paper mounds against the wall. Alex felt something inside him lurch out toward him.

The seventh circle was complete.

The tall man stood over the coffin inside his flickering dome. The whistling noise fell to silence. There came a great cracking, like something huge and made of stone breaking open infinitely far away.

The thunderous storm sound slammed down again, louder now, a deafening howl. The room vibrated to the noise, shifting, changing.

Alex looked up, felt his mouth fall open. The roof was gone, ripped away.

Vaults of clouds towered above, lit silver by the moon, stretching up into forever. The clouds were moving, ranks of them slowly circling around a single, small black point. Now they moved faster, as though being pulled into this lightless center, murky water draining upward into the plughole of the universe. This black whirlpool was growing, reaching down over them, a wormy tunnel descending through the night sky.

Far, far up there, flashes of white-blue lightning lit its swirling edges. Higher up, Alex thought he could see things moving, tiny in the distance. Flying things, things with wings, black flocks passing over.

In the room, the dome of light started stretching up to meet the lowering vortex. The nature of the light changed again, the translucent wall growing increasingly transparent, glassy. Inside, the hooded man stood erect, arms raised. Tongues of white fire played over his robe without burning it, hundreds of living flames licking over his skin. More of the stuff leapt from the coffin.

He stretched out an arm, reaching one flaming hand through the near-invisible barrier toward the girl. As his hand emerged from the light, Alex saw one of the thin black lines shoot hungrily up from beneath the floor, looping in a delicate, snaking circle around his wrist.

The girl raised the old robot. Hard light blazed out through its eye sockets. Forgetting everything else, Alex was on his feet, moving toward the end of the shelves, driven by a powerful desire to grab the toy.

She lifted the key.

"No!" Alex's grandfather cried from where he lay. He seemed unable to move. Beckman lifted his gun, pointing it straight at the old man. Alex halted in his tracks. His longing for the old toy, his thoughts about the tall man, all washed away. All that mattered was saving his grandfather. His head was ringing. He had no answer.

The girl turned the key, seven times.

The tin robot's little chest opened, folding back in a series of concertina panels. Alex caught sight of a complicated skein of thin silvery wires uncoiling before he had to shield his eyes from the glare of white light that came blasting from inside.

The girl picked this light out from inside the robot, dropped the toy to the floor, forgotten. The tablet blazed between her fingers. Flashing a victorious glance at Alex's grandfather, she held it high, touched it to her forehead. For a second, it was as if she was lit from within, the light pouring out of her. Then she handed her prize reverently to the tall man. He pulled the tablet inside his circle, blindly drawing some threads of blackness with it.

The ancient clay burned brighter and colder in his hands, like a piece of a star brought into the room. Raising it to his forehead, he began chanting again, words long unheard. As he closed his eyes, thin black veins uncoiled from his wrist and wrapped around the tablet, unnoticed. He bent over the coffin, reaching down. He brought his hands back empty.

The casket blazed. White flame burned all around the tall man, all over him.

And then it was burning him.

Alex smelled it before he saw it. Singed cloth. The man's robe was properly on fire, in the humdrum, earthly, lethal way. The howling sound stopped. Something made Alex look up. The vortex above was slowing, dissipating, falling apart. The darkness at its center came falling, forming into a single long black line, plummeting down. At first it fell loose, tangling, like a rope that had been untied and let go, but it was growing solid as it fell.

The tall man looked up in confusion, to see what was now a great spear of darkness streaking down upon him. As he raised his arms in defense, it struck, breaking over him in a blinding wash of black light that rippled through the room in silent, concussive waves, knocking everyone to the floor.

"My face!"

The tall man was shrieking, writhing on his back. The flames on his gown swarmed eagerly over him, seemed to move with a single will, pouring inside his hood.

"My face!"

The old attic was suddenly very ordinary. The roof was there above them again, fully intact. With a cry, the girl grabbed a coat from the floor and ran to the tall man, now curled in a ball, clutching and slapping at his hooded head, screaming terribly. She bent over him beating out flames, wrapping his head in the coat.

"You," Beckman hissed, lifting the gun to Alex's grandfather.

Bursting from behind the shelves, Alex was upon Beckman before anyone realized he was there. With a savage chop, he knocked the gun from his hand, saw it skidding off among the ancient piles of paper. In the same movement, he shoved the little man, sending him staggering, cowering, in the other direction.

His grandfather was on his feet, already moving, heading toward the attic door.

"You," the old man said to Beckman as he passed, "would be better off helping put that out."

He pointed back with his cane. The papers on the floor around the tall man and the girl had caught fire. Drawn by deep instinct, Alex began moving toward them to help.

"Alex," his grandfather's voice halted him. "Come on."

The old man was at the door. Von Sudenfeld cowered on his knees there, hands over his face, gibbering.

"It *touched* me . . . It made me *see* . . . The things it made me *see* . . ."

"Alex," his grandfather snapped, stepping out the door. "No time to waste. Chop-chop."

"Where are we going?"

"After the golem, of course."

"What?" Alex spun back to the casket.

Beckman was stamping desperately at flames around the old box.

The coffin was empty.

Alex looked back to see his grandfather's hat disappearing down the ladder. He scrambled after him, stopped, turned back. The girl sat staring vehemently at him, cradling the tall man's head in her lap.

For a second, Alex hung torn. Then he bent to pick up the discarded toy robot and its box, stuffed them inside his jacket, and threw himself down the cold iron rungs, after his grandfather, back out into the dark Prague night.

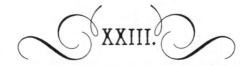

XXIII.

TO CATCH A MONSTER

A METAL LADDER had been placed against the synagogue, beneath the iron rungs in the wall. At its foot, the old man stood leaning on his cane, studying the snowy ground.

One of the bald men lay close by. He didn't move. The snow around his head was red.

The night had grown stormy. Snow stung Alex's face as he jumped from the ladder. His grandfather pointed with his cane. Huge footprints led off into the shadowy alleyway.

"I didn't even see it," Alex said. He trailed off, gestured up toward the attic. "I didn't even see it."

His grandfather crouched, examining the tracks. The feet that had made them had been blocky, almost rectangular, the toes stubby and crudely shaped. Straightening, he placed a foot inside one of the prints. It looked tiny by comparison.

"Yes, well," he muttered. "Quite a lot going on."

"What happened in there?"

"Hmm? Oh, combination of things, I suppose," his grandfather said. "For one thing, I rather suspect he wasn't quite as *pure in spirit* as he thought. For another, he might have made a certain mispronunciation saying the name. And for another, well . . . *you*, I think. Your blood, anyway. Tablet's been corrupted. Or claimed. Something like that. Ah, no offense, Alex."

Alex looked at the man on the ground. Both eyes were open, sightless and unblinking. Snowflakes landed on them without melting. Alex turned away.

"Is he . . . ?"

"Ah, yes. Yes he is."

"Did you . . . ?"

"Not me." The old man shook his head. "Come on."

He strode off quickly, following the prints.

Rounding the corner, Alex stopped in fright. Seven lifesizers hulked in the dimness of the alley, ranked from one wall to the other. The nearest robot's head had been smashed to a flattened circle.

His grandfather seemed unfazed.

"Don't worry about those." He lifted his cane and pushed gently at one of the machines. The robot rocked, then toppled backward, crashing to the ground with a resounding *clang*.

"No one telling them what to do. For the moment. Now."

He nodded at the ground. The tracks led the other way. He set off after them at a jog.

The night raged high above. Snow bit at them as they ran through old, empty streets. The moon appeared in a brief, hazy break in the clouds, beaming bright, full, and cold, then it was gone. Dark buildings loomed in, a black jumble of twisting angles. The place was a maze. The footprints led the way through it.

At the end of one street a huge chunk of rubble lay in the road. Opposite, the corner of a building bore a scarred dent the same size and shape, as if the stone had been ripped out of it.

They crossed an empty bridge. Black water ran high and fast beneath, restless with broken reflections of the lamps along the banks. Into another warren of alleyways. Back over another bridge. Many lampposts had been torn up, lay scattered across the road. Others had been bent to precarious angles. Another pile of debris at the corner. Snow swirled. The few working streetlights flickered in the flurry.

Coming out into a larger thoroughfare, the old man stopped.

"There." He pointed.

Off ahead, Alex could see a junction where another road cut across the street they were on. Something stood in the middle of the crossing.

Something big, shining pale gray under the streetlights.

His grandfather set off at a sprint. At his heels, slipping in the snow, Alex stared at the creature. From the corner of his eye, he saw the hoods of several parked cars had been crushed.

The golem stood motionless ahead of them. It was shaped more or less like a man, but not quite finished. It looked around seven feet tall, limbs blunt and thick, skin puttylike. As they drew nearer, Alex could see it was blurring at the edges, its shape changing slightly all the time, rippling, in flux.

A movement to the left drew his eyes away from the thing. A lonely late-night tram coming along the other street, windows glowing warmly. A few sleepy passengers inside. It was heading straight for the golem.

The golem didn't move.

The tram kept coming. Nearer. Nearer.

Suddenly, the golem did move, and quickly: running straight at the tram.

As Alex watched in horror, it grabbed the front car with two enormous trunk-like arms, wrenching the vehicle up off the tracks.

Alex felt his grandfather grab his arm, pull him down behind a parked car. Lifting the tram, the golem tossed it away with a single heave that sent it sailing into a building across the street from them. Shop windows smashed. Showers of sparks fell over the tracks, cascading among the snowflakes like snowflakes on fire. The other tram carriages were sent scattering across the road.

A migraine chorus of shop and car alarms went up. The golem ran, disappearing down a side street.

Alex and his grandfather sprinted through the wreckage. Passengers were staggering from the battered tramcars, dazed and shocked, some bleeding, reaching out to one another for support.

Alex could see faces appearing in the dark windows above,

curtains pulled back, blurry hands rubbing bleary eyes. A new sound joined the howl of alarms: sirens, coming closer.

"No one can see this," the old man said as they ran. "No one. We have to get to it. Get it away. The golem, it's wrong. The ceremony, it shouldn't have worked, but somehow it has—but it's wrong."

They rounded another corner. The footprints led down a flight of stairs. The old man took them two at a time. Alex's lungs burned, but his grandfather ran easily, spoke without even seeming to breathe heavily.

"The thing is quite mad, I should say. Insane. But it's still not fully here, you see, not properly awake. Our one hope is we can get to it before all its energy and power come together. It could tear this city down, and that wouldn't be the worst . . . Oh."

He pulled up short. Sheltered by the buildings above, the narrow street they stood in had largely escaped the snowfall. There were no footprints to follow.

Smaller streets led off left and right. In the sudden still, they could hear alarms wailing in the distance. As his grandfather paced around, searching for a clue to the golem's direction, Alex bent over, retching for breath. His head began to clear. Began to tingle weirdly. He looked up and panted:

"Left."

The old man spun. "How's that, now?"

"Left," Alex gasped, nodding in that direction. "It's gone down that way. Not far ahead. I can . . . you know. Feel it."

"Uh-huh. Well. Lead on, then."

They moved off at a run, Alex a step ahead, sensing more than seeing the path to take. Up stairs. Along another little street, another larger. Blunt footprints dotted the way now. Alex realized they were back on the same street as the old synagogue. And then all the lights went out.

They stopped, stumbling into each other. The night was solid black.

"Is that . . . ?" Alex asked the dim shadow that was his grandfather.

"Probably."

A few lights came weakly on, then went off again. Then on. Then off. On and off, rapidly, without rhythm, strobing the street in flickering light, interspersed with long periods of total darkness. Snow came storming around them, wild.

Alex nodded along the empty street ahead. He had to shout above the whipping wind. "It's heading toward the square."

They looked at each other in the glimmering silence. Then both cried simultaneously:

"The Christmas market!"

XXIV.

RIOT, SPIRE, VISION, MOON

THEY RAN, FASTER, jerky in the light, like a series of still images, the old man and the boy flashing in and out of existence as they moved.

Alex didn't need to see where he was going, anyway. He could sense the golem, the tablet, ahead. He could feel it reaching out to him. Feel what was inside him reaching back. And even if he couldn't, he could still have found the way. Simply by following the screams.

As they drew near, they ran into a panicked group of people rushing blindly in the opposite direction. Pushing their way through, Alex and his grandfather stumbled to a halt in the snow piled up around the edge of the square. Alex tried to take in the scene.

With the frail light flashing, harsh snow slashing his eyes, it was almost impossible to make sense of what was going on. The Christmas market had degenerated into a swarming arena of chaos, all flickering, stuttering black confusion. Several of the buildings lining the perimeter were damaged, windows smashed, walls ripped and torn.

A ragged mass of people was in constant motion around the square, a strange parade of festive figures going nowhere, panicking and pushing, running into one another, reaching out to one another for help. Throwing one another to the ground.

More and more were fighting, Alex realized. They seemed increasingly senseless, lost in the weird current of dread coursing through the place.

People crashed into him as they passed, and he felt himself suddenly caught up in the tide of heaving bodies, drawn helplessly away from his grandfather. Struggling to turn, he dimly glimpsed the old man, striving to reach him.

Several figures had turned on Alex's grandfather—men, women, and children, screaming in their merry hats and scarves. The old man was trying to fend them off without harming them. But more kept piling in, arms and legs swinging, teeth biting. Alex saw his grandfather look up, raise his cane to him, wave it in an obscure, frantic signal. Then he was gone, lost beneath his assailants.

Pulled and pushed farther and farther away, Alex called out, tried to force a path back. It was useless. Carried along on the panic, he had no choice but to turn and go with it, trying to keep his feet.

A cacophony of screaming roared above his head. He could really feel it now. The sensation inside him had swollen. The pressure was enormous. And the people around him were completely in the grip of the same feeling: drenched and deranged by waves of fear, grief and loneliness, giant, nameless horror. They no longer knew where they were, what they were doing. As they circled faster around the square in their terrible conga line, Alex caught glimpses of more figures being drawn to the turmoil from the streets beyond, pulled helplessly in, like leaves into a whirlpool.

Stumbling in the wild stampede, he could now see a great commotion at the center of it all, some great thrashing of darkness. The eerie feeling in his head shifted to a new pitch, pointing toward it.

He looked back in the direction he had last seen his grandfather.

"This isn't a good idea," he said.

He ignored himself. He started forcing his way through the seething mob toward the disturbance at its heart.

Ahead, in the middle of the confusion, a huge, shapeless mass churned in the flickering light, like an intense chunk of a storm that had become trapped somehow. It took him a few seconds to work out what it was.

A great number of the little wooden kiosks lay smashed and broken around it. As Alex looked, the enormous black thing reared up and lashed out, sending another small cabin flying through the snow in a rain of splinters and glass.

Ducking, Alex realized he was looking at the enormous Christmas tree, ripped free from its foundations and whipping madly around, flaying at the crowd. From the confusion of cables that hung from it like tangled roots, it looked as though half the city's electrics had been pulled up with it.

And there, among the wires, wielding the tree as its weapon, stood the golem, tearing the square apart.

Alex gagged at the force of the horrific vibration emanating from the thing. He could barely make the creature out, but the golem had grown taller, over eight feet now, whirling the mighty tree as though it were weightless, flattening a circle around itself.

It brought it smashing down, then whipped it savagely at the people struggling to get away. Alex saw some get hit, sent sprawling, senseless, to the ground. Unable to take his eyes from the creature, he moved tentatively closer. As the golem thrashed around, he could make out a curious detail, an almost delicate tinkling sound mixing with the harsh noise of screaming and weeping: the smashing of the thousands of tiny Christmas lights strung through the tree's branches.

As he stood gawping, it turned, saw him. Then it came rushing. Slipping in snow and broken glass, Alex backed away but found himself pushed forward again by the raging crowd. The creature was upon him now, barely six feet away. It raised the tree high, ready to smash him—and it stopped.

They stood stock-still in the maelstrom, watching each other through the precarious light. A boy and a shadow monster holding a Christmas tree. Alex felt the eerie, invisible current flowing between them reach a new intensity.

Snow came down, wild on the wind. Flakes settled on the golem's shoulders. They disappeared instantly, as if absorbed. The shuddering gray flesh was mottled with countless dents, like finger marks. Its face blurred constantly in and out of focus, one second bearing traces of features—a nose, cheeks with a hint of red, even a mustache—then just a claylike lump, with sad eyes like holes pushed by thumbs into putty.

At times, the creature seemed almost to vanish. Alex recalled something his grandfather had told him. *It was supposed to have access to all these great powers and knowledge: invisibility, the ability to raise the dead, all sorts.*

From the maddened throng behind him, someone shoved Alex roughly, knocking him to the ground at the golem's huge, half-shaped feet. The monster flinched. Its face flickered into a vicious grimace as it struck out furiously with its tree, smashing at the wall of bodies.

Crushed by the vibration howling in his head, Alex sensed rather than saw the creature come closer, dragging the tree behind it. Now it stood over him. He could barely see it, just rumors of its outline, a strange empty space carved out in the falling snow.

Then he felt it touch him, and the unnameable feeling in his head sharpened painfully and burst apart, like a radio signal coming into full reception, sudden silence amid all the roaring static.

The wavering lights of the square pulsed faster, fusing into a solid blaze. Something went off deep inside him, a flash of unearthly sheet lightning breaking across his being. For a moment, he could see nothing but a blinding blue-white glare, veined by thin, wriggling black lines. The black lines joined up, a writhing mass of roots, growing rapidly, growing blacker, until black was all there was.

Black.

Silence.

Black.

Faint screams, growing louder.

Gradually, his senses returned. He felt he was in motion. He opened his eyes. The sky was moving over him. He had been lifted. The golem cradled him tightly but gently in one huge arm. Half-visible, the creature charged through the crowds, stamping out a violent path, swatting bodies aside with the tree.

"C-careful." Alex croaked the words out past his heart, hammering in his throat. "You're hurting them."

He heard the thing grunt, a noise like gravel pouring down a well. The migraine feeling in Alex's head remained clear, but now he detected something else coming over the wavelength: the uncanny sensation of a thought forming in his mind that was not his own.

"You . . . think they're trying to hurt me? No, listen . . ."

The golem grunted again. It battered determinedly through the square toward a building ahead. Throwing the Christmas tree violently away, it leapt, smashed a blunt fist through the wall, and started pulling itself up, ripping out chunks of concrete for handholds.

In an instant, they were on a roof, then across it, heading toward another, more massive wall ahead. The thing jumped and began climbing again.

Alex realized they were scaling the face of the huge gothic edifice he had seen looming over the square. The golem climbed fast, heading up through shadow toward one of the tall, spiky towers. The creature had become visible again. Bundled in its arm, Alex could smell a cold, old smell. Damp, not quite unpleasant. He craned to look down.

The ground was far below. The square writhed in dread and confusion, but the effects of the field of fear that the golem generated seemed to be lessening as it moved away. Freed from its grip, people were no longer attacking each other. Streams were pouring out of the square in all directions. Aside from the unconscious bodies littering the ground, the smashed Christmas market soon seemed almost empty.

As the few flickering lights struggled on and off, Alex thought he could see his grandfather, a small gray figure, running from body to body, now looking up. He started to call down to him but gave up as the bitter wind ripped his breath away.

Up and up. High enough now that he could see the parts of the city where electricity still flowed, clustered around the darkness that rippled out from the square. Flashing lights moved through the streets, closing in. Police, ambulances. Sirens whooped, sounding small.

The golem had stopped climbing. They were among a cluster of spires at the top of the tower, beside one of a number of small windowed turrets that clung to a central spire. Bracing itself, the golem reached out and casually ripped an opening in the turret, gently placing Alex inside the ragged hole.

Sitting gingerly on serrated old bricks, he looked at the monster beside him. Snow danced between them.

The square below was strafed by the lights of police cars and ambulances. Flashlights flitted. Two larger, harder lights blazed to life. Spotlights being set up, directed across the carnage.

He turned back to his strange companion. The holes in its face blinked at him with strange sadness. A hint of a bright, cold blue light glimmered in their depths, then was gone.

Words formed shapelessly inside Alex.

"You're . . . *scared?* Confused," he said, hearing himself speak without knowing what he was going to say. He leaned toward the thing, and, before realizing what he was doing, reached out, touched its arm. The golem didn't move. Alien emotions swarmed Alex's mind.

"It's the city. The city isn't right. Things aren't where they should be. Things are where they shouldn't be. It's like the city, but it's not. You can hear the river. You have thoughts coming back. Memories. Work, so much work. Violence, so much violence, a world full. You're . . . lonely."

The thing shifted, an oddly pathetic movement. Its head hung, gazing below. Alex strained to pick up its thoughts. Nothing. He sighed.

Far beneath them, there was a new small commotion. A number of matchstick figures had gathered around one of the spotlights. They seemed to be arguing animatedly with the policemen operating the lights. Several were pointing up. Up toward Alex and the golem.

With a sickening feeling, Alex saw the light turn slowly toward them, the bright white circle beginning to climb the tower.

The golem moved quickly. It swung deftly up to the nearest spire. The point tapered into a long silver spike. The creature snapped it off, hefting it like a spear. Before Alex could get out the word "No!" it hurled it earthward.

Even with the wind storming around it, the spike struck down in a straight, deadly line. It hit the spotlight dead center, the lamp exploding with a concussive bang that threw those standing nearest to the ground. The explosion was loud even up at Alex's perch.

Figures were running to the other spotlight. It started to turn. The golem swung to another spire, ripped off its spike, and launched once more. There came another huge bang as the second light vanished.

The creature climbed up again. With a violent heave, it tore off the massive tip of the tower itself. Its eyes blazed. Bolts of blue light shot out, setting the chunk of roof burning with a ghostly fire. It flung the blazing heap downward. When it struck the ground, waves of the blue light rippled out. Alex could hear people screaming as the pale flames touched them.

"Stop!" The word ripped out of him. The golem stopped. Images poured from it into Alex.

He saw bodies now. Mounds in many uniforms, piled along the sides of a bare road cutting through the rubble of a devastated city. Fires at the far edges. The rim of the world burning, red, black, and blue.

He saw the golem, forty feet tall, straight, sleek, dark, finished. Muscles rippled as it strode through the ruins. Its eyes blazed a strong, hungry blue light. He saw himself riding on its shoulders, silhouetted against the burned sky, pointing the way ahead, pointing to the next task.

He leaned forward, pushing further into the pictures in his mind. Now his perspective shifted. He was looking out from his place high on the golem's back, watching everything fall before him.

Kings, queens, princes, presidents, prime ministers, and all their anonymous advisors. Billionaires, business tycoons, terrorists, religious leaders, military masterminds, media moguls. Teachers, doctors, bullies, Kenzie. All of defeated humanity lined up behind him and his beast, terrified, keeping their eyes down. Back along the line, he thought he saw his mother and Carl. Behind them, a tall man in black, a small girl. An old man in gray, head bent in sorrow.

He leaned forward again, felt himself lurch, almost fall. He grabbed at rough brickwork, opening his eyes. Beneath his wrecked tower, the vortex of Prague yawned up at him. He pulled back, panting.

"No." Alex shook his head, trying to dislodge the dissolving pictures. "No, no, no, no, no."

He tried to keep his voice calm, make it strong. The golem hulked beside him, impatient after centuries of sleep. A stray thought of Alex's own popped into his head: a time a few years before, when he had been cornered by a snarling dog. The memory was quickly followed by another: a scene from an old black-and-white movie, a woman soothing a giant monkey atop a tall building. Little planes were shooting at them.

Hungry for work, Alex thought, recalling his grandfather's words. He gazed at the night spread under him, thinking fast. Power, knowledge, secrets, questions.

"I know," he said. "I'll give you a question, just to give us something to do. Okay? So: where is my dad?"

He waited. Nothing happened. The golem sat motionless.

From his jacket, Alex pulled out the photograph. He held it up, one finger pointing at his father. He tried again. "Where?"

For several seconds, the golem remained still. Then it stretched one thick arm out, pointing in a definite direction.

Alex could barely breathe. He felt certain the creature was gesturing back toward the old synagogue. A moment later, it moved its arm through a forty-five-degree arc, then stopped, pointing in that direction. Then it turned forty-five-degrees again, pointed that way. Then again. It pointed straight up into the sky. Then straight down. Finally, it pointed straight at Alex. It dropped its arm.

It was Alex's turn to blink. He thought about it.

"Garbage in, garbage out," he muttered. More sirens were sounding below. The golem shifted restlessly.

"Okay," Alex said. "Forget that. We need to get you out of here. Away from here. Somewhere quiet."

The golem blinked, pointed below. Police were hauling another, larger, spotlight from a van. Another brief but very bloody image flashed into Alex's head.

"*No*. We need to get away. Now."

The golem blinked, loomed over him, raised an angry arm—then scooped him up. He had the clear sense it had gone into a mood. It swung to the far side of the tower, stepped to the edge.

"Wh-what?" Alex stammered. The sheer fall stretched sickeningly beneath them. "No, don't do . . ."

Too late. The golem, ignoring him, leapt. Stomach lurching, Alex watched the night streaking up past them in a lethal blur.

The creature landed with a crash that pulverized the cobblestones of a dark little street and tossed Alex's bones around in his skin. A strange, fast trip through dark Prague followed, the surly monster running, climbing, leaping. Hunting and hiding in empty streets. Occasionally smashing parked cars, tearing lampposts from the ground. Over roofs, along alleys.

Carried in its arms, Alex watched the unknown city slip by in shapes and shadows. His mind churned. Sirens shivered in the night, sometimes coming nearer, sometimes going away. He had the idea they were moving in circles. Eventually, he lost all sense of time and direction. Maybe he slept, or passed out. When he became aware again, he felt that the creature was growing calmer, placid. He had no idea how long they had been running.

They crept into a dim alley. The wind had dropped. Snow fell softly. Faint shouts, siren sounds from the square. The golem slowed. It moved cautiously along the darkened street, stopped beside a tall arched doorway set into the wall. The wooden doors were closed. It pressed at them, strangely gentle. Locked. Held in the creature's embrace, Alex saw the old stonework around the entrance was intricately carved. Two bears were sculpted directly above the doorway, facing each other. A man in armor sat before each, offering the big animals leafy branches.

The golem pushed on the doors again. For a moment, Alex had the terrible feeling it was going to smash them open. But it finally dropped its hand, turned, and padded sadly on.

After a while they came to a still and quiet section of town, another arched gateway. These gates hung open.

The creature stepped in, treading softly through an unlit passage. They came out into a silent courtyard, lined on all four sides by the blind windows of tall, sleeping tenements.

Snow lay deep in here. The moon broke through the clouds, very bright. The place lit up silvery blue.

At the center stood a small space for drying clothes, black poles strung with empty washing lines hanging thick with snow. The golem dropped Alex gently to the ground, then walked into the middle of this drying area. It stood there, staring up at the moon.

"Right," Alex said shakily, checking himself for damage. "Okay."

The thing turned its rough head to him. The blue light had vanished from its eyes. For a moment, they just looked at each other. Snow drifted softly around them, deepening the quiet.

Alex fought to remember anything else his grandfather had told him about the golem's story. "Uh . . . So, you've woken up too soon? See? It was a mistake. There's no work that you need to do now. You can go back to sleep. You don't have to worry about the city. The city's okay."

The thing blinked. A vague thought slipped into Alex's mind, the face of an old man he had never seen before.

"You're wondering where the rabbi is. Well, he's not around just now. He's away on business. But he asked me to let you know everything's okay. You can just go back to sleep again. And, uh, he'll wake you if he needs you."

The golem looked away. It stretched one thick arm up and out, pointing at the moon. After a few seconds gazing up, it turned back to Alex and blinked.

"Right. You recognize the moon. You like the moon. Okay, good."

A siren started up, startlingly close. The golem reared back in fright. A savage snarl on its face, the creature began fading before Alex's eyes.

"No, no," Alex said urgently, soothingly. "No turning invisible, now. It's okay."

The thing stood blinking. It stopped fading. The siren was moving away.

"Come on now. Come back."

The golem flickered back to full visibility.

"Good . . . er, good boy." Alex puffed in relief, scratched his forehead, screwing his eyes shut behind his mask in thought. "Okay. We need to get you back to sleep," he went on in as calming a tone as he could manage. He ransacked his memory for information. "And the way we do that is, we take the tablet back out of your mouth. Okay?"

The creature looked dumbly at him. Alex couldn't see a mouth. He broke off, at a loss. In the still, he began to remember how cold the night was. Hunching into his jacket, he dug his hands deep in the pockets. His fingers brushed small, unfamiliar objects. He pulled them out, idly curious.

In his palm lay three of the peppermint humbugs his grandfather had given him in the attic. Alex stared at them in the blue moonlight. Unwrapping one distractedly, he put it in his mouth, rolled it around, thinking. He recalled another phrase his grandfather had used: *dumb as a rock.*

He thought about the tablet in the golem's mouth. He rattled the humbug against his teeth. Like all the old man's candies, it was excellent. He thought about the candy, about the tablet. He thought about the old carving of the men holding out their leafy branches to feed the wild bears.

A dim plan struck him. It was ridiculous. It was the only one he had.

"Here, look" he said, suddenly sounding very cheery. He stuck the humbug out between his teeth, sucked it back in, and slobbered happily at it, making a satisfied sound. "Mmm-mmmm. When was the last time you had a sweet? Not for ages, I bet. Here, I'll unwrap one for you."

He removed the plastic paper, held out his hand. The golem blinked at him, then down at the little black-and-white lump lying in his palm. It lifted its head and blinked again.

Alex sighed. "Okay," he muttered, "okay."

He thought hard. *It's made a connection with you* . . . It could send ideas, feelings to him. He must be able to send them back, make it understand. How?

He closed his eyes. He concentrated on the candy in his mouth. He sucked at it, trying to make himself conscious of exactly how it tasted. He concentrated harder. He focused on the way the candy interacted with his tongue. He explored its precise shape and feel, noted how different clusters of taste buds responded to it in different ways.

Minutes went by in the silent courtyard. Alex's world shrunk to the shrinking candy in his mouth, and nothing else. A small black-and-white planet in an empty universe. All other thoughts dissolved. He found himself trying almost to build a picture of the taste, then enter the picture. There was nothing but the taste and how good it was.

After a while of this, Alex had almost forgotten where he was. He had almost forgotten *that* he was. The taste of the candy was all. He had never thought so deeply about anything. So deeply that he had become unaware he was thinking.

And just as he sunk to that deepest point, he felt it happen. It happened quickly, so quickly that by the time he became aware of it, it was over, and he had no idea how it had happened: he felt the thought go from his head. He felt his thought actually move out from him, toward the golem.

As soon as he thought about it, it was gone. His trance snapped instantly. The golem blinked down at him. He held out the candy again.

After a moment, hesitantly, the creature reached out an arm. A crude hand grew from the blunt stump, fingers forming. It lifted the candy to its face, blinked at it some more.

A mouth appeared. It placed the candy inside. The mouth closed.

"So . . . what do you think?" Alex asked.

The golem stood, face moving vaguely, as though it were rolling the candy around.

It blinked at him.

"Oh, hang on," Alex said. "You can't really taste it, can you? I think you've got something else stuck in there. Do you want to open up, let me look?"

The golem blinked again. It took a step forward, bent, and opened the hole in its face. Alex moved closer, peered in.

The mouth yawned before him like a small cave. The damp smell came at him. Huge teeth-like lumps rippled, rising and falling along gray gums, some blunt as boulders, some sharp as saw blades. He could see the forlorn little humbug. And there. Lodged at the back. The tablet. Its outline glowed with a faint blue-white light.

"U-u-h-huh. Yep. You've got a bit of clay stuck in there. I think I could get it out for you. Would that be okay?"

The golem bent closer, opening its great mouth wider. Alex rolled up his sleeve and reached delicately in. Teeth rubbed his skin.

"Hold steady," he grunted, straining to reach. "I think I've got it. Bingo."

He pulled his hand out carefully but quickly, holding the ancient tablet up so the golem could see it.

"There you go."

It blinked.

For a long second, or two, or seven, some force of life lingered on inside the huge stony creature. It had time to close its mouth and straighten. It stood tall, framed in empty washing lines, gazing up at the moon, and it made a noise that sounded very much like sucking. And for one final, fleeting moment, with the familiar moonlight on its face, the golem seemed to smile.

Then a deserted stillness came over it. The moon passed behind a cloud.

It was early morning. Alex stood in a dark courtyard beside some empty clotheslines and an old lump of clay shaped roughly like a man.

XXV.

THE RIVER

ALEX GAZED AT the lifeless creature.

"Sorry," he whispered.

He jumped at a noise from behind. A single pair of hands, clapping softly.

"Very sweetly done, Alex. Couldn't have done better myself."

His grandfather stood by the entrance to the moon-washed courtyard in his bowler hat and mask.

"Really," the old man went on, speaking quietly, "that all went much better than I'd anticipated. I had rather feared it would have ripped your head off by now. So, you could really feel it? I mean, you could talk to it, make it understand what you wanted?"

"Uh, yeah," Alex whispered. Then: "Uh, no." He shook his head. "Not really. Kind of. Sometimes. I'm not sure how I did it. How long have you been there?"

"Just a minute. I was standing here trying to work out the thing to do, but then it looked as though you were handling things rather well, so I thought I'd let you get on with it, see what happened."

"The police," Alex said in panic. "What'll we do? They must be coming."

"No, I don't think so," his grandfather said. "I had quite a job tracking you down, and I knew what I was looking for. No, I should think they'll be busy mopping up around the square for a while yet. What's left of the square, I should say."

Stepping into the drying area, the old man took the last candy from Alex's hand, popping it in his mouth.

"Don't mind if I do. No. We got lucky. What with the storm and the snow and the blackout and the general hypnotic confusion, very few people would have actually seen the golem, and none clearly. Of course, a few people were trying to tell the police they had seen *something* in the square, and they'd seen *something* climbing the church tower. But the police didn't really seem to credit them. Panic, you know. Does strange things to the mind. They turned the spotlights up after you pretty much to humor them."

"But the golem was throwing bits of the roof at them—"

"No, it wasn't. It was a bad storm, and it's a very old building. That's all. These things happen. Church spires go down in gales all the time. Maybe there was a spot of lightning. And that Christmas tree, well, I mean, that's collapsed before now. It went over in a storm around New Year's a few years back; lots of people were injured."

"But people saw . . ."

"Up until it's staring them in the face, Alex, people tend to see what they're attuned to seeing, or what they're told they have seen. And you couldn't see very much back there at all. And now, so."

Alex's grandfather held out his hand, raising his eyebrows expectantly above his mask. Alex realized he was looking at the clay tablet he still held.

The faint light he had seen glowing around the stone had disappeared. It felt cold, dead. As he considered it, the tablet seemed very heavy. All the same, it felt like part of him. He was loath to give it up. His fingers curled tighter around it. His mind itched. Remnants of pictures the golem had shown him, the two of them striding over the broken world.

"Alex." The old man straightened. His tone changed subtly. His voice surrounded Alex. The words came straight at the center of his mind. "Not for you."

Alex swallowed hard. The old man was smiling, but the eyes behind the mask bored into him. Alex started to say something, realized he couldn't, didn't know what to say. *The only question that matters is: do you trust me?*

He sagged, held out his hand. His grandfather took the tablet. Alex felt it go with a heavy sadness. At the same time, he felt a weight lifting. He was very tired. The night was very cold.

"And that," said the old man, pocketing the tablet quickly, "is that. Or almost, anyway."

Alex turned back to what had been the golem and placed

a hand gently on it. His grandfather looked around the court-yard.

"Wait here a minute." He hurried off into the shadows of a far corner.

Alex stood with his hand resting on the great clay lump beside him. He patted it softly, leaned his forehead against it.

"Where did you go?" he murmured. The night hung silent.

His grandfather came striding back across the snow.

"There's a bin shed over there. Bins look quite empty, so they're probably not due to be collected again for another few days. I've cleared some space at the back. We'll stow the old fellow in there for the time being, then we can come back with Harry and a van late tonight and get him back to his attic."

"What?" Alex gestured at the enormous rocky lump. "How are we supposed to get him over there?"

"Oh, there'll be no weight to him now; come on, grab an end."

Alex found he was right. The golem weighed hardly any-thing as they shuffled with it across the yard.

The old man dusted his hands as they stepped out from the shed. He pulled the wooden doors closed behind him.

"What if someone sees him?" Alex said.

"Hmm? Oh, they won't. There's no light, and he's up at the back. Think about it. If you came down from your flat in the snow and rain to take out your rubbish, you wouldn't want to hang about in there. Doesn't smell too rosy. And even if you did notice it, all you would see is a big old hunk of clay. You'd just suppose it was something someone from another flat had left in there. One of your messy neighbors, doing some decorating, or taking up sculpting. The chances of someone thinking, 'My goodness, there's the golem of Prague standing in my bins,' are fairly remote, I should think. Anyway, we won't leave him there long. This time tomorrow, he'll be back in his box."

They were in the street now. A distant siren started up and faded away. Alex lifted his hands to untie his eye mask.

"Leave it on awhile yet," his grandfather said. "We're not quite done." He produced the tablet, tossed it gently in his hand. "Time to take it to the river."

They walked in silence through slumbering snowy streets. Alex pulled the old robot from his jacket. Its chest still hung open. Hundreds of hairlike silver threads coiled around the insides.

"At least we'll be able to keep that," the old man said, nodding at the little toy. "One of a kind now."

"The golem stopped at a building," Alex·said, staring at the old toy. "It was like he wanted to get in." He described the creature's strange behavior, the carved doorway.

"Ah," his grandfather said. "The House at the Two Golden Bears. Yes, makes sense, I suppose. That's a place that has a very old and very strange history, Alex. All sorts of magic and rumor. Story goes there are secret tunnels from the basement that run all over the city and—"

He broke off abruptly. Alex frowned up at him.

"Oh," his grandfather said, staggering. "Ow."

Alex stared in confusion, then fright, as he saw a straight, bloody, red line open up across his forehead.

The old man stumbled back, shaking his head. He grabbed Alex by the arm, pulled him roughly down. This time, Alex heard it, the vicious whine as a flier shot over them, inches above.

"Rats," the old man said. He scooped up snow, rubbed it quickly across his face, pressing it into the gash on his forehead. "Don't know when they're beat. Can you see them?"

Alex started to shake his head, but then something caught his eye. He pointed.

"There."

A cloud of darkness moved among the streetlights. A swarm of fliers. Alex counted eight or nine, but then made it ten as he heard another whine swooping from behind. Shielding his head, he received a slicing cut across his wrist. Blood sprang out, black in the lamplight.

A small figure turned the corner back there. The girl, stalking furiously toward them. The flock of fliers grouped around her head, a hellish halo. Their hungry droning could now be heard.

Behind her, a curious, shambling tangle appeared. After a moment, Alex realized it was the tall man, being held up on either side by Beckman and von Sudenfeld, both struggling to support him.

His grandfather tugged Alex to his feet, pressing the tablet into his hands.

"You know what to do. Get to the river. Head for the Charles Bridge. You'll know it when you see it. Footbridge. Lots of statues along the sides. It's another powerful old place, Alex. It'll help you. Go."

The old man straightened, unbuttoned his coat, and stepped into the road, facing down the coming convoy. He suddenly leapt, swinging his cane like a baseball bat. Alex heard a crack, saw one of the flying robots sent crashing into the wall beside him, land stunned in the snow.

The girl recoiled but kept coming. She lifted an arm, pointing. Two more fliers rocketed through the air.

"I'm not leaving you!" Alex cried.

"Get to the bridge," his grandfather called back. "That's the best way to help me. Get it to the river and this is over."

The surviving bald man appeared, sprinting past the girl. As he came, he wrapped his arms around his body as though hugging himself, brought them back, a serious dagger in each.

"Take it to the river, Alex," the old man called again. He started running to meet his charging opponent.

Alex wavered, took a few steps after his grandfather, stopped. He looked off at the tall man, struggling forward. He stared at the clay tablet in his hand. He heard the angry clatter as the old man's cane and the bald man's knives met. He turned and started running.

He had charged around two corners before he remembered he didn't know where he was going.

The tablet felt heavy again. As he ran, he turned it over.

Smooth on one side. Indecipherable markings etched into the other. He pulled out the robot. He considered the things he held in either hand. Making a decision, he pressed the tablet back inside the toy.

With a small, delicate sound of ticking and whirring, the silver wires uncoiled, arranging themselves hungrily around the stone, a tight, complex embrace. He felt the robot vibrate slightly as its chest folded out, sealing completely over, without leaving a trace of a gap or a hinge. The tin seemed to grow infinitesimally colder in his fingers.

He raced blindly through the unknown city. Streetlights trembled in the falling snow. Dark streets slanted at shaking black angles. Images, memories swarmed at him. Golem thoughts. A terrifying, sickening, comfortable feeling. He sensed hidden tunnels beneath his feet. He was aware of tiny windows far above. Candlelight. All the secret lives, lonely in the night. The city changing. The night black and yellow. He knew the city. He didn't know the city. Things weren't where they should be. Things were where they shouldn't be.

He remembered patrolling long ago, long nights of work. Hunting. Fighting. Being hunted. Men with torches. Flickering light. Screaming faces. He heard the river. He felt the river. He knew where the river was. The stone bridge singing silently. The clay riverbed. His feet taking a familiar path through unfamiliar streets. Centuries rising and falling around him.

Alex shook his head, panting. He was here and now, a boy running on this dark street, on this cold night, this old toy robot burning icy in his hand. He saw he had come to a tall archway and raced on under it, coming out onto a wide stone bridge carpeted in snow, lined by soft lamps and black statues hunched in patience.

High on a hill to his left, a castle glowed like a stern fairy tale, lit up warm golden-white in the night. Its reflection shuddered in the rushing water. The black river was wild and high, overflowing its banks.

When he reached the center of the bridge, he stopped. Ahead, a tower loomed hazily above another archway, marking the opposite end. He looked back, saw nothing, no one. He moved to the side, looked over. The water wasn't far below. It coursed in a lethal torrent, foaming furious white where it smashed around the bridge's stone buttresses and arches. He looked at the water. He weighed the robot in his hand.

A noise made him glance up. An unsteady, unrhythmic sound, echoing and amplified by the archway ahead. Like the marching feet of a broken army.

Tramp. Tramp. Tramp. Tramp.

He stepped to the center of the bridge, peering toward the tower ahead. The stuttering marching grew louder. Then he saw. At first it looked like just one figure—tall, wearing a long black coat, a hat—but as Alex watched, six more life-sizers spread out from behind it, forming a ragged line from one side of the bridge to the other. The head of the machine at the extreme right was squashed flat. Still it stumbled on with its brothers.

One by one, the robots raised their arms. Depleted as they were, they still seemed deadly enough. Alex turned, began running for the other end. Coming from that direction, tiny in the archway, was the lone, sullen figure of the girl, walking fast.

Alex skidded to a halt, turned again.

The robots were very close now.

Spinning around in desperation, he found he stood at the base of a statue: a tall bearded man in a hooded robe loomed sternly over him, flanked either side by sad angels with huge stone wings. He heard the terrible noise of the river.

A thought seized him. He searched in his jacket until he found the robot's old box. He dug out his ruined phone. He looked at the robot, at the box, at his phone.

He pushed the lid closed on the robot's box, then hauled himself up onto the bridge's parapet, feet sliding dangerously in the snow, then up again, until he stood on the plinth at an angel's feet. The angel held a massive book. For a stupid second, he caught himself wondering what it was. He heard the robots suddenly stop.

"Alexander!"

The voice sounded sharp, and very close. He looked down. The girl stood directly beneath him. Her huge dark eyes burned hatred. Her face bleakly fascinated him. Sister.

Alex hoisted the box. The thing inside rattled feebly.

"Don't come any closer, I'll throw it in!"

"Now, now, little Alexander." She suddenly smiled a smile that failed to reach her eyes. "Let's not be foolish. Now, look."

Rolling her head as though trying to ease an ache in her neck, she lifted both arms, held them cruciform. Her coat moved strangely and the button at her throat fell open as a flier came crawling out from inside, followed by another, then another, eight in all. As they emerged in a small silver swarm, they split in two directions, until four apiece stood perched along her outstretched arms.

Simultaneously, they swung down their hooks, piercing the heavy fabric of her coat. The girl fluttered her eyes up at Alex. The fliers' wings started beating in a blur. Slowly, she came rising into the air.

"Now, wouldn't you like to learn?" she said as her head drew level with his. She hovered motionless, effortless before him, the straining little machines sounding like distant dentists' drills. Alex leaned back until he pressed against the angel's cold hard wing.

"Tricks and toys and techniques, and all the time in the world to learn," she went on. "Oh, the places you'll go! Oh, the things you will think! No more dreary little rabbit boy running away all the time, hop, hop, but Alexander—the Great! You can keep your little toy and come with us, and we'll teach you how to play with it properly. You won't believe how easy it all is, bunny. All the secret things. Secrets about you, too, maybe, eh?"

She cocked her head.

"Would you like to know a secret now?"

Alex swallowed.

The girl whispered something he couldn't make out.

She giggled and whispered again. He leaned forward, straining to hear. Her mouth moved. Alex stretched farther, trying to catch her words.

". . . *my favorite boots for kicking.*"

She jerked back, bringing one large boot up in a wild, balletic swing that hit his elbow with crushing force. The box spun from his grasp. They both lunged for it, Alex managing to grab it a fraction before her. The fliers made a grinding noise and she twitched violently, aiming another heavy kick at his side, another at his arm.

"Steel toes. See?"

The boot just missed his jaw as he ducked back.

"Zia!"

The girl froze, hung scowling in the air. Beneath them, the tall man and Beckman were approaching, moving painfully, but moving fast. The tall man was practically dragging himself, staggering on his cane, leaning heavily on Beckman's shoulder.

The girl spun with another high, swiping kick.

"Zia," the tall man shouted again. "Down. Now."

"But . . ."

He moved a finger slightly on his cane. Instantly the fliers responded, dragging her downward as she frowned furiously up at Alex. The man patted her head weakly as she landed, the small robots burrowing back inside her coat.

"Come down now, Alexander."

It sounded as though it was costing him a great effort to

speak. In the lamplight, Alex could see that, beneath his hat, his entire head had been hastily wrapped in white bandages. One red, weary, yet furious eye stared out from the mummy-like mask, hints of raw skin around it.

Alex opened his mouth. A mass of emotions stuck in his throat. His head rang. "Are—" he managed. Then: "Who are you?"

"Come down," the man said in his exhausted croak, "and then let us talk."

"*Alex!*"

The voice came from behind them. Looking off, Alex could see his grandfather's dove-gray figure running onto the bridge, sprinting toward them.

"The *river!*"

"Listen to me, Alexander," the mouth behind the bandages hissed. "Don't listen to him." Alex saw the eye wince shut in painful concentration. Two life-sizers lurched off from the line, staggering toward the old man.

"He's had long enough with you," the tall man gasped bitterly, almost spent. "And what has he done for you? What has he taught you? He has only kept things from you, eh? Things I can teach you, things you could not begin to imagine. But you will imagine them. Now. Listen."

"Shut up," Alex shouted. "Stop talking to me. Don't you say my name."

He turned to the angel, grabbed at the book in its arms, and used it to clamber higher. Now he sat perched on its shoulder, leaning exhausted against its snowy stone wing. The water churned and roared beneath him. Looking around desperately, his eyes stuck on another statue, not far away, a man with a staff, carrying a child on his shoulder.

"*Alex!*" His grandfather was getting nearer. He stopped to swat savagely in the air with his stick at something Alex couldn't see. The girl turned toward him, tracing strange patterns in the air. Another flier emerged from her coat. The old man lifted his cane to meet the whipping arm of the lumbering life-sizer bearing down on him.

"All the things you could see," the whisper hissed on from below. "Don't let him stop you. Don't let him stop you from being who you could be. Who you should be. Who you are."

"Shut up!" Alex yelled.

"Don't let him close your world down. Don't let him hold you back."

"*Shut up!*"

Alex heard the roaring water. The sharp sound of his grandfather's cane snapping in two.

"Come down, Alexander."

"Leave me *alone!*"

He saw the old man hit hard, knocked down, scrabbling desperately backward through snow, pressed by the life-sizer, pecked and buzzed by the flier.

"Alexander. You know us. You have always known us. Inside you."

"I said *Shut UP! STOP!*"

Alex felt it. He felt his shout move out, straight toward the toy robot. Felt it drawn inside. And he felt the robot move, just once.

He felt his shout absorbed by the tablet, the clay growing heavier and colder and burning blue inside its awkward little container. He felt the light. Then he felt his shout sent back out into the flickering world, a fury on the wing. His voice, his command, bursting over the bridge in a cold, lightless wave. It rolled out, breaking across everyone and everything.

The force stunned the world. Time slowed, the river slowed, everything stopped. Everything but him. He had been trembling, but now he moved surely, in full control, the only thing left moving anywhere. He grabbed the angel's somber head, pulled himself up, leaned far out over the frozen, boiling river. All the statues watched him.

He held the robot's old box at arm's length. The river responded. The waters parted before him, rolling back and up into two towering black walls to reveal the scarred clay river-bed, littered with centuries of junk, hungry to take back what had been removed from it long ago.

His senses were intensely sharp. He studied the picture painted on the box. The dark streets. The jaggy buildings. The robot marching, comically angry, looking for work. Then he pulled back his arm and threw the box as hard and far as he could, threw it forever away.

Things now happened at once, the planet spinning, the tides turning again. Alex saw the robot's box leave his hand, saw it arc up and out toward the waiting river, saw it turn, fall, and disappear as the churning waters smashed violently together to receive it.

At the same time, he saw the girl break away from the tall man. He saw the flier drop from the air, saw her leap onto the side of the bridge and extend her arms, coat sleeves falling back, the dark map of scars catching the light. He saw her dive, plummeting into the water. He saw her sink, rise again, saw her look suddenly desperate, saw her pulled helplessly away, fast, caught in the raging current.

At the same time he heard the tall man cry after her in purest horror—"*Zia!*"—saw him cast away his cane and crouch painfully. He heard the creaking mechanical crank, saw the heavy old springs working at his heels, and saw him sent leaping high off the bridge after the girl. He saw him hit the river hard, saw him strike out toward her.

At the same time, Alex felt something inside lurch after him, a sharp bloom of fear and loss that swelled and burst around his heart. He saw his hand reach out as the word he had been fighting was torn from him, a whisper he barely heard.

"*Dad?*"

But he remained clinging to the statue, staring down at the water. The tall man's bandage must have come off. It unfurled in a long snaking white coil on the seething black surface.

His grandfather appeared at the foot of the statue, leaning out over the water, gazing after them. Beckman went scurrying along the side of the bridge, stopping every few steps to look down, then hurry on. *"No, no, no, no, no, no . . ."*

In the darkness it was difficult to see. They were far out now, moving swiftly. It looked as though maybe the two small heads came together. Then they were gone, pulled down, pulled away.

Alex stared off down the river, straining to catch any further sign. But all there was to see was the Vltava, running high and black and very fast, catching the reflections of Prague and throwing them back, just as it has always done.

He was shaking again. A torrent of things ripped through him, burned his throat. He looked down at his grandfather, still staring out over the empty black water. As if sensing his stare, the old man turned, looking very grave.

"Alex." He sounded tired. "Come down."

"Are they . . . ? Is he . . . ? Is it over?"

"Yes, well—" The old man stopped. He was staring intently at him, head cocked, studying him seriously. He opened his mouth as if to ask a question, then seemed to change his mind.

"It would appear to be over, yes. Unless there's anything you want to tell me now. Or . . . ask me?"

Alex clung to the cold stone, considering the old man. His mind had been raging like the river, but now it felt stunned, drained. He was exhausted.

"I . . . Not now. Maybe later. I think . . . I'd like us just to have some normal time. If we can. Just me and you, like it used to be. I mean, just for a little while? I need time to think."

His grandfather sighed. "I would like that very much." He

reached up a strong, friendly hand. "Come on down, Alex. Let's leave the saints and the angels alone."

"So what now?" Alex said as he jumped weakly to the bridge.

Lifeless life-sizers stood around like strange new statues waiting to be hoisted up to join the others. A flier lay smashed near his feet. Beneath the high tower at the far end, he could see figures in shadows: a bald man, a small man, a chubby man. They looked lost.

"Ah, well." His grandfather kicked sadly at the broken pieces of his cane in the snow, then bent to pick up the one the tall man had thrown away as he jumped. He held it up to a lamp, weighed it, and swiped loosely at the air.

"Hmm. Not a bad stick. Not a patch on mine, of course. But it'll do until I can see my man about fixing me up another."

He placed an arm around Alex's shoulder, steered him firmly around so his back was to the robots and the men. They started walking toward the archway at the other end of the bridge.

"I think the first thing to do now," Alex's grandfather said, removing his mask, "is find ourselves a spot of breakfast. Ah, do you fancy trying to give Harry a ring?"

"Oh, I . . ." Alex patted his jacket pockets. "My phone. I've lost it. It must have fallen out. It was broken, anyway."

"Uh-huh." His grandfather spoke without looking at him. "Well, no matter. We'll find another somewhere. I think you should call your mother, too. Do you good to hear her voice. Although, ah, we should probably work out what we're going to tell her. Get our stories straight.

"I'll have to buy you a new phone, I suppose," the old man went on after a moment. "Harry was telling me he's got one of those things now. Says he can't live without it, although, if you ask me, he managed fine for long enough. Now he's on at me to get one. And Anne, she's another one. In fact, most people I know."

The light was changing. Morning breaking.

"I don't know, though. I just *don't like them*. I mean . . . Anyway. Now, tell me this, Alex: have you ever tried Turkish coffee? Tricky stuff. But worth the effort. There's a knack to drinking it, you see . . ."

They passed beneath the old stone arch, the old man casually twirling his new cane.

THEY STAYED ON in Prague two more days. They maintained the strange silent pact and refrained from discussing much that had happened. Instead, they explored the city, and they ate some incredible dumpling things in a small restaurant not far from the Old Town Square.

Still, Alex was aware that, sometimes, when he entered a room, Harry and his grandfather would stop their conversation. And aware of the clamor building again in his mind that he had decided not to think about. Not yet.

Meanwhile, his grandfather scoured newspapers and listened to local radio news. But there were no reports of bodies in the river. There was, however, a great deal about the tramcar crash, and lots more about the blackout and what was described as "the freak localized storm" that had ripped through the Christmas market, snapping spires from the Church of Our Lady before Týn. Many people had been injured by the huge tree when it fell.

Accounts of all these incidents were hazy and varied, the details confused and confusing. All the newspapers noted one particular detail, however:

The police were seeking two masked men for questioning.

AFTER THE END

SNOW IS FALLING on the islands of Britain.

It falls gently on the Palace of Westminster and the standing stones of Wiltshire; on Manchester's soccer stadia and the great iron angel at Newcastle; on the columns of the Giant's Causeway and the high castle in Edinburgh. From John o'Groats to Land's End, the entire country lies blanketed in white, everywhere, all at once.

It is a dim afternoon, a few days after Christmas. Snowmen stand in streets and gardens, silent sentinels of a scattered and crudely shaped army. They leer stony smiles, wink coaly eyes, test the air with carroty noses. No one counted, but, for one moment, there were exactly seven hundred and seventy-seven thousand, seven hundred and seventy-seven of them.

In a humdrum park in a humdrum town, small children in bright winter clothes squeal happily as they slip and slide. Old people stand around telling one another they remember how it always used to snow like this.

Out of their sight, away in a lonely corner of this park, a boy of around fifteen lies on his back in the snow, breathing hard, holding his jaw.

A circle of other, older boys looms over him. The boy on the ground has been hit and is about to be hit again. Were anyone to ask, none of them could give a reason for it. It is just how it is.

Another boy, younger, thirteen perhaps, stands outside the park railings, watching. After a moment, he climbs the fence, drops down on the other side, and begins walking toward them, leaving fresh tracks in the snow.

As he walks, he hunches against the cold, tugs up his hood, sticks his hands deep into his jacket pockets. Approaching the circle of boys, he speaks quietly.

"Leave him alone."

The teenagers turn. One steps toward him:

"And what—" he begins. But he doesn't finish.

"Just leave him alone. Go home."

The older boy's face falls. He looks around in sudden confusion. His friends, too, seem stricken, sadness passing over them like a wave. They stare at one another, looking lost. Then, without speaking, they drift away, drift apart, eager to be home.

The boy on the ground looks after them in puzzlement, then stares up at the hooded boy. "Thanks," he says. His face clouds.

"Go home, Kenzie," Alex says.

Kenzie scrambles up, begins walking fast, actually runs.

Alex watches him go, turns away. He stands alone, looking

up at the trees. He has spent a lot of time these past few days thinking of his father. He thinks about him again now, uncertain as to what it is he thinks.

Bare black branches rattle against low gray clouds. The sky hangs heavy, as though something were pressing behind it. Soon it will be dark.

His hand closes again around the old toy robot he carries in his pocket. His thumb rubs softly over its jagged little head.

It feels good.

ACKNOWLEDGMENTS

THIS BOOK WOULD not have existed as this book without the faith, vision, and energy of Catherine Drayton, whom I'm lucky to have as an agent, and in whose debt I will always remain. Equally, this book wouldn't be this book had it not been for the belief, encouragement, hard work, and seemingly unshakable cheerfulness of Alex Ulyett at Viking, an editor with a sharp eye and an unfailing ability to ask the right questions in a nice way.

My thanks to Ken Wright and the entire extraordinary team at Viking who had a hand in making *Monstrous Devices*, not least Janet Pascal and Jody Corbett at the copyediting stage. I'm especially indebted to Sam LeDoyen, who provided the kind of cover that can set you dreaming and an illustration with the hint of nightmare, and to Jim Hoover, whose beautiful design makes you want to spend time inside the pages. My thanks, too, to Catherine's colleagues at Inkwell Management for all their work, and to Mary Pender at UTA.

A lot of friends and family provided support, encouragement, and general comradeship along the way: Thank you. And a particular thanks to Peter and James Ross, who were among the first readers, and the best kind. Alison, again. All these people made things better. The bad stuff is mine alone.

Damien Love was born in Scotland and lives in the city of Glasgow, where, even as you read these words, it is raining. He has worked as a journalist for many years, writing about movies, music, TV, and other things for a variety of publications. He has the ability to talk to cats, but there is no evidence that they understand him. *Monstrous Devices* is his first novel. Learn more at damienlove.com.